MURDER IN
PERSPECTIVE

MURDER IN PERSPECTIVE

An Architectural Mystery

Keith Miles

WALKER AND COMPANY

NEW YORK

First published in the United States of America in 1997 by
Walker Publishing Company, Inc.

Published simultaneously in Canada by Thomas Allen & Son Canada,
Limited, Markham, Ontario

Library of Congress Cataloging-in-Publication Data
Miles, Keith.
Murder in perspective: an architectural mystery/by Keith Miles.
        p.   cm.
ISBN 0-8027-3298-4 (hardcover)
1. Wright, Frank Lloyd, 1867–1959—Fiction. I. Title.
        PR6063.I3175M87   1997
    823′.914—dc20   96-35898
                CIP

Printed in the United States of America
2 4 6 8 10 9 7 5 3 1

With love and thanks
to
Barbara Peters
who took me to lunch at the Arizona
Biltmore and inadvertently set this
novel in motion. It was a great meal.

Foreword

AFTER ALMOST SEVENTY years, the Arizona Biltmore is still one of the finest resort hotels in the whole of America. Built as a jewel in the desert, it is now a haven of peace and opulence in the huge urban sprawl of Phoenix. Who designed it? Albert Chase McArthur was the architect, but the influence of Frank Lloyd Wright is so great as to be overwhelming. Arguments about which of them deserves the real credit have added to the mystique surrounding the hotel. This novel is a fanciful exploration of that mystique. The ideal place to read it is in the beautiful lobby of the Biltmore itself. Sit there long enough, and the ghost of Frank Lloyd Wright will brush gently past your shoulder.

Acknowledgments

FRANK LLOYD WRIGHT first walked into my life in 1954 when my elder brother, then an assistant at an architectural practice in South Wales, came home with wondrous tales about the great man. The interest that was kindled that day has remained with me ever since, and the flames of curiosity have been constantly fed with books, memoirs, and photographic records of Wright, supplemented by visits to the surviving examples of his work in Illinois, Wisconsin, California, Arizona, New York, Florida, and Pennsylvania.

For striking that initial match, I must thank my brother Alan Miles, a former president of the Society of Welsh Architects.

Special thanks must go to Bruce Brooks Pfeiffer, director of the Frank Lloyd Wright Archives, who gave generously of his time when I visited Taliesin West and whose anecdotes about life as one of Wright's apprentices were fascinating. At the same location, I received kind help and encouragement from Suzette Lucas, director of external affairs; and from Indira Berndtson, administrator, Historic Studies, who grew up in the long shadow of Wright because her mother, Cornelia Brierley, joined the Taliesin Fellowship in 1934 and worked with Wright for many years.

I must also thank Doug Collier for facilitating my visit to

Taliesin West and Marjorie Lord Westphal for driving me out there and accompanying me on the tour. My wonderful hosts in Scottsdale, Barbara Peters and Rob Rosenwald, kindly provided me with a base from which to make recurring visits to the Arizona Biltmore.

Belated thanks go to Mary Helen Becker of Madison, Wisconsin, who traded a Frank Lloyd Wright sweater for three of my golf mysteries and whose husband, Brooks, kindly drove me to Spring Green, where the tours of Taliesin and Hillside Home School were inspiring.

Frank Lloyd Wright has spawned a huge literature, and in the course of writing one book, I have consulted well over a hundred others. The most useful for my purposes were the biographies by Meryle Secrest, Brendan Gill, and Finis Farr; the excellent *Wright in Hollywood: Visions of a New Architecture* by Robert L. Sweeney; *Years with Frank Lloyd Wright: Apprentice to a Genius* by Edgar Tafel; and the *Frank Lloyd Wright Collected Writings*, volume 2 (1930–32), edited by Bruce Brooks Pfeiffer and containing the lyrical and idiosyncratic autobiography of Wright.

Finally, my sincere thanks go to Michael Seidman and George Gibson of Walker and Company for their faith in this idea and for giving me the opportunity to put flesh on its bones.

MURDER IN
PERSPECTIVE

1

WALES. AUTUMN, 1928

E V E R Y M A N I S entitled to one act of madness in his life.
That was too meager a ration for Merlin Richards. With the hot
blood of idealism in his veins, he went for a hat trick. He resigned from his job, he decided to go to America, and he elected
to take the harp with him. Lunacy in triplicate.

His father gave a clear diagnosis.

"It's insanity, Merlin!"

"Not to me, Dad."

"You can't just walk out on us like this."

"If I don't make the break now, I never will."

"Why make it at all?"

"Because I must."

Daniel Richards winced. He was a tall, thin man with ascetic
features and a voice so rarely raised in anger that it was out of
practice. When it hit a higher octave, it cracked into falsetto.

"Have you taken leave of your senses, mun?" he demanded.
"People have been dragged off to the asylum for less than this.
You've got everything—and you're throwing it away! It's mad-
ness. Go on like this, and you'll end up in a straitjacket."

"I'm already in one," said his son reasonably. "Don't you
see that?"

"No, I don't."

"I have to escape."

His father was incredulous. "From what? The practice? The town? The family? Architecture? What the hell are you supposed to be escaping *from*, Merlin?"

"Us."

"Us?"

"Yes, Dad," he said softly. "You and me."

There was a hurt silence. Merlin hated having to wound his father so deeply. Daniel Richards was the senior partner in the largest architectural practice in Merthyr Tydfil. His dearest wish had been fulfilled when his only son joined him at the drawing board, forging another link in the Richards family chain. The thought that Merlin now wanted to walk out of the practice induced a glassy-eyed disbelief.

"You and me?" repeated Daniel. "All this?"

His gesture took in the entire room and—by extension—the whole relationship between father and son. They were standing in Daniel's office, a place as piously neat and symmetrical as the man himself. Desk, chairs, cupboards, and cabinets were set at perfect right angles to one another. Every drawing was in its portfolio, every scrap of correspondence filed away, every pencil sharpened and ready for the morrow. A ruler had been used to draw a straight line through each dead day on the calendar. The sense of organization was overwhelming.

That holy lust for order could be seen most clearly in Daniel's work. All over the Welsh valleys, residential housing, civic buildings, commercial properties, and recreational facilities designed by Daniel Richards attempted to impose shape and definition on the topographical anarchy surrounding them.

Merlin nodded. "All this," he confirmed.

"But I thought you liked it here."

"I do. It's one of the reasons I have to go."

"Your career is just starting to open up."

"I know, Dad."

"I've got wonderful plans for you," said Daniel. "The practice is ready to expand. When you've had a few more years' experience, I intend to open that branch in Cardiff that we've always talked about. That's why I'm grooming you so carefully, Merlin. To run the Cardiff office as smoothly and efficiently as I run this one." He smiled, a little hopelessly. "It would be a challenge for you."

"No, Dad."

"Don't you like the idea?"

"For the practice, yes. You should have opened a branch in Cardiff years ago. That's where the money is and where the real development is taking place. Merthyr is on the slide. Don't miss out on opportunities elsewhere." Merlin gave an apologetic shrug. "But what's good for the practice is not good for me. I just can't stay, that's all."

"Why not?"

Merlin hesitated, searching in vain for words. There was no way that he could let his father down easily.

"Why not?" Daniel, wounded, asked again.

"Because I don't want my future to be so predictable. I want to live my own life, Dad. Not have it designed on the drawing board by you. I'm a human being, not another commission for the practice. Your way is too safe and linear. It leaves me no room for mistakes or adventures or real growth. Yes," he continued quickly as his father tried to protest, "I know that you've given me an enormous amount of help, and I'm grateful for that, believe me. You gave me a wonderful start. But I must strike out on my own. Don't you understand that, Dad? I must find my own voice."

Daniel Richards, his tongue turned to paper, had lost his. Merlin's decision was a blow to him both as a father and as a professional colleague. An architectural practice that he had inherited from his own father might now be heading for extinction. There was nobody else in the family to carry on the tradition.

Merlin, seeing his pain, fought to hold back tears. A big, broad-shouldered young man with the physique of a miner but the sensitivity and soft hands of an artist, he had a round face, a strong chin, a crooked nose, and short fair hair that spilled from a wayward center parting. Though he wore a suit, he looked somehow slovenly. Pencils and pens jostled for space in his top pocket. His tie was loose, one cuff smudged with ink. His trousers were baggy. There was an amiable chaos about Merlin Richards.

It was not appreciated at that moment by his father. When his voice came back, it was dark with rancor.

"You're leaving us in the lurch. Do you realize that?"

"You'll soon find someone to replace me."

"Not from the family!"

"I can't do anything about that."

"Of course you can, Merlin. You can do what I've done for the last thirty-five years. Stay here to do your duty."

"I need to spread my wings."

"I wanted to do the same at your age."

"Then why didn't you?"

"Because it wasn't appropriate."

"You always say that."

"Somebody has to set the standards around here."

Merlin smarted beneath the rebuke. "This is not a wild decision taken on impulse, Dad. I've been thinking about it for a long time. Thinking about it and saving up for it. I know it's the right thing to do."

"It's sheer idiocy!"

"All right, it's idiocy. But it's given me the greatest excitement I've had in years. This is what I want. What I *need*."

"To get away from us."

"To stand on my own two feet at last."

"You could do that in Cardiff," argued his father. "When we open the new office. You'd call your own tune."

"No, Dad. I could never have real independence while I'm working with you. I have to get right away. To America."

"Why there?"

"Why do you think?"

Realization hit Daniel Richards with the force of a blow. He reeled visibly. When his head cleared, he glanced at the architectural magazines arranged neatly and chronologically on the shelf beside his desk. One American architect featured more often in the magazines than any other.

"Frank Lloyd Wright."

"I think he's a genius, Dad."

"He's behind all this nonsense, isn't he?"

"Indirectly."

"I should have spotted the signs when you wrote off for that American magazine. What was it called?"

"*Architectural Record.*"

"All that fuss over Frank Lloyd Wright."

"He's their leading architect."

"That's a matter of opinion," said Daniel sharply. "He doesn't rate highly in my book, I know that. But you worship him. A man you've never met, who designs buildings you've never seen."

"I've seen the drawings. That's enough."

"Enough to make you turn your back on all of us?"

"There's a bit more to it than that, Dad."

"Oh?"

"I wrote to him."

Daniel goggled. "You wrote to Frank Lloyd Wright?"

"Yes," said Merlin. "I told him how much I admired his work and asked him for advice about my own career. I also told him that I'd always wanted to visit America. To be honest, I never expected to get a reply. He must have hundreds of letters from

young architects all over the globe. But he *did* write back."
Merlin took an envelope from his inside pocket. "He only scribbled a sentence, but it helped me to make up my mind." He
offered the letter to his father. "Do you want to see it?"

"No!"

"But it's in Frank Lloyd Wright's own hand." He took a thin
sheet of paper from the envelope. "Listen to this. 'If you make
it to America, come and see me.' That's what he says. It's an
invitation. I'll actually get to meet him."

"And then what?"

"I'll be face to face with the finest architect in America. In
the whole world, probably. Just think, mun. I'll shake hands
with Frank Lloyd Wright."

"And then what?" said Daniel skeptically. "Where will you
live? Where will you work? How will you feed yourself?"

"I'll manage somehow."

"You could end up in the gutter."

"I'm ready to take that chance. Mr. Wright has shown an
interest in me. That's all I need to know. I'm off." He held out
the letter once more. "Here. See for yourself, Dad."

"No, thanks."

"It's got his signature."

"That's the last thing I want to see."

Merlin held up the letter. "This is my talisman."

"Well, it's no talisman for me," said his father bitterly. "It's
a death warrant for this practice. So don't expect *me* to lead three
cheers for Frank Lloyd Wright. I don't give a damn about American architecture. I'm only concerned with what happens here
in Wales."

"Mr. Wright has Welsh ancestors."

"So do you!" He turned on his heel and strode across the
room to stare unseeing through the bay window. Merlin was
stung by the harshness of his tone. He could understand his
father's acrimony, but that did not lessen its impact. Putting the

letter back into the envelope, he slipped it into his inside pocket. Then he stood a couple of paces behind his father.

The practice was housed in a large Victorian dwelling that stood, grimly solid, at the highest point of the town. Daniel's office occupied the master bedroom on the second floor. Over his father's shoulder, Merlin looked out at the drab panorama of the town itself, huddled against a persistent drizzle, the valley below, twisting its way south through the mountains like a long black serpent.

It was a view that Daniel Richards loved, but one that his son had come to hate. A beautiful landscape had been scarred beyond redemption. Industry had declared war on nature, attacking it relentlessly with ugly ironworks, blazing steel plants, clanking collieries, and all their associated pollution. A bleak and functional architecture marked each triumph on the battlefield. Instead of blending harmoniously into the environment, buildings were alien and hostile, giant gravestones in the undulating cemetery that was South Wales.

"This is your world, Dad," Merlin said gently. "I need to search for one of my own. I'd hoped to go with your blessing, but I can see that that was too much to ask."

"What am I to tell your mother?" said Daniel forlornly. "And your sister? You may have no consideration for me and the practice, but didn't you stop for one minute to think about them?"

"Of course."

"Well?"

"I've already spoken with Mam and with Eirwen." His father spun around to glare at him, aghast. "They weren't happy about me leaving—Mam especially—but they came to accept that I had to go."

"You spoke to them before me?"

"Sorry, Dad."

"Don't I count for anything around here?"

"I felt that they needed to know first."

"So that you could get them on your side. Is that it?" He shook his head ruefully. "My own wife and daughter. All part of the conspiracy against me."

There was no point in further argument. Merlin had nerved himself to announce his decision, and his father had taken it as a personal insult that no amount of apology could excuse or soften. It was time for Merlin to put space between himself and his father. Before he left, however, there was one more blow to deliver.

"I'm taking the harp with me," he said.

"To America?"

"Yes, Dad."

"But you can't," said Daniel, scandalized at the notion. "That harp is ours, in the Richards family for generations. It belongs here in Merthyr. As an heirloom."

"It was left to me."

"You don't need a harp in America."

"Yes, I do."

"Why?"

"Frank Lloyd Wright loves music."

Merlin gave a sad nod of farewell, then let himself out of the room. Daniel Richards, caught between rage and despair, was furious at what his son was proposing yet powerless to do anything to stop him. At a single sentence from a faraway architect, Merlin had rejected all that his father had worked for.

Daniel was now able to make a more specific diagnosis of his son's insanity. Resignation. America. The harp. Three separate types of madness. Each had a name. Daniel linked them together and spat them out like venom.

"Frank Lloyd Wright!"

2

THE CAR WAS picking its way between the tents when a
burly figure stepped casually out in front of it. The girl jabbed
her foot down hard on the brake, and the vehicle came to a
sudden halt in the dust. With a lazy grin, the man flicked the
brim of his battered fedora by way of greeting. There was a
teasing note in her rebuke.

"You might have gotten yourself killed, Pete Bickley."

"Can't think of a nicer way to go."

"Run over by a Chevy?"

"Mowed down by a beautiful gal."

"You're crazy!"

The grin broadened. "When I'm around you, I guess I am."

"Out of my way," she said with a laugh.

"Not till you agree to have that drink with me."

"Intoxicating liquor is illegal."

"Then they oughta throw you in jail," he said with a wink.
"You're just about the most intoxicating liquor I ever tasted. One
look at you, I'm drunk for the rest of the goddamn day. Yessir!
You're a walking violation of the Eighteenth Amendment."

Rosa Lustig laughed again. She was slim and dark-haired,
with features that needed no makeup. She wore denim pants, a
check shirt, and an upturned straw hat. The morning sun gave
her complexion a rich glow. Pete Bickley feasted his eyes on

her for a few seconds. Tall, rangy, and in his late twenties, he wore the light blue uniform of the site guards. A gun was holstered at his hip. He looked as if he knew how to use it.

"Where you running off to?" he asked.

"Only into Phoenix."

"I've a mind to hop in that car and come with you."

"You're supposed to be on patrol here."

"They won't miss me for an hour or two," he said as he ambled around to her. "Wouldn't you like some company, Rosa?"

"No, thanks."

"I could show you a real good time."

"I'll bear that in mind, Pete."

"You do."

"It's a promise."

"I'm counting on that."

He flicked the brim of his hat again and stood back a yard. Rosa gave him a cheerful wave and drove off down the track. Fondling the butt of his gun, Pete watched her until the car vanished around a bend in the distance.

MERLIN HAD WALKED almost two miles before he saw the car coming toward him. Trudging along the desert road, he was a strange sight in his three-piece suit and flat cap, a portfolio tucked under one arm, a small bag in the other hand. Spiked with cactus and studded with sage, the landscape was inhospitable. Even in winter the sun could pack a punch for someone so fair-skinned, and its glare made him squint.

As the car approached, he scurried a few yards off the road and waited for it to pass. Instead the vehicle slowed to a halt, and a pair of curious eyes appraised him.

"I may be a lousy driver," admitted Rosa, "but I don't usually hit people. Not all that hard, anyway."

"Good," he said with a cautious smile.

"Why did you jump out of the way like a jackrabbit?"

"The other drivers weren't as considerate as you."

"Other drivers?"

"Lorries, heading the way you've just come. They seemed to take a delight in forcing me off the road and covering me with dust. Those men in the back of the lorries thought it was a great joke."

"That'll be the guys driving out to the site."

"The Arizona Biltmore?"

"Yes, just left there myself. Most of the workers stay on site in tents, but the ones who live in Phoenix go to and fro each day. They're a rough-and-ready bunch."

"I noticed."

Rosa took a closer look at him. Merlin was not in good shape. He had a two-day growth of beard and the remains of a black eye. His body was slack with fatigue, his suit caked with filth. He was either a well-dressed hobo or a gentleman down on his luck. The portfolio told her which.

"You're not from around these parts, are you?" she said with a warm smile.

"How did you guess?" He grinned and walked across to her. "Good to meet a friendly face at last. My name is Merlin Richards. I'm Welsh."

"I'd worked that bit out. I'm Rosa Lustig."

"Hello," he said, touching his cap politely.

"So what are you doing here? Nobody walks along this road unless they're drunk or lost."

"I feel as if I'm both. I was on my way to the site."

"Why not take a taxi?"

"They cost money, Rosa."

"Are you that short of cash?"

"Afraid so."

"You must have a pretty strong reason to get out to the site if you're prepared to walk eight miles across a desert. I mean, you're not exactly dressed for hiking."

"I found that out."

"So what's out at the Biltmore for you?"

"Frank Lloyd Wright."

"Ah!" She nodded as she began to understand. "Of course."

"He is there, isn't he?" asked Merlin, eagerly.

"Not at the moment."

"But they told me that he would be."

"Who did?"

"The people up in Spring Green."

She was astonished. "You've come from Wisconsin?"

"I've come all the way from Wales to see him. I was hoping this would be the last leg of a very long journey. They assured me that he'd be in Arizona."

"He is, Merlin. The question is—where?" She gave a shrug. "Mr. Wright may be on-site today or tomorrow. Who knows? He's a law unto himself. My guess is that he may still be in Chandler."

"Chandler?"

"He's designing another resort hotel over there."

"How far away is Chandler?"

"Over twenty miles south of Phoenix, so don't even think of walking. It would finish you off good and proper." She studied him quizzically. "When did you last eat?"

"Yesterday," he said. "I think."

"Well, I think otherwise. Hop in."

"Why?"

"Because you need some food inside you. Come on. I'll drive you into Phoenix and buy you some breakfast."

"But you don't even know me," he said, overwhelmed by her generosity. "I'm a complete stranger."

"Not exactly, Merlin. We're two of a kind."

"Are we?"

"Yes," She opened the door on the passenger side so that he could get in beside her. "I came down here in search of Mr. Wright as well."

"Have you found him?"

"Now and again."

"What sort of a man is he?"

"Elusive."

The car shot away in a cloud of white dust.

THREE CUPS OF coffee and a plate of eggs and bacon put some color back into Merlin's face and some animation into his body. Rosa enjoyed watching the transformation.

"You were hungry."

"Starving."

"Now that you've got your strength back, tell me why."

"It's a long story."

"Give me the short version."

"Right," he said, wiping his mouth with a napkin and pushing his plate aside. "How far did I get?"

"They finally let you off Ellis Island."

"Yes, Rosa. I had no idea it'd be so difficult to get into America. I mean, I'm a professional man. Qualified and that. They treated me like I was some sort of foreign spy." He gave a hollow laugh. "And I was one of the lucky ones. No sooner had some of the poor dabs stepped onto the immigrant landing stage than they were hustled back onto their boats to be sent home. I've never seen people herded like that."

"They let you in, that's the main thing. Then what?"

"New York!"

"It's some city, isn't it?"

"Amazing! I've never seen anything like it. All those people, all those big cars. It's so dynamic, Rosa. Really pulsing with life. Makes even London seem provincial. As for the architecture—" He rolled his eyes in wonderment. "I spent the first couple of days in a dream, just walking around and staring up at the skyscrapers." A rueful note intruded. "That was how it happened."

"What?"

"I had my wallet stolen."

"Oh, no!"

"Outside the Woolworth Building," said Merlin. "I must've spent an hour just gazing up at it. All sixty stories. Sixty! It's phenomenal. The tallest structure we ever designed was a warehouse with four floors. It's like a garden shed compared to the Woolworth Building. Honestly, it was almost worth being robbed to see that."

"Who took the wallet?"

"No idea. Some clever pickpocket, I expect. People were brushing past me all the time. Stupid tourist with his head in the clouds. I was an easy target."

"Did you go to the cops?"

"Of course."

"What did they say?"

Merlin grimaced. "They suggested that I keep my eyes open in the future. Only they put it a bit more bluntly than that. Anyway, that was my first disaster."

"When was the next?"

"In Chicago. My luggage was pinched from the hotel."

Rosa listened with interest and sympathy. The more he talked, the more she was drawn to Merlin Richards. He told his tale simply and without any trace of self-pity. America had both entranced and shocked him. While two of its cities had mesmerized the newcomer, two of its citizens had taken his money and his luggage. Rosa was surprised at his resilience. He was even able to laugh at himself.

"They saw me coming, Rosa," he said with a chuckle. "I was so green, they must've thought it was their birthday."

"How can you joke about it?"

"What else can I do?"

"I'd be livid. You lost everything, Merlin."

"Not quite," he corrected. "I still have the two most valuable things. One is right here," he said, indicating his portfolio. "Fortunately, no thief is going to be interested in my work as an architect in Merthyr. And the second thing they couldn't steal was my harp."

"Harp?"

"Too heavy for one person to carry on his own."

She grinned. "You brought a *harp* to America?"

"Well, I wasn't going to leave it at home. Only instrument I can play. Inherited it from my grandmother. Along with the money that paid for my voyage. That harp simply had to travel with me."

"Where is it now?"

"In a pawn shop in Madison, Wisconsin," he said. "It was the only way I could raise the money for the train fare down here. That's why I'm traveling so light. There's hardly anything in my bag." Another wry chuckle. "Though that didn't stop someone trying to steal it."

"When?"

"First night of the ride down here. But I learn fast. I was ready for him. We had a rare old fight. I had to take a couple of punches to the face, as you can see, but he came off far worse. Those years playing rugby came in useful."

"Playing what?"

"Rugby. A violent game we have back in Wales. Like a second religion to me. I pretended that my bag was the rugby ball, and nobody—but *nobody*—was going to take it off me."

She gave an admiring nod, then glanced at the portfolio.

"Do you think I could take a look at those drawings?"

Merlin was touched. "Please do."

"I'm not an architect, mind you," she said. "I'm only an interior designer, but I can recognize talent when I see it."

"I'd value your opinion."

He handed the portfolio to her and watched carefully as she sifted through his collection. They were in a large café near the center of the city. A waitress came to refill their coffee cups and to clear away his plate, but Merlin did not take his eyes off his companion's face. He was thrilled when she began to murmur her approval. Rosa Lustig was turning out to be the best thing he had so far encountered in his new country.

"They're good," she said simply. "Real good."

"Don't be afraid to criticize."

"As far as the draftsmanship goes, there's nothing to criticize, Merlin. You've got technique. It's just that some of the buildings are a bit, well—"

"Humdrum?"

"Conventional."

"They're the only sorts of commissions we get," he said with a sigh. "Safe and solid architecture. Stone boxes. No room for flair or imagination. It's one of the reasons I decided to leave the practice and come to America."

"I'm glad that you did."

"Thanks. I appreciate that."

She tied the ribbons on the portfolio and handed it back to him before sipping her coffee. Her eye caught his beard.

"Do you have a razor in that bag of yours?" she asked.

"I do, actually."

"Could I suggest that you have a shave before you meet Mr. Wright? Turn up like that, and he won't know whether to look at your portfolio or spare you a dime." Merlin laughed. "There's a washroom out back. When you've finished your coffee, why not clean up a bit? A clothes brush would do wonders for that suit."

"I know. I feel embarrassed to be seen like this."

"Ten minutes in the washroom will make a new man of you. Besides, I have to go to the bank and make a couple of other calls. There's a drugstore on the corner of the street. Why don't we meet up again in there?"

"I won't be long, if you'd rather wait."

"Not here, Merlin," she said, briskly. "To be honest, I've had about as much of that guy as I can take."

He was mystified. "What guy?"

"The one who's been staring at me since we came in."

Merlin looked around and soon identified the man in question. Seated at a table in the corner, he was a short, stout individual of middle years in a smart white suit and a red tie, his thinning hair graying at the temples. He had a quiet, watchful authority about him. A lawyer, perhaps, or even a doctor. What made him slightly sinister was the intensity of his gaze. It was fixed immoveably on Rosa and seemed to contain both fascination and hostility in equal parts.

Merlin's protective instincts were aroused at once.

"Like me to go over there and speak to him?" he said.

"No, no. Don't do that."

"But if the man is bothering you—"

"Forget him. He's nothing."

"Rosa—"

"I'm leaving now, anyway," she said, rising to her feet. A teasing smile surfaced. "You haven't learned quite as fast as you thought, Merlin."

"What do you mean?"

"You never even noticed the guy."

"No, that's true," he confessed. "I was hypnotized by fine architecture once again. You put even the Woolworth Building in the shade, Rosa." She acknowledged the compliment with a grin. "But you're right. I should've kept one eye open for trouble."

"He's no trouble."

"Then why are you running away from him?"

"I'll see you in the drugstore."

"Do you know the man?"

"No," she said, crisply. "But I know his type."

And she was gone.

3

WHEN HE FIRST looked in the washroom mirror, Merlin got a profound shock. A disheveled tramp stared back at him. He was ashamed to be seen in that condition and staggered that Rosa had been so friendly toward such a ravaged and wild-eyed creature.

The train journey had been largely to blame. It had taken him the best part of three days to reach the Union Depot Railroad Station in Phoenix. Trying to shave on board the jolting train had been akin to flirting with suicide as his cutthroat razor did its best to live up to its name. Since his face was tender after the bruising encounter with the nocturnal thief, Merlin had simply eliminated shaving from his daily routine.

But America itself was the main culprit. Openmouthed with awe, Merlin had wandered around the architectural splendors of New York and Chicago like a child in a colossal toy store. He thought he had exhausted his sense of wonder. Then came the long journey south, and his red-rimmed eyes widened anew at the changing vistas. Huge lakes, mighty rivers, vast plains, immense forests, towering mountains, and—stretched magnificently over them all—the vivid hues of the sky. Even the cloud formations were objects of veneration to an artist.

Sleep was fitful in a sitting position, and the rattling carriages made few concessions to comfort. Fresh days brought fresh demands on his attention and his energy. He was still trying to absorb the subtle magic of the Sonoran desert when the train finally steamed into its destination. Merlin's strength had been sapped by his own curiosity. That was why he was looking in the mirror at an escaped convict.

Stripping down to his shirtsleeves, he shaved himself with great care, then washed his face and hands. By the time he had slicked his hair into place with a wet comb, he bore a faint resemblance to the handsome young man who had set out from Wales weeks earlier with such high hopes.

Vigorous use of the clothes brush made dust billow and restored his suit to something like its original color and texture. A sheet of paper wiped the grime from his shoes. Stuffing his cap into his bag, he took a final glance at himself in the mirror and decided that he was now presentable.

Then he remembered someone. The man in the café had been annoying Rosa. In return for her generosity, the least that Merlin could do was to speak to her unwanted spectator and put him firmly in his place.

He came out of the washroom in a combative frame of mind and headed for the table in the corner. But it was now empty. The man was no longer there. Merlin felt cheated.

He went out into the street and crossed it diagonally to reach the drugstore, so unlike the dispensing chemist he knew so well back home. Ewart Morgan's aromatic establishment in the Merthyr Tydfil high street ran simply to medicines, soap, toothpaste, and shampoo. The drugstore was substantially larger, and the first thing that Merlin saw was a rack of magazines. Toiletries, greeting cards, stationery, soft drinks, confectionery, and many other small items were also on sale. Once again, he felt that he had been living life in miniature back in Wales.

The pharmacy was at the far end of the store, and a couple of people were waiting for their prescriptions to be made up, but no sign of Rosa. Merlin was shaken. Had she cut and run? Had she sent him to the washroom to cover a hasty departure? Why, after all, should she bother about a stray hitchhiker? Another thought nudged him. Had she been frightened away by the man at the corner table?

Fearing the worst, he swung round to peer out through the window and was relieved to see that her car was still parked in the street. Perhaps she had not finished making her other calls yet. Or had bumped into friends with whom she was now still chatting. Merlin had not been dumped.

The sound of her voice made him spin around again. She had been in the drugstore all the time, hidden behind a shelf on which an array of cosmetics was displayed. The pharmacist handed her a small paper wallet, and Rosa paid him. She was about to open the wallet when Merlin bore down on her.

"There you are!" he said, beaming.

Rosa was defensive. "I'm sorry. Do I know you?" Then she recognized him and let out a whoop of surprise. "Oh no! I don't believe it! It's *you!*"

"How do I look?"

"Almost human."

She ran a frank eye over him, delighted with what she saw. After straightening his tie, Rosa caressed his cheek with the back of her hand.

"Smooth as silk."

"I feel so much better."

"It shows, Merlin."

"Good."

Emboldened by her candid admiration, Merlin was able to take a fuller inventory of her charms. Rosa Lustig had a kind of natural, unforced beauty that crept up quietly on a man. The denim pants and shirt served to accentuate her shapely figure, but it was her sophisticated pertness that really hooked him. He studied her left hand for the first time. She wore no rings.

"I'm not married," she confirmed, reading his mind. "Nor even engaged. Not that I'd wear rings even if I were."

"Why not?"

"I sculpt. You need clean hands for that." She nodded toward the door. "Ready for the road?"

"Have you got everything you need?"

She grinned. "I have now. Let's go."

He followed her out into the street, and they headed for the car. Her manner had changed into a kind of affectionate familiarity that put even more spring into his step. When they clambered into the Chevrolet, her questions were both casual and searching.

"What about you, Merlin?"

"Me?"

"Married or engaged?"

"Neither."

"Divorced, maybe?"

"In a community like the one I lived in? Divorce is not an option. You're either shackled by the church or fettered by the chapel. However bad it gets, married couples just have to stick it out."

"Did that scare you off?"

"It did. I came close a few times. At least, the girls in question *thought* I came close. That was the problem. Marriage wasn't just high on their agenda—it *was* their agenda. Take a girl out, and she started to look in the jeweler's window. And while she was sizing up the rings, her parents would be touring the furniture shops."

"No wonder you picked up your harp and fled."

"I'm hoping things'll be different here."

"What's the verdict so far?"

"The jury's still out."

She switched on the ignition. After a glance over her shoulder, Rosa swung the car around in a graceful arc and set off down the other side of the wide street. Merlin caught a glimpse of a figure standing in the doorway of the bank, watching Rosa with the same cold intensity he had shown at the café.

"It's that man again," he said.

"Ignore him."

"He seems to know you, Rosa."

"I hate guys like that."

"Are you sure you've never met him before?"

"Oh, I've met him," she said with studied indifference. "In just about every town I've ever lived in. And he doesn't improve on acquaintance."

It was all she was prepared to say on the subject.

JOE SANTANA WAS just coming out of the site office when he saw his visitor approaching. He let out an audible groan. Tom Vernon was amused by his reception.

"That's not the way to welcome a friend, Joe," he said.

"I'm busy."

"So am I. But I always find time for you."

"What do you want this time?"

"To see that big warm smile of yours."

Santana scowled. "Don't bullshit me, Tom. You're here to watch over my shoulder again. To chivvy me along."

"Would I do that to you?"

"Every time."

Tom Vernon chuckled and used a finger to push his glasses up the bridge of his nose. A lanky man in his early thirties with an intelligent face and an easygoing manner, and dressed in casual clothes, Tom was one of the draftsmen who worked with Frank Lloyd Wright.

Even someone as short-tempered as Joe Santana found it difficult to remain irritated by Tom for very long. His visitor was so relaxed and affable that a business meeting with him was always more like a social call.

"How's it all going, Joe?"

"Don't ask."

"Will you meet the target date?"

"No chance."

"What are the problems?"

"When you've got a week to spare, I'll tell you."

"That bad, huh?"

"Worse."

"Maybe you should crack the whip over them."

"I've been doing that from the start."

"So why the delays?"

"You tell me."

Joe Santana was a compact, well-muscled man of forty with a gleaming bald head above a swarthy face. He had the harassed look of a man under continuous pressure. While his companion was patently at ease with his work, Santana seemed to be suffering from his. He had enjoyed far easier jobs than being site manager on the Arizona Biltmore.

Tom spared a moment to gaze quickly around the site.

"Is Mr. McArthur here?"

"Which one?"

"Albert, of course," said Tom, pointedly. "The architect. His two brothers merely raised the cash for this project. Albert Chase McArthur is the important member of the family. Architects always come before money men."

"That's not the way I see it."

"The contractor has to work from plans."

"Some poor bastard has to foot the bill for them."

"Money spent on a true artist is never wasted."

"You sound like Mr. Wright."

Tom grinned. "Yeah. I've been working on it."

"At least your boss is not here to pester the living daylights out of me again. That's some consolation."

"Mr. Wright may be along later on, Joe. He sent me on

as a sort of advance guard. To get a progress report."
"I can give it to you in one word."
"Go on."
"Slow."
"You've been behind schedule at every stage."
"I blame the architect."
"Is that so?" mocked Vernon.
"He's more than doubled the cost of this hotel."
"Only the best will suffice, Joe."
"The best takes time."
"Now *you're* starting to sound like Mr. Wright."

Santana gave a grudging smile and fell in beside him. They walked toward the building to scrutinize it properly.

The site comprised over six hundred acres of land with the Arizona Canal running straight through it. Squaw Peak loomed in the background, with the even more impressive Camelback Mountain to the east of it. Two hundred acres had been set aside for the hotel itself, with the remaining tract earmarked for residential development at a future date.

With so much land at his disposal, the architect had been able to spread the Arizona Biltmore out at will. Fronted by the canal, the main building was well over a hundred yards long and rose to a height of four stories. The first floor was occupied by the main lobby, dining room, sun room, bar, and service areas. Guest rooms were directly above.

Two single-story wings had been added to the south, one at right angles to the main building and the other at a sixty-degree angle. While the former contained shops, the latter wing boasted a polygonal ballroom and lounge. Two further guest wings extended to the east, and fifteen detached cottages were set on the grounds behind the hotel. To provide vertical contrast, a hipped roof over the ballroom was topped by a festive spire, and the elevator tower was given bulk and height.

Building was at a fairly advanced stage, but scaffolding was still up, and construction workers were swarming all over the main structure. As materials were being winched up to the roof, fresh supplies were arriving in trucks. The whole building was faced with decorated concrete blocks, and it was over these that Tom Vernon first ran an expert eye.

"The other blocks would have worked better, Joe."

"Too late to change them now."

"Mr. Wright recommended a sixteen-inch module," reminded Vernon, "and you can see why. I still think that McArthur was wrong to select the eighteen-by-thirteen blocks."

"What's the difference in a couple of inches?"

"Ask any woman."

"We just do what the architect tells us."

"I'm not blaming you or your men. It's just a pity that the architect can't follow the advice of his consultant."

"Except that Mr. Wright doesn't consult."

"What do you mean?"

"He bullies, Tom."

"*Persuades.*"

"That's not what I'd call it."

"He has a true vision of how it should be."

"So he keeps telling us."

"An artist must fight to preserve his conception."

"Who needs Mr. Wright when we've got *you* around?"

Vernon chuckled. "That's the closest to a joke that I've ever heard you get, Joe. This job is obviously doing wonders for your sense of humor."

"Oh, sure. I laugh my head off all day long."

"Think how proud you'll feel when the hotel is finally completed. The Arizona Biltmore. The Jewel of the Desert. That'll be one hell of an achievement."

"If we ever get there."

"Have you never heard of optimism?"

"Not in this game."

They went in much closer to carry out a more detailed survey of work in progress. The two men studied the hotel from different perspectives. Tom Vernon was pleased to see how much had been done since his last visit, but Joe Santana was exercised by how much still remained. Like so many major buildings, the Arizona Biltmore was an uneasy compromise between artistic imagination and the practicalities of construction.

Tom Vernon was determined to take a positive view.

"It's going to work, Joe."

"Is it?"

"Not as well as it should, mark you, but I think it will pass muster. Only the trained architect will spot the mistakes and the shortcomings. *I* wouldn't mind staying here, I know that."

"I couldn't afford to."

"Resort hotels are for the very rich."

"Maybe that's why I don't enjoy building them."

The approach of a car interrupted their discussion. They turned around to see the Chevrolet heading toward them. Tom Vernon grinned when he saw Rosa Lustig behind the steering wheel and semaphored a welcome. She waved back at him.

Joe Santana was less sociable. He curled his lip.

"Here comes trouble," he sneered. "I'm off."

4

R O S A   B R O U G H T   T H E   car to a juddering halt some thirty
yards away.

"You're in luck, Merlin," she said.

"Am I?"

"That's Tom Vernon. One of Mr. Wright's boys."

His interest quickened. "Does that mean that Frank Lloyd
Wright is here himself?"

"He won't be far away."

"Great!"

They got out of the car and strolled toward Vernon.

"Who was that other man?" he asked.

"Oh, that was Joe Santana. Site manager."

"See that look he gave us before he stalked off?"

"That's his way."

"He didn't seem to like us at all."

."Joe doesn't like anybody," she said dismissively. "Tom is
the opposite. Friend to all the world. Terrific guy."

"Hi, there!" said Vernon.

He gave Rosa a kiss on the cheek, then shook Merlin's hand
warmly. Vernon was torn between amusement and approval when
she had reduced Merlin's travels to a few graphic sentences.

"You came all this way just to see Mr. Wright?"

"Yes."

"And you brought a *harp*?"

"Sentimental reasons."

"Mr. Wright will be tickled to hear about that."

"Is he going to be here today?"

"Possibly. It depends how long his meeting with Dr. Chandler drags on."

"Dr. Chandler?"

"He's the client who commissioned the other hotel."

"I thought Rosa told me that Chandler was a town."

"It is," she assured him. "Named after Dr. Alexander Chandler. He was a vet at one time, wasn't he, Tom?"

"That's right," said Vernon, primed with all the relevant information. "Born and brought up in Canada. Came down here all of—what?—forty years ago, it must be, as veterinary surgeon to the Territory of Arizona. Settled in Prescott."

"The territorial capital in those days," added Rosa.

"That was before Arizona became a state. Dr. Chandler hated the place. The drought was so unbearable that he resigned his post after a month. On his way to Los Angeles, he stopped off in Phoenix at the very moment when the drought broke. They reckon that it rained for almost three weeks."

"Did that change his mind for him?" asked Merlin.

"You bet," said Vernon. "He saw just how fertile the Salt River Valley might be when it had plenty of water. So he stayed in Arizona, continued his work as a vet, and got himself involved in large-scale irrigation. He managed to accumulate a lot of land along the way, and that became the Chandler ranch. Out of that, in time, grew Chandler itself. Small town with big ideas. So far, the San Marcos Hotel is the only building of any distinction there. That's where Mr. Wright is at this moment."

"Designing another hotel, you say?"

"Yes, Merlin. San Marcos in the Desert."

"It will compete with this place," observed Rosa.

"That's the hope," agreed Vernon. "Eastern millionaires like to spend their winters in the sun, and Arizona has got just as much to offer as Florida or California. All that it lacks are sufficient resort hotels."

"So Mr. Wright is building two."

"One," emphasized Vernon. "One hotel. San Marcos in the Desert. Mr. Wright is only working on the Biltmore in an advisory capacity."

"Albert Chase McArthur certainly *needs* advice," Rosa said, tartly. "Without help, he'd never have got this project off the ground."

"Give him his due," said Vernon, tolerantly. "Mr. McArthur is a good architect. Ought to be. He was taught by Mr. Wright himself. Spent two years at the Oak Park studio. But you can see for yourself, Merlin—" He stood back to allow the newcomer an uninterrupted view of the building. "You're a fellow architect. What do you think?"

Merlin spread his arms in a gesture of admiration.

"Amazing!" he said. "As we were driving up just now, I was bowled over by it. I mean, I've spent most of my working life visiting building sites, but nothing on this scale. It's a revelation!" Face aglow, he surveyed the building with keen interest. "Are you sure Mr. Wright didn't design it?"

Vernon was adamant. "Quite sure."

"It's so reminiscent of his work."

"His influence rubs off on all his pupils."

"Those concrete blocks are astonishing," said Merlin, pointing to the facade. "Such simple and yet striking patterns. I had no idea that concrete could be so beautiful."

"That's Mr. Wright's real contribution to the hotel."

"How many blocks will be needed?"

"A quarter of a million."

"You're pulling my leg!"

"At least that number. The contractors had to set up a small factory on site just to produce the blocks. Works twenty-four hours a day."

"I can vouch for that," said Rosa, jerking her head toward a rudimentary concrete building off to the right. "Some nights I can't get a wink of sleep because of the sound of those mixers. They never let up, and the noise is worse because there's no roof on the factory to hold it in."

"Sorry about that, Rosa," said Vernon. "But those blocks are a vital feature of the Biltmore. Try wearing ear plugs."

"They don't work."

Merlin was still enraptured by the art deco formalism of the building, the perils and misadventures of his journey forgotten. This was what he had come to see: Frank Lloyd Wright made manifest.

Tom Vernon knew exactly what he must be feeling.

"Would you like to take a look inside?" he offered.

"Would I!"

"Unless Rosa has other plans for you—"

"No, no. You go ahead, Tom. Show him all the sights. And don't rush. I've got some work to do, anyway. When you've finished, Merlin, find your way to my tent."

Vernon grinned. "That's an invitation no man could refuse."

Rosa blew him a kiss and strode back toward her car.

"What about my portfolio?" called Merlin.

"I'll guard it with my life."

"Thanks."

They watched her climb into the Chevrolet to drive the short distance to the site camp, a large cluster of tents and makeshift shacks. Tom Vernon gave a low murmur of pleasure.

"You struck oil there," he said.

"Oil?"

"Rosa. Great girl. Talented designer as well."

"She told me that she once worked with Mr. Wright."

"She did. Briefly. Up in Spring Green."

"Rosa's hoping to team up with him again one day."

"I'm sure she is," sighed Vernon. "Unfortunately, she's one of many with that ambition. They buzz around him like moths around a flame. Rosa may have a long wait, I'm afraid." He looked Merlin in the eye. "I daresay you have vague hopes of your own regarding Mr. Wright."

"Shaking hands with him will be enough for me."

"That's what I thought."

"You?"

"Yes," admitted the other. "I was a fresh-faced idealist who once came in search of my hero. Like you, I was ready to settle for a handshake and a kind word from the master."

"What happened?"

Tom Vernon gave a philosophical chuckle.

"You'll find out," he said.

AS SOON AS she got back to her tent, Rosa went inside and took out the small wallet that she had collected from the drugstore in Phoenix. She was still examining its contents when she heard footsteps outside. Rosa quickly hid what she was holding under a blanket.

The flap was pulled back, and the raw-boned features of Pete Bickley intruded a few inches. He gave his lazy smile.

"Saw you come back," he said.

"Not now, Pete. I'm busy."

"What did you get up to in Phoenix?"

"Some shopping, that's all."

"Where did you buy him?"

"Who?"

"That greenhorn in the suit. Is he your new beau?"

"Of course not!"

"Then who is he?"

"That's none of your business."

"I figured it was."

"Then you figured wrong, mister!"

"Did I?" he said, stepping into the tent and crouching down to avoid knocking his head against the canvas. "Maybe I just got a better memory than you, Rosa."

"Get out!"

"Now, that's not very hospitable. Is it?"

"I don't want you in here."

"You've changed your tune, lady."

She took a deep breath and tried to compose herself. Manufacturing a smile, she gave an apologetic shrug. Then she touched his arm with an offhand affection.

"Look, I'm sorry. Didn't mean to bite your head off."

"Bite all you want, Rosa. I like it."

"This really isn't a good time for me, Pete."

"When is?"

"I'll let you know."

"Seems to me I spend most of my time waiting for you to let me know." His smile vanished. "I saw the way you was talking to that guy when you drove up. Real friendly. And he was taken with you. That was obvious. I put the hours in on this, Rosa. Now, you wouldn't let a dude like that jump to the head of the class, would you?"

"I hardly know him."

"So who is he?"

"A hitchhiker I picked up. An architect."

"Big step up from a site guard."

"Don't be silly, Pete. There's nothing like that going on. I only met the guy a couple of hours ago."

"That's time enough."

"Not for me."

"So what's his name?"

"Does it matter?"

"Just like to know, that's all."

"Pete—"

"I'm curious."

Another deep breath. "Will you go if I tell you?"

"I might. Now, who is he?"

"Merlin Richards."

"Has he come from back East?"

"Much farther away than that. All the way from Wales. It took him five days just to reach this country. He's had a pretty raw deal here so far. I took pity on him."

"What's he doing in Arizona?"

"Looking for Frank Lloyd Wright."

"That all he's after?"

"Of course."

He studied her shrewdly for a moment, then reached out to fondle a wisp of her hair between tobacco-stained fingers. Rosa was polite but firm.

"It's time for you to go, Pete."

He nodded. "I'll be back."

"Only on my terms," she warned.

"Suits me fine."

He flicked the brim of his hat and ducked out of the tent. She relaxed. His face reappeared almost instantly.

"I'll be waiting, Rosa."

"I'm counting on it."

He took his grin back out on duty again. Rosa waited a few minutes, then peered through the flap to make sure that he had gone. Confident that she was now alone, she lifted the blanket to examine the contents of the wallet once again.

MERLIN RICHARDS WAS in his element. The tour of the hotel was fascinating. Each corner they turned threw up some intriguing design feature or some daring use of basic materials, and his mental dossier was soon crammed with exciting detail. Tom Vernon was a patient and supremely well informed guide, who relished Merlin's educated comments on the building.

It was well over two hours before they completed the tour. Vernon turned to his companion.

"Well?" he said. "Give it to me in a word."

"Breathtaking!"

"I guess you don't have too many hotels like this in Wales."

"None at all."

"Go back and build one."

"If only I could! But there's no chance of that. Who wants a resort hotel in the middle of an industrial area?"

"This one is in the middle of a desert."

"It's like a palace."

"What would you be doing if you were back home now?"

"Shivering in the cold."

"On the drawing board, I meant."

"Working with my father on a new Methodist chapel in Pontypridd. I'm so glad to have escaped that chore."

"Never despise religion. It brings in commissions."

"Not the kind that inspire."

"Didn't you see Unity Temple when you were up in Oak Park?" Merlin nodded enthusiastically. "Mr. Wright built that for the Unitarian Church. You can't say there's no inspiration there. Those poured-concrete exterior walls and columns were a radical innovation at the time."

"It's wonderful," agreed Merlin, "but then the architect was allowed to express himself. We're not. To be honest, I'm not sure that Dad could now. He's spent so many years giving the clients exactly what they want that his creative juices have dried up."

"I can see why you got out from under him."

"It wasn't easy. I still feel guilty."

"That'll wear off."

"Everything here is so different." Merlin looked up at some figures moving about on the roof. "The construction workers, for instance. You've got such a rich mix."

"We have to take what we can get," said Vernon. "Some of the guys are local, but we have a lot of immigrant labor as well. Mexicans, Cubans, Chinese, Hawaiians, Europeans of various kinds." He gave a teasing wink. "We might even have an odd Welshman somewhere in amongst them."

"I thought I noticed a couple of Indians."

"More than a couple, Merlin. We've got Navajo, Hopi, Pima, and Papago. No Apache, luckily. This hotel is being built by an international labor force." He saw a figure walking toward them. "Here's another member of it. Joe Santana. That's right, isn't it, Joe?"

"What is?" asked the site manager.

"Where were your parents born?"

"Tijuana."

"I rest my case."

"But they were brought up in L.A.," stressed Santana. "So was I, Tom. I'm an American citizen."

"We believe you." He indicated his companion. "Meet another architect. This is Merlin Richards."

"How do you do?" said Merlin, offering his hand.

Santana ignored it. "We got all the architects we can handle around here. I sometimes wish they'd just let us get on with building the damn place."

"You've done pretty well so far."

"Thanks."

"I gave him the grand tour," said Vernon.

"So I noticed."

"We've seen everything but the concrete block factory," said Merlin. "I'm dying to take a look around that."

"It's out of bounds," warned Santana.

"Oh."

"Remember that."

"If you say so."

"And don't get under our feet. We got work to do."

He walked off in the direction of the site office. Taken aback by the abrupt departure, Merlin raised an inquisitive eyebrow.

"Joe is a bit short on social skills," said Vernon, drily. "You have to get to know him before he begins to loosen up."

"I'm not sure I want to make the effort."

"Can't blame you for that." He looked across at the parking area. "No sign of Mr. Wright yet. My guess is that he probably won't make it out here this afternoon." Merlin's face crumpled with disappointment. "Don't worry. He'll be here tomorrow. I can almost guarantee that."

"Then I need to find somewhere to stay."

"Rosa will fix you up," he said, airily.

"We've only just met. I hate to impose."

"You want to see Mr. Wright, don't you?"

"Yes," affirmed Merlin. "Somehow or other, I'll be here tomorrow. Even if I have to sleep out in the desert."

"Not for long. It gets real cold out here at nights. And the first howl of a coyote would send you scurrying for cover. No, you speak to Rosa. She'll help." He pushed his glasses up the bridge of his nose again. "Oh, and one last thing."

"Yes, Tom?"

"Don't expect too much."

"From what?"

"Your meeting with Mr. Wright. He may be a little preoccupied. Apart from anything else, he'll probably have his wife with him. And the children."

"I see."

"I don't think you do, Merlin." He stepped in closer and lowered his voice. "How much do you know about Mr. Wright?"

"I've read everything I could about his work."

"His work, yes. You've obviously studied that and were

able to see examples of it up in Illinois and Wisconsin. But I was talking about his personal life."

"I know next to nothing about that."

"Then it's high time you learned a few facts."

"Why?"

A long pause. "Let's take a stroll," said Vernon.

5

WHEN HE FINALLY met up with her again, Rosa Lustig was sitting on a folding stool outside her tent. There was a sketch pad across her knee, and her pencil moved fluently. A coat around her shoulders kept at bay the cool breeze that had sprung up. Engrossed in her work, she did not hear Merlin come up behind her.

"What are you doing?" he asked.

She cried out in surprise and sat upright.

"I'm sorry," he said, stepping around to face her. "Didn't mean to startle you like that."

"It's okay."

"Stupid of me."

"Forget it."

"What were you working on?"

"Oh, I was just playing around with an idea."

"May I see?"

"Sure." She handed over the sketch pad. "It's very crude at this stage, so don't be too harsh."

Merlin studied the design. It was made up of a series of overlapping chevrons, carefully shaded to throw them into relief. He gave a quiet whistle of appreciation.

"This is great!"

"You don't have to flatter me, Merlin."

"No, I mean it. I really love this motif. It's got the power of true simplicity."

"Imagine four of them together, each set at a different angle to vary the pattern. Can you visualize that?"

"Easily. It'd be very effective."

"I think so."

"Same principle as some of the concrete blocks here."

"Yes," she said, evenly. "There are similarities."

He gave her the sketch pad. "This is good. But what about those other designs you promised to show me?"

"You'll see them."

"I insist, Rosa. Where do you get your ideas?"

"Anywhere and everywhere."

"Just like me. Pick up a good thing where you find it."

"Exactly." She held up the pad. "This came out of a trip I made to a Hopi reservation."

"Tom Vernon mentioned that name. It's an Indian tribe."

"That's right. I spent some time with them and with the Navajo. Most people think their art is very primitive, but I still believe they can teach us something about symbols."

"No question of that."

She got up from her seat. "So? How was the tour?"

"A joy from start to finish. Tom was marvelous."

"I knew he would be."

"He must've been bored stiff with all my questions, but he never showed it. Tom knows *everything* about that hotel. He kept telling me that the architect is Albert Chase McArthur, and maybe he is. But I know one thing. Frank Lloyd Wright was holding his hand when he designed it."

"Did you say that to Tom?"

"Four or five times."

"What was his answer?"

"That Mr. Wright is far from happy with the result. If he *had* designed the Arizona Biltmore, there would have been substan-

tial differences. Tom listed some of them." He gave an involun-
tary yawn. "Oh, excuse me."

"You're dead beat."

"No, I'll hold out for a few more hours yet."

"Give up any hope of seeing Mr. Wright today."

"That's what Tom said. He won't come now." He put up a
hand to stifle another yawn. "By the way, Tom's invited me to
have breakfast with him tomorrow."

"Oh?"

"If I can hitch a lift into Phoenix, that is."

"I'll take you myself."

"I couldn't put you to that trouble, Rosa."

"It's no trouble. Besides, I'll have a couple of letters to mail,
so I'll need to go into town again."

"We'd have to be back here by noon," said Merlin. "According to Tom, that's the most likely time for Mr. Wright to show
up. The warmest part of the day."

"We'll be back." She saw his eyelids flicker. "You're almost
out on your feet, Merlin. Call it a day."

"I'm fine, really."

"Don't argue. You need to catch up on some sleep."

"This early?"

"It'll soon be dark, believe me. Sun's already sinking right
down. And there's nothing much to do around here at night.
Unless you want to play cards with the guys from the construction gang. No," she said, pulling back the flap of her tent, "you
can get some shut-eye in there."

He was astounded. "With you?"

"Well, I wasn't planning to sit out here all night."

"Are you sure you don't mind, Rosa?"

"Why should I?" she said, easily. "As long as you understand that all I'm offering you is a couple of blankets and the
chance of a long rest."

"Fair enough."

"Not that you'd have much strength for anything else."

He was almost bashful. "That's true."

"What's the matter? Have you never spent a night in a tent with a woman before?" A mocking grin appeared. "Oh, I forgot. You're Welsh. They're very religious, aren't they?"

"That's right. We always say our prayers before we make love." A third yawn caught him unawares. "Maybe I do need a short nap."

"You need much more than that, Merlin."

She took him into the tent and showed him where he could sleep. As he accepted the blankets gratefully, he noticed the large portfolio propped up against the tent pole.

"Could I take a peep at your designs?" he asked.

"There's not much light in here."

"Leave the flap open, and I'll manage."

"I doubt it." She kissed him softly on the cheek. "Goodnight, Merlin."

"Goodnight—and thanks."

Rosa stepped out of the tent and tied back the flaps before settling down on her stool. Her pencil was soon at work again. Ten minutes later, she peered into the tent and saw exactly what she had expected. Still wearing shirt and trousers, Merlin was fast asleep under his blankets.

The portfolio lay unopened beside him.

IT WAS WELL past midnight before the recurring dream sharpened its terror. Clothes in tatters and money all gone, Merlin returned to Merthyr Tydfil to confess his failure. Daniel Richards was in his customary posture at the drawing board.

He did not even look up when his son went meekly into his office. Merlin stood there, a bedraggled penitent.

"Hello, Dad," he said.

"I knew you'd come crawling back sooner or later."

"It didn't work out."

"What did I tell you?"

"I had a run of bad luck."

"No more than you deserve."

"Aren't you pleased to see me?"

Daniel lifted his head for the first time. His eyes were full of disgust as he appraised his son's wretched condition.

"You *dared* to come home in that state?"

"I had to, Dad."

"Where's your self-respect, mun?"

"I lost it along the way."

"No fame and fortune in America, then?" gloated his father. "No glorious career alongside Frank Lloyd Wright?"

"He wouldn't even see me."

"Why the hell should he?"

"Everything depended on that."

"So much for spreading your bloody wings!"

"Don't be sarcastic."

"Be glad that I'm not foaming at the mouth," snarled his father. "You betrayed us. Now, where is it?"

"I was robbed in New York, and again in Chicago."

"Where's the harp?"

"All I had left were the clothes I stood up in."

"Where's my mother's harp?"

"I was reduced to begging in the street."

"It was the only thing of value to leave Merthyr. A cherished family heirloom, and you took it all the way to that godforsaken country. What have you done with it?"

"I sold it to get the fare home."

Daniel was enraged. "You what?"

"I'll buy another one, Dad. I promise."

"You *sold* our harp?"

"It was the only way I could get back."

"But we don't want you here," howled his father, rising

from his chair. "Don't you understand that? I don't want you, and your mother thinks you're a disgrace, and your sister can't even bear to hear your name. We knew a Merlin Richards we could love and respect. Don't try to palm this sniveling ragamuffin off on us. Take him away! Take him away!"

Seizing the drawing board, he used it to belabor his son's head. Merlin cowered beneath the onslaught.

"Get him out!" roared Daniel. "He's no use to this family. Drive him away! We disown him! Drive him away! Get rid of him once and for all!"

As the blows grew harder, Merlin's ears were suddenly filled with a deafening series of chords played on a harp. The instrument seemed to be inside his head. Its strings were his brains, plucked by white-hot fingers. Merlin realized that his father was trying to smash his way through to the coveted harp with his bloodstained drawing board.

Music and pain blended in such searing agony that his skull seemed to be splitting apart like an apple cleft in two. Instantly awake, Merlin sat up with a silent cry of horror. But the nightmare continued. Instead of escaping his father, he was still at his mercy. Daniel Richards was standing over him in the darkness to resume the vengeful punishment.

Merlin put his hands up instinctively to ward off blows that never came. The figure in the tent was not his father at all but some voiceless stranger, seen only in hazy outline, staring out of the gloom at him. Before Merlin could challenge him, the man slipped quickly away through the gap between the flaps and merged with the darkness of the night.

Still groggy with fatigue, Merlin was not sure if the anonymous visitor was real or imagined. He leaned over to look down at Rosa. Wrapped in a blanket, she was fast asleep and breathing steadily. No harm had come to her. He had sensed menace, but it had not been directed at Rosa. He fumbled his way to the tent flaps and tied them together again. Then he lay down once more.

Within seconds, he was spiraling into another dream.

INGRID HANSA WAS in a testy mood. She sipped her coffee without really tasting it, then put her cup back in the saucer.

"Why did you invite him in the first place?" she said.

"I took a liking to the guy," replied Tom Vernon.

"Does that mean you have to have breakfast with him?"

"He's broke, Ingrid. It won't hurt me to put at least one decent meal inside him. He deserves a break."

"Don't we all?" she murmured.

"Nobody forced *you* to come along."

"I was hoping we'd be alone, Tom."

Ingrid Hansa was a plump woman in her mid-twenties with plain features and blond hair swept back severely, imprisoned with a tight bow. Large earrings dangled from pudgy lobes. She wore a light blue velour blouse above a dark blue cotton skirt. A red scarf was knotted loosely just above her ample bosom.

"Look," she said, making a conscious effort to relax, "I don't mean to crowd you, but we have lots to discuss."

"There'll be time."

"Not if this guy is going to barge in on us."

"His name's Merlin. Who knows? You might go for him."

"Don't hold your breath."

"He's Welsh."

"So what?"

"I thought you liked the Celtic strain in a man."

She shot him a glance of reproof and snatched up her cup again. Tom Vernon chuckled and put a consoling hand on her arm. When he whispered soothing words in her ear, she began to relax again. He even coaxed the beginning of a smile out of her.

"Well," she conceded, "I don't suppose it'll hurt us to be nice to the guy for an hour."

"He's harmless enough, Ingrid."

"Not if he's got stars in his eyes about Mr. Wright."

"We all started out that way," he reminded her.

"How will he get into Phoenix?"

"He'll find a way."

They were seated at a table against the far wall. Ingrid had her back to the door, but Vernon made sure that he could keep it under surveillance with the occasional glance. He checked his wristwatch and saw that Merlin was now twenty minutes late. He was about to express mild irritation when the Welshman came into the café and looked around. Spotting his friend, he headed for their table.

"Sorry to have kept you waiting, Tom," he said, shaking his hand. "I overslept."

"No problem. Take a seat."

"Thanks."

When Merlin had settled down, he was introduced to Ingrid. She gave him a firm handshake but a tepid smile. Merlin was slightly unsettled by her. There was a tomboy bluntness about her he had never met in a young woman before, and her aquamarine eyes had a piercing coldness.

"Ingrid is a colleague of mine," said Vernon.

"Ah," said Merlin, interest sparked. "You work with Mr. Wright as well, then?"

"Occasionally. In the drafting room."

"That must be a real honor."

"It's no rest cure, I know that. He's a slave driver."

"Art is never easy," said Vernon with a grin. "Did you sleep well last night, Merlin?"

"Eventually."

"Too noisy?"

"I wouldn't have heard a steamroller passing over me."

"You certainly look a lot better."

"I feel it."

Merlin had washed, shaved, and smartened himself up as best he could. His coat had been left back at the camp, and he wore the waistcoat over an open-necked shirt. The black eye had surrendered even more ground, and his face had regained something of its old charm.

Vernon picked up the menu and offered it to him. "Why don't we order?"

"Could we hang on a few minutes for Rosa?" said Merlin. "She only went to post some letters."

Ingrid bristled. "Rosa Lustig is with you?"

"She drove me into town."

"I had no idea that *she* was invited."

"She wasn't," said Vernon, calmly. "Not directly, that is. But she's welcome to join us. There's plenty of room at the table."

"There'd be even more if I'd been warned about this," she snapped at him. "You know how I feel about Rosa."

"What's the trouble?" asked Merlin.

"There isn't any," assured Vernon. "All four of us are going to have a nice, civilized meal together. It's what adults do. Isn't it, Ingrid?"

She said nothing, but her anger visibly subsided. Merlin did his best to translate some of the glances and gestures passing between the two colleagues, but their private language was too obscure for him. In the mirror on the wall, he caught sight of Rosa in the doorway.

"Here she is now," he said with some misgiving.

Vernon was on his feet. "Over here, Rosa!"

"Hi!" she said, crossing to the table. "Hi, Ingrid."

"Hello, Rosa."

"Good to see you again."

Notwithstanding her earlier protest, Ingrid was on her best

behavior. She even allowed a token hug. Merlin saw no animosity toward the other woman in Rosa's manner. The latter settled down happily beside Ingrid, reached for the menu, and scanned it avidly.

"What's everybody having?" she said.

When the orders had been given to the waitress, they pushed around some neutral topics amicably enough. Merlin noted that Tom Vernon steered the conversation subtly away from potential areas of friction between the two women. All four of them were given the illusion that they were actually enjoying themselves.

Ingrid waited until the food arrived before she fired her question, with a sweetness that failed to conceal the underlying malice.

"What exactly are you doing here, Rosa?" she asked.

Rosa stiffened. "Doing here?"

"Trying to eat her food in peace," said Vernon.

"In Arizona, I mean," continued Ingrid, impervious to the sharp nudge from her colleague. "There's no work to keep you out on that site, is there? Mr. McArthur turned down your designs weeks and weeks ago. So why are you still hanging around?"

"Ingrid!" chided Vernon.

"I just want to know, that's all."

"Then you're going to be disappointed," said Rosa quietly. "So why don't you fill that evil mouth of yours with food and let it do something useful for a change?"

"What's going on here?" said Merlin in some discomfort.

"Nothing," soothed Vernon.

"Why this atmosphere?"

"She started it," said Rosa levelly.

Ingrid smirked. "All I did was ask a simple question."

"Wrapped in barbed wire."

"Ladies—*ladies.*" Vernon held up both hands. "Merlin is our guest. What's he going to think if you two start bickering in front of him?"

"That's not going to happen," said Rosa.

"So what *are* you doing here?" pressed Ingrid.

"Taking a vacation."

"Who is he this time?"

Rosa picked up her cup and tossed her coffee down the front of Ingrid's blouse. As the other woman shrieked in pain and dabbed at her breasts with a napkin, Rosa got to her feet with great dignity and turned to Merlin. Her voice was calm.

"Take your time," she said. "I need some fresh air. I'll wait for you in the car."

6

S A I L I N G   S E R E N E L Y   O U T the door, Rosa left chaos in
her wake. Ingrid's scream reached a new pitch. Jumping up in
alarm, she shook the whole table and knocked over her chair.
The commotion brought two waitresses and the manager running
out from the kitchen. Other customers stood up to see what was
going on. For a few seconds Merlin was too embarrassed even
to move, not knowing whether to follow Rosa or stay to placate
her victim.

Tom Vernon came to the rescue. He put his arm around
Ingrid and gave her his own napkin to push down inside her
brassiere. The coffee had been hot, but not scalding; the hys-
terical screech was really a cry of humiliation. Vernon managed
to pacify her slightly, then guided her toward the washroom at
the rear of the building. By the time he handed her over to one
of the waitresses, Ingrid's wail had become a wild sobbing.

Glad that the incident was over, the manager gestured the
other customers back to their seats and waved away Vernon's
profuse apology.

"If that's the worst that happens in here," he said with an
indulgent smile, "I'll be a very happy man."

"It was an accident," lied Vernon.

"It always is, sir. Jeannie will move you to another table."

He flicked his fingers at the other waitress, and she moved

swiftly into action, clearing an adjacent table for occupation before inviting the two men to sit there, and they were soon reunited with their breakfasts. Everything else was taken off into the kitchen with the coffee-stained tablecloth.

"The show's over," sighed Vernon. "Sorry about all that."

"It's not your fault."

"It is. I should never have brought Ingrid. But she only arrived in Phoenix last night and asked if we could have breakfast together this morning. What could I say? Besides, I thought you might enjoy meeting another of Mr. Wright's faithful acolytes."

"I did," said Merlin. "While she was here."

"Truth is, I had no idea you'd turn up with Rosa."

"She sort of invited herself along."

"Rosa does that."

"Do you think I should go after her?"

"No," insisted Vernon. "Stay and eat your food. Don't let a little catfight like that put you off." He glanced toward the washroom. "Ingrid will be cleaning up in there for ages. Much as I like her, I'm bound to say that she asked for it. I did my best to head her off, but Ingrid was determined to put the knife in."

"Why did she goad Rosa like that?"

"Long story."

"Seemed to be some professional jealousy between them."

"It goes deeper than that," said Vernon, tactfully. "But I'm not one to tell tales. You'd have to ask Norm himself."

"Norm?"

"Norm Kozelsky. Another one of Mr. Wright's boys. He was up at Taliesin when Ingrid and Rosa were both around." He picked up his fork. "But let's forget them. They've caused enough trouble for one morning. I invited you here for breakfast. Eat up."

"Oh . . . yes."

Merlin reluctantly took up a knife and fork, picking at his

food without conviction. He was troubled to have been the cata-
lyst for the argument between the two women. Ingrid had been
pleasant to him until she realized that he was with Rosa Lustig,
when her attitude had shifted dramatically. He, in turn, was now
forced to reevaluate his erstwhile friend. Rosa had not struck
him as the kind of person who'd throw a cup of hot coffee over
someone, least of all another woman. It was disturbing.

"Still with me?" asked Vernon, jokingly.

"What?" Merlin came out of his reverie. "Yes, Tom."

"So what would you like to know?"

"Is Mr. Wright definitely visiting the site today?"

"I wouldn't swear to it. You can never use a word like 'definitely' about Mr. Wright. He's far too capricious for that. What he
likes to do is to make an unannounced visit to a site. To catch people
off guard. That way he gets a truer picture of what's been going on."

Merlin was deflated. "So he may not turn up at all?"

"In all probability, he will. But that's as high as I'd put it."
He began to butter some toast. "Mr. Wright *has* to inspect the
Biltmore at some stage. It's one of the main reasons we made
this sudden dash to Arizona."

"Good."

"You'll get to see him, Merlin."

"I won't leave until I do." He sprinkled some salt on the
edge of his plate. "Tell me some more about his private life."

"Maybe I've told you too much already."

"No, no," said Merlin. "It was fascinating. It's helped me to
understand him. I had no idea that he'd led such a—well, such
a tempestuous life."

"There are no half-measures with Frank Lloyd Wright."

"Such astounding vitality!"

"That's one word to describe it, I guess."

"He must be nearly sixty."

"At least. But he can still run rings around the lot of us."

"You were telling me about his second wife. Miriam Noel."

"Sad case!"

"Did their divorce finally go through?"

"It was a difficult business," said Vernon discreetly. "I wouldn't care to know the full details. According to the rumors, Miriam got pretty desperate in the later stages."

"But she's gone now."

"In the legal sense."

"Mr. Wright is married to his third wife."

"Yes, Olgivanna. A delightful lady."

"She must be."

"They're very happy together. And they're devoted to Iovanna, their child. Mrs. Wright also has a daughter by her first marriage, Svetlana."

"It's so complicated," said Merlin. "This sort of thing just never happens where I come from. Divorce is a real stigma."

"It is here—in some people's eyes. He's spent a whole lifetime battling against prudes. They've said some scathing things about him." He winced slightly. "But then, so has Miriam Noel. And she goes on saying them."

"Even after the divorce?"

"Miriam hasn't exactly bowed out gracefully. She's dead, but she won't lie down. Whenever she can, she still tries to stir up trouble for them."

"How?"

"I daren't ask."

INGRID HANSA NEEDED over twenty minutes to recover from the shock of the attack upon her. She took great pains with the choice of her clothing and cosmetics, all too aware of her physical shortcomings. Now she was mortified to see herself in the washroom mirror. The velour blouse had a hideous stain down the front, the coffee had also spattered her skirt, and tears had ruined her makeup.

When she finally emerged, the damage had been partially repaired, but her pride was clearly still in tatters. She mumbled an apology to the two men, then headed for the door.

"I'd better go," said Vernon, on his feet at once. "I think Ingrid may need me."

"Time for me to push off as well."

"This wasn't the way I'd planned it."

"I know," said Merlin with a grin. "Thanks, anyway."

"If I get the chance, I'll put in a good word for you with Mr. Wright."

"That'd be great, mun."

Vernon left some money on the table and led the way out. After a brief handshake, he went trotting off along the sidewalk to catch up with Ingrid. Merlin watched him go, then turned to cross the street. He halted in his tracks. Rosa's car was no longer parked on the opposite side. In its place was a Plymouth with a damaged headlight. He looked up and down the street, but her Chevrolet was nowhere to be seen.

Mild panic seized him. Had she abandoned him? Had the row with Ingrid made her flee? It would be a cruel irony if Frank Lloyd Wright chose to visit the Biltmore site at a time when he was stranded alone in Phoenix. He put a hand into his pocket to finger his last few dollars, so carefully harbored against a dire emergency. Had that emergency come? Should he invest some of the money in a taxi or attempt a long and dusty walk?

He grasped at a wild hope. Rosa had merely driven around the corner to avoid the danger of another brush with Ingrid. She would be waiting in the intersecting street. Merlin ran to the corner and scanned it. No Chevrolet. He sprinted back in the other direction in case she had simply gone three-quarters of the way around the block. Plenty of cars were parked in the side street, but Rosa's was not among them.

Merlin tried to reassure himself. A woman who had shown such kindness to him would hardly forsake him now. If she let him share her tent for the night, she would not deny him a lift back to the site. Yet where could she be?

A toot on the horn put him out of his misery. The Chevrolet came around a corner two blocks away and accelerated toward him. Merlin sighed with gratitude. When the car stopped, he leaped straight in.

"Where were you?"

"Just cruising around," she said with a shrug. "When I was parked across the street, two guys stopped by to hassle me. I don't have to put up with that kind of thing anymore, so I just went for a little drive."

"They hassled you?"

"It was nothing serious."

"Where are they?" he said, angry. "Point them out to me, Rosa."

"They've gone now."

"I won't let anyone hassle you. Who were they?"

"The sort of guys who give me that look."

"Like the one who was staring at you yesterday?"

"Yes."

"I should've punched him on the nose!"

"That wouldn't have helped," she said with a wan smile. "In a town like this, there are too many of them. It was almost like being back in Indiana."

"Is that where you grew up?"

"Yes, Merlin. Real fast."

She drove away from the curb in a way that told him the subject was now closed. Also on the prohibited list was any mention of the incident at the café. Rosa was patently in no mood to discuss Ingrid Hansa.

Merlin held his peace. It was her car. He waited for her to set the agenda. They were a mile out of town before she broke the silence.

"You can stay again tonight, if you like."

"Tonight?"

"In my tent."

"Oh . . . thanks, Rosa."

"But that's it, I'm afraid."

"Whatever you say."

"I have to leave tomorrow."

"Where are you going?"

The question hung unanswered in the air. For the rest of the journey, Rosa was too enmeshed in her own thoughts to speak to him. Merlin was not offended. He had plenty to reflect upon.

When they reached the site, she drove on past the parking area and snaked through the tents. The Chevrolet squealed to a halt, and she killed the engine. As if to signal that communication lines were open again, she patted Merlin's knee and gave him a token smile.

"Help me with the food," she asked.

"Food?"

"I bought a few provisions for us."

She hopped out of the car and opened the trunk. When Merlin joined her, she handed him two tall brown paper bags. As he put them down gently inside the tent, he glimpsed an assortment that included bread, cheese, fruit, soft drinks, and a jar of pickles. His guilt stirred, he went back out to her.

"You ought to let me contribute something toward all this," he said, putting his hand into his pocket. "I can't go on sponging off you."

"Keep your money," she insisted, happily. "You may need it. This is on me. My farewell treat."

"But you've done so much for me, Rosa. I was struggling until you came along. What can I do for you in return?"

"You've already done it."

"Have I?"

She gave him a kiss on the cheek, then took a camera out of the trunk before closing the lid. When she disappeared into the tent, he hovered uncertainly outside it, his eye traveling across to the hotel. It was more imposing than ever.

"Come on in!" she invited. "No charge."

"Can I ask you a favor, Rosa?"

"Sure." Her head popped out. "What is it?"

"I wondered if you could spare a sheet or two of that cartridge paper. I'd like to do some sketching."

"Take the whole pad. I've finished with it now."

"A couple of sheets will do. And a pencil."

Rosa put her head to one side and looked at him with a sudden fondness. Merlin felt a rustle of affection for her without quite knowing what to do about it. There was a directness in her gaze that excited him, but it was tempered by a deep sense of regret, as if she felt they had met too late for anything but the most casual friendship. Merlin put out a tentative hand.

"I'll get the paper," she said.

And she vanished into the tent.

THE ARIZONA BILTMORE Hotel was throbbing with noise and alive with activity. Construction workers were crawling all over the main building, adding refinements, glazing windows, and putting the last sections of the dazzling copper roof in position. Armies of gardeners were planting countless eucalyptus saplings. Trucks were tipping loads of topsoil to create an eighteen-hole golf course that would be dotted with long-established giant saguaro cacti and newly imported trees. Water was already playing in the fountain. The Biltmore was a huge artificial oasis in the desert.

Yet something was amiss. As he sat on an upturned crate and used his portfolio as his drawing board, Merlin was struck by a sense of unease. Mistakes were being made before his eyes, and yet he was somehow unable to identify them.

His artist's impression of the hotel included none of the

teeming hordes who labored on it. He was visualizing the Arizona Biltmore in its completed state, supplementing what he could actually see with what he knew of Frank Lloyd Wright's celebrated theories of form and function, his exploration of texture and pattern, his gospel of organic architecture.

There was something wrong. When Merlin compared his own sketch with the reality that was mushrooming before him, he began to understand what it was. His version—inspired by Wright—was smaller, more compact, and more wedded to correct proportion. The real version was vitiating some of the master's basic principles. Compromise was a cunning saboteur.

A surly voice broke in upon his meditations.

"What the hell are you doing here?" demanded the guard.

"Sketching the hotel," said Merlin.

"Who gave you permission?"

"Well . . . nobody."

"What right have you got to be on this site?"

"I'm not doing any harm," said the Welshman, standing up to face a glowering Pete Bickley. "I just wanted a quick sketch as a memento, that's all."

"You're trespassing on private property."

"I'm an architect."

"Not one employed on this project."

"I'm waiting to meet Frank Lloyd Wright."

"Then wait somewhere else," ordered Pete, jerking a thumb toward the site entrance. "Get off this property, or you'll be prosecuted. As for that—" He snatched the paper from Merlin. "I'll have to confiscate it."

"Give it here!" yelled Merlin, trying to grab it back. "That's mine."

"Not anymore."

"I've worked hard on that."

He lunged at the sketch again, but Pete pulled it away. Merlin was furious. He bunched an angry fist, but the punch was never thrown. Instead, he found himself staring down the barrel of a revolver.

"Want to argue about it?"

"That's my sketch."

"Disappear."

"I want it."

"Then take it off me."

Pete dangled the sketch invitingly in one hand while holding the gun menacingly in the other. Merlin was smoldering with rage, but there was nothing he could do. The tense pause lasted for several minutes, until Rosa came striding quickly up to them.

"Put that gun away, Pete."

"Keep out of this."

"You've got no call to draw it."

"This guy is an intruder."

"Merlin is with me."

"So what?"

"Let him have his sketch back."

She stood between the two men so that the weapon was pointed at her. Pete Bickley glared defiantly at Rosa before slowly capitulating. The lazy smile oozed back into place. The gun was dropped into its holster. Pete threw a contemptuous glance at the sketch, then handed it over.

Merlin put it quickly into his portfolio and retied the ribbons. He was baffled by the exchange between Rosa and the guard, at whom she was still looking steadily. All three of them remained in a silent tableau.

The roar of an approaching vehicle jerked them back into life. They turned to see a Packard straight-eight touring car speeding through the site entrance.

"It's Mr. Wright," Rosa said.

7

FRANK LLOYD WRIGHT was behind the steering wheel
of the elegant monster as it swept into the car park and skidded
to a halt. His wife, Olgivanna, was beside him, his daughter and
stepdaughter in the backseat. All four wore protective helmets
and goggles for the dusty drive across the desert. It was a dra-
matic entry, and it served its purpose. Almost everyone on-site
was staring at the newcomers.

One hand on the tonneau windshield, Wright stood erect in
the open-topped convertible and gazed at the hotel like an
explorer surveying newly discovered land from the prow of a
sailing ship. He wore a loose-fitting white shirt with a high,
starched, detachable collar, a flowing tie with ambitions of
being a scarf, and a pair of tweed trousers. Designed by
himself, his apparel was made up by a tailor in Chicago. It
had undoubted style.

Merlin was hypnotized. He was looking at a legend. The
sense of exhilaration was almost overwhelming. A journey that
had taken him several weeks and cost him almost all that he
possessed had come to fruition. The setbacks, the doubts, the
delays, and the embittered parting with his father faded completely away. This moment justified everything that Merlin had
believed and done.

The feeling of euphoria did not last long. As soon as the

architect stepped out of the car, Merlin felt a lurch of disappointment. Frank Lloyd Wright was relatively short. Expecting him to have the giant proportions of his artistic reputation, Merlin was taken aback to see the rather stocky figure strutting gracefully toward the hotel with a cane in his hand. As people began to converge on him, Wright stopped to remove his goggles and helmet, allowing wavy white hair of bardic luxuriance to tumble out.

Joe Santana and the others surrounded Wright, shielding him from view. Rosa sounded oddly nervous.

"Let's hope we've caught him on a good day."

"What do you mean?" said Merlin.

"He can be very spiky with strangers."

"Tom warned me not to expect too much."

"I'd go along with that," she said. "Just remember. You may have traveled all the way here to meet him, but Mr. Wright didn't come to Arizona just to meet you. He has a lot of other things on his plate. We'll have to bide our time."

"Will you introduce me?"

"If I get the chance."

It was a long wait. Wright was involved in an earnest debate with his impromptu welcoming committee. One by one, they peeled away, allowing Merlin by degrees to see more of the great man. In the end, only Joe Santana remained. He nodded in the direction of the main building, then walked toward it, Wright doing all the talking beside him.

They passed within a few feet of Merlin and his two companions, but Wright did not even notice them; he was too absorbed in his monologue. Santana was showing a grudging respect. Pausing some thirty yards closer to the hotel, Wright used his cane to point to various features and to draw fresh plans in the air.

Rosa nudged Merlin, and the two of them moved stealthily toward the architect. Pete Bickley spat on the ground before sauntering off toward the concrete block factory. Merlin continued his vigil at closer quarters. His flickering disillusion had been completely extinguished. Proximity to Frank Lloyd Wright made him seem much taller than he was, and the deep, booming voice helped to increase his size even more. Wright was every bit the equal of his legend. His charisma was almost tangible. Merlin felt as if an electric current were passing through him.

Wright's sharp eye raked the building mercilessly as he fired rhetorical questions at Santana. The site manager finally broke in with a few defensive sentences, then excused himself and moved away. Merlin caught the full force of Santana's glare, but it bounced harmlessly off him. Nothing could hurt him now: His mission in life was standing only yards away.

Rosa decided that the opportunity had come. She ushered Merlin forward so that they were level with the architect.

"Hello, Mr. Wright," she said, chirpily. "Remember me?"

His whole body swung around as he looked across at her. A guarded smile. "Of course I do. How are you, Rosa?"

"Fine, thanks."

"Good."

"I'd like to introduce Merlin Richards," she said, motioning him forward. "He's a young Welsh architect. Came all this way just to meet you."

Frank Lloyd Wright turned a searching gaze on him, then gave a noncommittal nod of greeting. Merlin had rehearsed his speech for weeks, but the words would simply not come out in any intelligible order. All he could do was to stand there with a vacuous grin and let Rosa speak on his behalf.

"Merlin went up to Spring Green at first, but they told him you'd come down to Arizona. So he followed you to Phoenix." There was an awkward pause. "He's a great admirer of your work. He's read just about everything that's been written about you in European journals. Merlin's a disciple of your philosophy of architecture."

"So was Albert Chase McArthur! Once upon a time."

"He's brought his portfolio with him."

Merlin was fighting hard against his unexpected attack of shyness. He lifted his portfolio up to display it, but Wright had already turned back to continue his scrutiny of the building. Talking quietly to himself, the architect jabbed away with his cane once more, then clicked his tongue in irritation. After clearing his throat, he tossed a sudden question at Merlin.

"What do you think of the hotel, Mr. Richards?"

"Oh, well, I think it's wonderful," said Merlin with a tremble in his voice. "I congratulate you, Mr. Wright."

A stern face was turned instantly upon him.

"On what?"

"Your contribution."

"It was largely ignored."

"I didn't realize that."

"Then look at it properly, man!"

"That's what I tried to do, Mr. Wright."

"And didn't you *see*?"

"See what?"

"The Arizona Biltmore is an architectural disaster!"

Without another word, Frank Lloyd Wright marched off toward his family. The interview was decisively over. Merlin was in despair.

ROSA DISAPPEARED FOR most of the afternoon, and Merlin was left to brood on his failure. Had he come all that distance for this? To be slapped down with one astringent sentence? He was so disconsolate that he even began to wish he had stayed at home in Merthyr. His father might criticize him, but Daniel Richards did not have the power to crush his spirit so utterly.

Merlin did not blame Wright. When he put himself in the

architect's position, he saw how callow and unimpressive he must have appeared. Instead of presenting himself as an alert and promising young artist, Merlin came across as a tongue-tied bumpkin with no perception of quality in design. He berated himself for his incompetence.

There was not the faintest hope of repairing the damage. Frank Lloyd Wright had now left the site and would probably not return. Merlin Richards would already have been erased from his memory.

After walking aimlessly around the site, he made an effort to shake off his self-disgust and turn his attention to someone else. Rosa Lustig had taken the trouble to introduce him to his idol. Though the result had been devastating, she was not at fault. When he recalled her other acts of kindness, he saw how grateful he should be to her. Instead of wallowing in his own pain, he ought to find a means to repay her in some way, especially as she would be leaving the site on the next day.

Since he had no money, his possibilities were limited, but there was one thing he could do. Like any artist, Rosa thrived on praise. He could look at the designs in her collection so that he was able to give an informed judgment when she came back. Merlin was certain that he would like them.

The portfolio was still in the tent, propped up against the pole and bearing her full name. Rosa Judith Lustig. He brought it out into the daylight and sat cross-legged on the ground to sift through its contents. The designs, inspired by her travels in Arizona and New Mexico, were quite stunning. Simple motifs borrowed from Indian art had been transformed into something that blended the ancient and modern into a seamless whole. Whatever Rosa found, she had somehow made inimitably her own.

It was only when Merlin reached the last couple of drawings that he realized he was being watched. At first it was only a mild sensation of discomfort, but it soon grew into something more threatening. Merlin remembered the shadowy figure who came into their tent the previous night. Had the same man returned to continue his surveillance?

When he had studied the final design, he slipped it back into the portfolio, then quickly raised his eyes. He was just in time to see a head vanish behind the angle of a wooden cabin some twenty yards away. Dropping the portfolio on the ground, he leaped up and ran to the cabin with the burst of speed for which he had been renowned on the rugby field.

But there was no sign of the person he had glimpsed. Whoever it was must have been fit and lithe to hide himself so quickly in the rabbit warren of tents beyond the cabin. Merlin's dash was not in vain, however; it allowed him to witness something of great interest. Two figures were having an animated conversation outside the site office. The man was pointing toward the concrete block factory, and the woman was nodding gratefully. They seemed to know each other well.

Merlin told himself that Ingrid Hansa might have a perfectly innocent reason to talk to Joe Santana, but the sight of them together rang a distant bell of alarm.

"DID YOU REALLY like them?" she asked with an almost childlike need for approval. "Tell me the truth, Merlin."

"I loved them, Rosa."

"There's over a year's work in there."

"It's stupendous."

"Which did you like best?"

"The ones from the Navajo reservation."

"Those are my favorites as well."

"Did you do all that traveling on your own?"

"More or less."

"Wasn't it dangerous?"

"I've had to learn to look after myself."

Rosa had made a wood fire to cook them a meal, and they were eating it outside the tent in the fading light. A chill had come up on the desert now, and both had coats draped around their shoulders. The hot food was very welcome.

She looked across at him with a wan smile.

"I'm sorry things didn't work out for you, Merlin."

"I could kick myself."

"Don't give up hope."

"Mr. Wright will never let me near him again."

"We could have picked a better place and time," she decided. "He's feeling very touchy about the Biltmore. I should've realized that. Do you forgive me?"

"Of course."

"You did actually get to meet him."

"For all of thirty seconds."

"That's longer than some people have lasted."

They finished their meal and cleared the things away. He put all the rubbish in one of the trash bins that had been brought out to the camp.

"Where are you off to in the morning?" he asked.

"Back home."

"To Indiana?"

"No, no. I live in California now. I find the climate and the people a little more to my taste. What about you?"

He gave a shrug. "I'll just hit the road, I suppose."

"In which direction?"

"I haven't a clue. Suddenly, I've lost my compass."

"Compass?"

"Frank Lloyd Wright. He guided me here, Rosa. I took all my bearings from him." He shook his head sadly. "And what a mistake that turned out to be!"

"Merlin!"

"Let's face it, Rosa. It was a fiasco."

"No, it wasn't."

"Tom Vernon was right, you see."

"About what?"

"My secret ambition. To work alongside Mr. Wright. Deep down, I had this feeling that all I had to do was turn up and wave my drawings under his nose. Then he'd welcome me with open arms. Instead, he didn't even open my portfolio."

"Take heart." Her voice hardened. "You're not the only person to be rejected by him, believe me." Rosa brightened. "Anyway, enough of this breast-beating on our last night together. There've been some consolations."

Merlin rallied. "Yes—I met you!"

"It's been fun."

He felt another surge of affection and reached out impulsively to take her in his arms. Rose responded to his kiss at first, then eased him gently away.

"That was . . . very nice, Merlin."

"Why did you stop?"

"Because it would have got even nicer," she whispered, "and that's not part of the deal. Unfortunately." She gave him a peck on the cheek and broke away. "Besides, I have somewhere to go."

"But it's almost dark."

"It's not far to walk. Excuse me." She slipped into the tent for a few minutes to brush her hair, then reappeared, carrying something concealed in one of the brown paper bags. "If I'm late back, you turn in. I'll try not to disturb you."

"Where are you going?"

"To visit a friend."

"On the site?"

"More or less."

"Won't you need a torch?"

"I've left it for you. Under my blanket."

"Hang on a minute, Rosa."

"I can't."

"But I want to say something."

"It'll keep. I'm late already. Sleep well."

She went tripping off into the gloom and was soon lost from sight. There was such vivacity about her that it never occurred to Merlin that he would not see her alive again.

THE NIGHTMARE RETURNED to torment him, but the roles had been reassigned. It was not his father who spurned Merlin and assaulted him this time. It was Frank Lloyd Wright. Taking Merlin's portfolio from him, he tore it into shreds before throwing the pieces into the air to create a snowstorm of desecrated architecture.

As Merlin tried to protest, his hero started to bludgeon him with a drawing board made of decorated concrete. Each blow was a separate agony, and he was beaten almost senseless. When the drawing board turned into a harp, the punishment was accompanied by jangling harmonies as steel strings snapped and lacerated him all over. The harp was still pounding him into a discordant oblivion when he felt a rush of air so cold it woke him.

He opened his eyes to find himself alone in the tent. An icy wind was blowing the flaps open and shut. Merlin groped under Rosa's blanket for the torch and switched it on. The place was in disarray. A nocturnal visitor had called again, this time rifling Rosa's belongings, which were scattered all over the ground. When Merlin shone the light on the flaps, he saw that the canvas strips he had used to tie them shut had been sliced through.

His immediate concern was for Rosa's safety. Dressing quickly, he went out into the camp and began his search. The small torch was a poor assistant. There were lights in some of the cabins, and the embers of an occasional fire gave him some illumination, but he was really fumbling in a void. It was only when he got near the concrete block factory that he could actually see where he was going.

The factory was blazing with light and shuddering with noise as giant concrete mixers churned their contents to the right consistency to be poured into the molds. The resulting blocks were a decorative triumph, but Merlin had not been allowed to watch the process by which they were made.

Even in his state of high anxiety, he could not resist a peep through the window at the creative cacophony within. It was a remarkable sight: Bare-armed workmen in dusty overalls were laboring through the night to turn one of the lowliest and most despised of building materials into a thing of real beauty. Poured concrete was being treated with a respect that paid huge dividends. He was mesmerized by the whole process.

Merlin would have stayed there longer if he had not heard the voices of the guards on patrol. They came around the corner of the factory and swaggered toward him, briefly illuminated as they passed a window. Seeing the shotguns they were carrying, Merlin looked around for a place to hide. He was trespassing. If he could be upbraided for simply sketching the hotel, there was no telling what fate he would suffer if they caught him spying on operations in the factory.

Piles of concrete blocks stood nearby, drying out slowly for use at a later stage. Merlin dived behind the first pile and crouched low; but he was not alone in his refuge. His foot came up against something soft and bulky. He switched on the torch and directed its beam downward.

His heart became a drum, and his stomach rebelled, spewing up its contents. Merlin was looking at the blood-covered face of Rosa Lustig, her skull smashed to a pulp by one of the concrete blocks.

8

MERLIN RETCHED SO violently that he dropped the torch. As he lurched against the pile of blocks, he displaced several of them, and they fell to the ground with a loud thud. Even with the turmoil of the factory in their ears, the guards heard the noise and came running to investigate. The beams of their two flashlights met to illuminate the grisly scene.

Pete Bickley stared in disbelief at the murdered woman. "Jesus!"

"Poor kid!" said the other man, staring with ghoulish fascination. "Look at all that blood."

"It's Rosa." Pete was shuddering. "It's Rosa Lustig."

"I found her like this," explained Merlin, wiping his mouth with a handkerchief. "I just stumbled up against her."

"Shut up!" snarled Pete.

The other guard was a stickler for detail. "That block must've cracked her head right open. There's a hole big enough to put your fist in. One of her ears is hanging off."

"Call the cops," ordered Pete.

"I bet she didn't know what hit her."

"Do as I tell you, Dave!" Bickley pulled him away by the collar. "Call the cops. We got a murder on our hands."

"Oh boy! We sure have!"

Dave broke into a run and headed for the site office. Stom-

ach still churning, Merlin was finding it difficult to stand upright. He did not dare to look down at the corpse again.

"Come out of there!" yelled Pete.

"This had nothing to do with me."

"Come out!"

Peter grabbed him by the lapel and dragged him out from
behind the blocks. He then shoved Merlin hard against the wall
of the factory and leveled his shotgun at him.

"Why did you do it?"

"I didn't!"

"You killed Rosa!"

"She was my friend."

"Horseshit!"

"She was," pleaded Merlin. "She helped me."

"Is this how you thank her?"

"No!"

"Beating her brains out with a piece of concrete?" He put
the barrel of the weapon against Merlin's throat. "I oughta
shoot you down right here. It's no more than you deserve. A
man who can do a thing like *that*," he roared with a jerk of
his head toward Rosa, "shouldn't be allowed to walk above-
ground. I oughta do everyone a favor and pull this trigger.
Jesus! What kind of an animal are you?"

"It wasn't me."

"Save your lies for the cops."

"I didn't lay a finger on her."

"It looks like it."

"I only came out to search for Rosa."

"And you certainly found her!"

Pete forced himself to gaze down at the body once more. A
beautiful face had been turned into a hideous mess. The black
hair was matted with gore. Her neck had snapped. For a few
seconds, he was overcome with emotion. His shoulders sagged.
The shotgun hung loose in one hand. A tear began to form.

Merlin took a step toward him and widened his arms.
"I didn't kill her—I swear it!"
"You'll pay for this."
"When I found that she wasn't in the tent—"
"Shut your mouth!"
"But I'm trying to explain how I—"
"Shut it, I said!"

With both hands on the shotgun, Pete swung the butt upward with vicious force. It caught Merlin on the point of his chin and knocked his head back against the wall. As the blood began to seep out from his scalp wound, he fell to the ground in a heap. He was still unconscious when the wail of the police sirens battled with the howl of a coyote.

DELIVERED UP TO his dreams again, Merlin was beset by a series of images that repeated themselves with gathering speed. His father was slamming the door of the office in his face. Frank Lloyd Wright was tearing up his drawings. Rosa was hurling a cup of scalding coffee over him. Pete Bickley was firing his shotgun from close range. Joe Santana was smashing a concrete block over his head. Someone was destroying his harp with a sledgehammer. Ingrid Hansa was laughing hysterically at him.

Whichever way Merlin turned, he was met with pain and humiliation. As the images spun ever faster in his febrile imagination, a new and more immediate terror came. Someone was holding him down against his will and using a drill to bore a way in through the back of his skull. Too weak to resist, he moaned in pain and waited for the blessed release of death.

A faraway voice drifted into his ears.

"I'm done here. He's all yours, guys."

Rough hands were laid upon him to roll him over. Merlin raised leaden eyelids to get a hazy glimpse of a figure in a white coat, disappearing through a door. Someone lifted him so that he sat upright against a wall. The stinging pain at the back of his head was so intense that he put up a hand to relieve it. His fingers made contact with a pad, held in place with bandaging. When he tried to ask what they had done to him, Merlin learned that his jaw would not move. It seemed to be encased in solid concrete. His eyelids snapped shut.

"He's coming to at last," said a voice.

"About time," grunted another.

"Wake up, buddy." Someone shook him. "We need to talk."

"I could use another coffee."

"Lemme rustle one up."

Merlin heard footsteps moving away, a door opening, and a muted command. Another set of footsteps; two cups rattled in saucers as they were set on a table. Gratitude was mumbled. Footsteps departed. The door closed again. A match was struck. Heavy puffing.

As his hearing improved, so did his sense of smell. The acrid cigar smoke mingled with the pervasive stink of disinfectant and invaded his throat. He coughed himself more fully awake. His eyelids finally obeyed his instruction to open again.

He was propped up on an examination bed. The naked electric lightbulb showed him a small, featureless room with fading whitewash on the walls and a bare wooden floor. A glass cabinet was filled with elementary medical supplies. Two men sat behind a table on upright chairs, their eyes cold. One man was smoking a big cigar, the other had a pencil poised above a pad. Steam curled up from the two cups of coffee set out before them.

The cigar glowed as its owner inhaled deeply.

"The doc patched you up," he said hoarsely. "You got six stitches in that skull of yours, and you're lucky not to have that jaw wired up." He rolled the cigar across his mouth. "The doc says you must be a pretty tough hombre. Blow like that would have cracked most jaws open like a walnut. As it is, you'll just be taking meals through a straw for a coupla days."

Merlin used delicate fingers to explore the throbbing bruise that was his chin. It seemed to be twice its normal size. When he spoke, his jaw did not move, and the words dribbled out of the corner of his mouth.

"Where am I?" he asked.

"In police custody," said the man with the pad.

"Why?"

"You're being held as a suspect in a homicide inquiry."

"A prime suspect," added his colleague.

"Homicide?"

"The victim's name was Rosa Lustig."

It all came back with the force of a blow from the butt of a shotgun. Merlin recoiled from the gruesome memory and brought both hands up to his head.

"I didn't kill her," he cried. "I didn't touch Rosa."

"Calm down, son," advised the man with the cigar. "Before we go any further, you're entitled to know who we are. I'm Lieutenant Corbin, and this here is Sergeant Drummond." He turned to his colleague. "Do the honors, Walt."

Noah Corbin was a big, flabby man in his fifties with iron-gray hair. Although it was cold in the room, he had removed his jacket to reveal a white shirt stretched over a large paunch. Thick suspenders created depressions in his fleshy chest. His blue tie only ventured down as far as his sternum.

Walt Drummond was at least ten years younger, a slim, wiry man with dark hair and a neat mustache. Dressed in a crumpled suit, he was humming with nervous energy, constantly changing his sitting position. Both detectives were intimidating, but Merlin found the senior man slightly less alarming. Corbin had an avuncular expression and a measured croak. Drummond looked as if he was ready to use violence to speed up the interrogation.

Formalities over, Corbin opened a palm. "Tell it your way, son."

"I went out searching for Rosa and found her lying outside

the concrete block factory. That was all that happened, honestly. I was horrified when I saw her there. I threw up. Why should I kill her? Rosa was my friend. In fact—"

"Hold on, hold on!" said Corbin. "We want a statement, not a load of gibberish. Now don't rush. We got all night. Take it from the beginning. You say the lady was a friend?"

"Yes."

"How did you come to meet her?"

"She gave me a lift in her car."

"When?" pressed Drummond. "And exactly where?"

Corbin puffed nonchalantly. "Take it slow and easy."

Merlin collected his thoughts, then told his story with as much detail as he could recall. As he heard himself talking, he was surprised at how much had happened to him in such a short time. The only thing he omitted was his demoralizing encounter with Frank Lloyd Wright. In the circumstances, that seemed irrelevant.

While Drummond took notes, Corbin threw in the odd question to prod things gently along. When Merlin described how he had accidentally stumbled upon Rosa's dead body, the detectives exchanged a cynical glance. Corbin spooled back through the narrative in his mind.

"You mentioned a guy who was staring at Rosa," he said.

"Yes, that first time we drove into Phoenix. He was at one of the other tables in the café and hung about outside when we left."

"Did she know him?"

"Rosa said that she knew his type."

"Some kind of heavy breather, was he? Did the guy have his hand in the pocket of his pants while he was looking at her?"

"I didn't notice."

"Attractive girl. They always get pestered. But you said that Rosa handled the situation like she was used to it."

"Yes. It annoyed me more than it did her."

"Why were you annoyed?" asked Drummond.

"Because the man had no right to bother her like that."

"All he did was look."

"It was more than that," said Merlin.

"Most guys like to ogle a nice ass."

"Let's move on to that first night you spent together," said Corbin. "Both of you in the same tent. Right?"

"Yes."

"Side by side?"

"Yes."

"Alone in the dark with someone like that? You sure you didn't try to get more closely acquainted with her?"

"Quite sure!"

"Turn you down, did she?"

"No!"

"Then maybe she was the one who made the first move."

"Rosa wasn't like that."

"How do you know, son? According to your story, you met her less than forty-eight hours ago. You didn't exactly have plenty of leisure time to plumb her character, did you?" He dropped the cigar butt to the floor and ground it beneath his heel. "How many other women have picked you up on the road?"

Merlin shrugged. "None."

"And I bet none have let you sleep with them the way this one did. Hear what I'm saying, Merlin? We got our share of sassy girls around Phoenix, but very few of them would pick up a hitchhiker in the state you were in. Fewer still would come through with accommodation for two whole nights. This was one unusual lady you met out there in the desert." A deep chuckle. "I wish a few like that had crossed *my* path. Don't you, Walt?"

"Yep. Some guys have all the luck."

"You've got it wrong," argued Merlin. "Rosa wasn't that sort of girl at all."

"So why did she pick you up?" asked Drummond.

"Because we had something in common." He rode over the detective's snigger. "And I don't mean that. Rosa knew that the only reason I could be on that road was to get out to the hotel site. I'm an architect, she was a designer. We talked the same language."

Corbin grinned. "Especially inside a tent."

"No!" denied Merlin, vehemently.

"What's the matter? Didn't you like the girl?"

"Of course."

"Didn't you think she might warm up a cold night in the desert for you? Or did you leave your balls back home in Wales? What kind of a guy are you, Merlin?"

"Nothing happened between us."

"Did you *want* it to happen?"

"That's irrelevant."

"Did you?"

"It never crossed my mind."

"Did you?" pursued Corbin.

"I was there for other reasons."

A fist thumped the table. "DID YOU!"

"Yes!" confessed Merlin.

Corbin smiled complacently. "Now we're getting somewhere."

Merlin was furious. Wrongly suspected of the murder, he was now being accused of having lustful designs on Rosa as well.

"Rosa was a brilliant designer," he protested. "That was her whole life. She gave up everything for the sake of her art. That sort of commitment takes guts. I don't expect you to understand it—that's beyond you—but you might at least show some respect for her. Rosa was a marvelous girl." He jumped off the bed. "So stop making her sound like some kind of tramp!"

Walt Drummond was on his feet at once, easing his jacket open to show the holstered gun beneath it. Merlin stared back at him without flinching. Noah Corbin was unperturbed.

"Sit down again, son," he said.

"I'd rather stand, if you don't mind."

"We do mind. It irritates me, and it makes Walt nervous. You'd rather be cuffed and questioned in one of the cells, we can easily oblige you. It's much nicer in here, believe me." He put his thumbs behind his suspenders. "Do yourself a favor. Sit down."

Still fuming, Merlin eventually gave in. He hopped back up onto the bed and rested his back against the wall. Drummond let his coat fall back over the gun. Resuming his seat, he helped himself to a swig of coffee before picking up his pad again. Without taking his gaze off Merlin, the older detective reached out for his own coffee. He sipped it noisily.

"I believe you," he said at length. "I believe that nothing happened between the pair of you in that tent. You just didn't light her fire." He leaned forward. "That the reason you killed her, son?"

"No!"

"A thwarted lover. Happens all the time."

"I wouldn't have harmed Rosa for the world."

"Not deliberately, maybe," said Corbin, "but these things sometimes get out of hand. You pounce, she turns you down, rushes out of the tent. You give chase, try to persuade her. A struggle begins. Rosa screams. You want to shut her up before she arouses the guards. There's a concrete block nearby—"

"It wasn't like that."

"Then what was it like?"

"I've already told you."

"There're too many holes in your story."

"This is ridiculous!" said Merlin, hotly. "I'm a qualified architect. I've never been in trouble with the police for any reason whatsoever. I only came to this country in the first place out of professional curiosity. Do I look like the sort of person who could commit murder?"

"Yep," said Drummond, casually.

Corbin nodded his agreement. "We're all capable of it if pushed hard enough." He finished his coffee. "All you had in your pocket when we brought you in was three dollars and fifteen cents. No luggage, no fixed abode, no prospects. We could run you in as a vagrant, Merlin. Ever think of that? Now, see it the way it looks to us. Here's this bum, who wanders into town and hooks up with a girl because she's got a soft spot for guys down on their luck. He's got nothing, but she seems to have the lot—a car of her own, a tent, a purpose in life, money . . . That what you were after? Take the money and hightail it in the Chevy? Was that the plan?"

"There *was* no plan," said Merlin.

"It all happened on the spur of the moment?"

"I went searching for Rosa with the torch."

"Why?"

"Because I was worried about her."

"Wasn't it a bit late for that?"

"I was fast asleep."

"So you say."

"I was," insisted Merlin.

Noah Corbin put his hands behind his neck and leaned back in the chair, making it creak ominously and causing his shirt buttons to strain mutinously. He closed his eyes and seemed to doze off. He soon shook himself awake.

"I'm tired," he complained. "We're all tired. Why can't people get themselves killed in the middle of the day? It'd make our job a lot easier." He hauled himself to his feet. "Lock him up, Walt. We'll try again in the morning. After a night in the cell, he might be a bit more cooperative."

"I've told you the truth!" said Merlin.

"Your version of the truth, son. That's different."

Corbin took his jacket from the back of his chair and ambled out, leaving the door wide open. Drummond gestured for Merlin to follow. When they got out into the corridor, a uniformed policeman was waiting. He escorted Merlin to the cell block and opened the door of the cage with a key.

Merlin was pushed inside. As he looked around, he quailed. The cell was cramped, filthy, and full of aromatic memories of previous occupants. A cockroach scurried across the floor and vanished beneath the bunk bed. Spiders had staked out territories in the corners. A metal chamber pot stood in a corner.

Drummond enjoyed watching the prisoner's revulsion.

"Best room in the house," he mocked. "Just one thing. The last guy in here had a nasty habit. Used to split open the mattress so he could stick his dick into it." He gave a dull laugh. "I guess it's no worse than humping the old lady. And at least a mattress won't nag your ass off afterward."

The door clanged shut.

"Good night," Merlin said, absentmindedly.

"Yep," added Drummond. "Sweet dreams!"

9

M U R D E R   A T   T H E Biltmore site caused havoc and conster-
nation. The building of the hotel was an important undertaking
that would bring rich tourists and great prestige to the area.
Local businessmen and the Arizona newspapers supported the
venture wholeheartedly. Though work was behind schedule, the
contractor was confident that the original opening date would
not have to be postponed too drastically. Additional financing
had been poured into the project as its size increased and its
refinements became more grandiose. Nothing would be allowed
to dim the sparkle of the jewel of the desert.

Rosa Lustig's death was an ugly fissure in the precious
stone. It was vital that the case be cleared up as quickly as
possible so that the luster could return to the Arizona Biltmore.
Image was crucial. Since the site was just outside the city limits,
the responsibility for investigating the homicide lay with the
sheriff of Maricopa County, but Big Bill Ramsay—first on the
scene when the news broke—elected to combine forces with the
Phoenix chief of police. It was the most effective way to speed
things up, and it revived a partnership that had borne fruit on
previous occasions.

The camp was in a state of confusion. Armed police surrounded the site to prevent anyone leaving it. Bleary-eyed deni-
zens were roused from their slumber to answer questions put by

teams of detectives. Lights were set up around the scene of the crime, and the area cordoned off. As soon as the body was examined and removed, the forensic experts moved in to begin their painstaking work. Crime reporters arrived throughout the night in search of photographs and information.

Big Bill Ramsay gave regular statements at impromptu press conferences held on the hoof. A huge bear of a man with a white beard, he stomped around the site with his hands deep in the pockets of his thick coat. A clutch of reporters trotted at his heels like hounds.

"This won't look good on the hotel brochure," said one.

"No, sir," conceded the sheriff.

"Will this cause a further delay to the opening?"

"Not if we can help it."

"There's a rumor that you've got the guy who did it."

"A suspect is in custody and being questioned. Too soon to say if he's our man. As you see, we've hit this with all we've got. The hunt for clues will go on throughout the night. That's all I can tell you at this stage."

The questions came thick and fast from the darkness.

"What's his name?"

"Why did he do it?"

"Was there any sexual assault?"

"Where is he being held?"

"How soon can we get some shots of him?"

"Who was the girl?"

"What's the exact nature of her injuries?"

"Any evidence of a conspiracy?"

"Is this a deliberate attempt to smear the Biltmore?"

"You'll have to excuse me, gents," said Big Bill with a weary smile. "We still have a helluva lot to do out here, and you guys are holding me up. When we get more detail, you'll be the first to hear it. Okay?"

He broke away from the pack and ducked under the rope

around the scene of the crime. A uniformed sergeant joined him. Big Bill raised his voice above the noise from the factory behind him.

"It's like a three-ring circus out here," he moaned.

"Where did all these guys come from?" asked the other.

"They're vultures."

"The body left an hour ago. Don't they know that?"

"They can still smell the blood on the ground, Ed." The sheriff cupped his hands to speak into the sergeant's ear. "Let's hope they don't find out what else has been going on out here, or we'll have even more bad publicity. Give a place like this a good shake, and all sorts of things fall out."

"What d'you mean?"

"We found ten cases of bootleg liquor in one of the cabins. And we caught three hookers, working a shift system throughout the night in a tent. They come out on payday and clean up." He gave a philosophical shrug. "Can't blame the poor guys. What else can you do when you're marooned out here except drink and fuck? It must be hell." He scowled at the concrete block factory. "Especially with that din going on, day and night."

Inside the factory, the concrete mixers churned on remorselessly. Orders had to be met and quality maintained. Dozens of different molds were pressed into service to produce the decorated blocks, jambs, caps, bases, special corners, spandrels, half blocks, plain blocks, column blocks, and all the other subtle variations required. The machinery surged on with ear-shattering relish, quite undeterred by the fact that it had helped to set disaster in motion.

MERLIN RICHARDS SPENT a cold night in the police cell. There was a rough woolen blanket on the mattress, but its noisome odor made his stomach heave. Since the mattress itself was even less inviting, he wedged himself into a corner and crouched down, his arms wrapped around his body. He was aching all over. The scalp wound and the bruised jaw hurt most, but a general soreness spread through his whole frame.

Grief added a sharper agony. His own plight was nothing compared to the savage attack on Rosa Lustig. He would have been sad to part company with her in any case, but to lose her in such a grotesque and final way was shattering. Even in the short time he had known her, Merlin had become very fond of Rosa. It was difficult to believe that such a friendly girl could attract such a mortal enemy. Then the face of Ingrid Hansa flashed before him.

His sorrow was tinged with a deep anger. He had more reason than anybody to track down the real killer. It was pure chance that he had discovered the body, and he could not believe they would actually charge him with the murder. When his innocence was established, he would be released to begin his own inquiry. Having been so close to Rosa during the time leading up to her death, he felt that he must have picked up crucial information without even realizing it. Once he sifted through it, he might have a head start on the police investigation.

Fatigue and anguish slowly got the better of him, and he drifted off to sleep. No dreams brought further affliction. What frightened him awake was the creature that ran across his foot. A mouse? A rat? He did not pause to speculate. Dragging himself upright, he lumbered across to the door of his cage and put his arms through the bars. What little was left of the night, he spent in a standing position.

Merlin had no grasp on time. They had taken his wristwatch from him, and there was no window through which he could watch for the dawn. The cell was lit by a low-voltage bulb set into the ceiling and protected by a metal grill.

Wales seemed a million miles away.

BREAKFAST WAS A glass of water and an inedible bowl of grits. A uniformed policeman let Merlin out of the cell and conducted him along a corridor and up a flight of stairs. When he was shown into a room, he found Noah Corbin and Walt Drummond already there. Again in his shirtsleeves, the older man was looking out through the window while his colleague sat behind a table. Merlin was jolted to see that Drummond was leafing through the drawings in his portfolio.

"Where did you get that?" asked Merlin with righteous indignation. "They're mine!"

"Sit down," ordered Drummond.

"You've got no right to look at those."

"Shut up!"

"We have to examine all the material evidence, son," explained Corbin as he joined the other detective behind the table. "Besides, these drawings are good. They prove that you are what you say you are." He lowered himself into his chair and waved Merlin onto the seat facing them. "That's better. Daresay you need the rest. Get any sleep?"

"Not much."

"That's what most of our guests say."

Corbin had changed his shirt, tie, and suspenders, and he was clean-shaven. Drummond, too, had been home to wash, shave, and change into a pale gray suit. His mustache had been given meticulous attention. Merlin felt dirty and unkempt. There was a small mirror on one wall, but he did not dare even to glance in it; afraid that his unshaven face and staring eyes made him look like the killer they thought him. Lock any man up in those conditions, and he grows into the part.

Apart from a low cupboard, there was no other furniture in the room. The window was ajar to let in fresh air, which helped to revive Merlin. He was determined not to be cowed by the detectives this time. His jaw was still uncooperative, so he forced the words out between his lips like a stream of bullets.

"I demand a lawyer," he said, folding his arms.

Corbin burst out laughing. "A lawyer?"

"It's my right, surely?"

"Which lawyer did you have in mind?"

"What?"

"Phoenix is crawling with the guys. We got more lawyers than roaches. I just wondered which of them you had retained to give you legal advice."

"Well, nobody so far."

"Like us to recommend one?"

"No, thanks."

"Not that he'd bother to come down here," said Corbin with a grin. "Three dollars and fifteen cents don't even buy a smile from a lawyer. Unless you got other financial means that we don't know of. Have you?"

Merlin shook his head. "Not to hand."

"What about the money you stole from the murder victim?" asked Drummond. "Where did you stash that away?"

"I didn't steal any money."

"Someone did. Her purse was empty."

"Maybe that man took it."

"What man?"

"The one who came into the tent to search her things."

Drummond was skeptical. "Is this the guy you saw bending over you in the dark, or the one you never actually set eyes on?"

"He got into the tent last night by slicing through the canvas ties. Rosa's belongings were all over the place."

"Did you find what you were searching for?"

"I didn't touch her things. That man did!"

"How can you be sure it was a man?" asked Corbin. "What if it was a woman? Rosa herself maybe, coming back for something she'd forgotten."

"She wouldn't need to cut herself into the tent."

"Depends how tight you tied the knots."

It was hopeless. Merlin was up against a blank refusal to accept almost anything that he said. Gritting his teeth, he tried another tack.

"Have you identified her friend yet?" he asked.

"What friend?" said Drummond.

"The one that Rosa went off to see that night."

"We only have your word that he exists."

"Why else should she leave the tent?"

"Maybe the company wasn't to her taste."

"Rosa told me she was going to see her friend. On the site. No, wait a minute," he said as his memory was jogged. "What she actually said was 'more or less' on the site."

"More or less?"

"That doesn't make sense," remarked Corbin. "You're either on the site or off it. Step outside the perimeter, and you're in the desert. Is that what you're suggesting? That this so-called friend of hers had four legs? Did she seem the type to have the hots for a coyote?"

"This is serious!"

"Oh, don't worry, son. We're taking it very seriously."

Drummond looked at his pad. "I got him down as number four on the list."

"What list?" said Merlin.

"Of your invisible men. First, there's the guy you wake up and find in the tent with you. Then there's the one who's supposed to be spying on you. Next comes the thief in the night, and the phantom friend completes the lineup."

"They could all be the same man."

"Yes," said Drummond. "He's called Merlin Richards."

"No!"

"Walt has a problem with trust," explained Corbin. "It goes with being a cop. Now me, I'm ready to take a chance on a guy. As long as he doesn't lie to me, that is." He showed discolored teeth in a warning smile. "Yesterday—or maybe it was earlier today—I asked you a question. I need to put it to you again, because it's very important that I get the correct answer. Do you understand, son?"

Merlin nodded. "What's the question?"

"Did you and the lady ever get real close?"

"Of course not!"

"No farewell screw on the last night together?"

"Nothing."

"That's what you said before, but we got new evidence that makes me doubt your word. Now, let me give you one more chance to tell the—"

"I didn't touch her! That *is* the truth."

Corbin scratched his head. "Well, someone did. While you were having a nice restful night in a police cell, the medical officer and his boys were working like slaves over in the lab. They had a lot of questions to put to Miss Rosa Lustig, and it seems she answered most of them. Of course, all I've got is a preliminary report, and the details will have to be confirmed. But one thing is crystal clear."

"What's that?"

"Some time before she was killed, the victim had sex. Willingly, it seems. There were no signs of bruising or forced entry. She got herself well and truly fucked."

Merlin was shocked. "How can they tell?"

"By the presence of semen in the vagina." He shot a knowing glance at Drummond. "Not only there. There were traces in the throat and the stomach as well. Seems she gave some guy one helluva good time last night."

"Didn't she?" accused Drummond, glaring at Merlin.

"It wasn't me! And what sort of a man would make love to a woman and then kill her?"

"A pervert. We see a lot in this job."

"Are we looking at another one now?" asked Corbin.

"No!" said Merlin, rising to his feet. "Rosa was my friend. I liked her. I respected her. All right, I may have fancied her as well. What red-blooded man wouldn't? She was gorgeous. But that doesn't mean I'd have sex with her before smashing her head in! I did neither of those things. I'd take my Bible oath on it."

Corbin pulled an invisible string to make him resume his seat. Merlin's speech had the ring of truth. It let him off one hook, but he might still be impaled on the other.

"Okay," said Corbin, quietly. "It wasn't you that got lucky last night. I accept that."

"Thank goodness!"

"But it does give you a strong motive for murder."

"Motive?"

"It's bad enough to be rejected, but to watch the lady in question hop into the sack with someone else is far worse. That must really have stirred up your feelings of jealousy. What did you do, son? Watch them at it through a gap in a tent? Wonder why she couldn't put on a show like that for you? Wait till she finished, then ambush her?"

"It all adds up," agreed Drummond.

"I had no idea where she was," said Merlin.

"You did. With a friend."

"She told you that," added Corbin. "And now we know what kind of friend. Rosa wasn't just going to discuss the weather with the guy. It was an assignation."

"At least you believe that he exists now. That's a big advance. Cross number four off your list of invisible men. He's real. He walks, talks, and makes love to a woman. Maybe *he* gets a thrill out of murdering her straight afterward. Ask him when you find him."

There was a long pause. Noah Corbin ran his tongue over dry lips, then let out an admiring cackle.

"He's got a point, Walt."

"I don't buy it," said Drummond.

Merlin felt encouraged. "One invisible man down, only three to go. Unless all four are the same person, as I suggested earlier. Instead of barking up the wrong tree with me, you ought to be out looking for him. I know you want a medal for a quick arrest, but you'll look pretty stupid when you realize that I'm not involved in this murder in any way."

"Watch your mouth!" ordered Drummond.

"That's *all* I need to be told!"

He pointed to his jaw. Noah Corbin was the first to respond, with a throaty chuckle that soon matured into a full belly laugh. Even though it was painful, Merlin himself shook with ridiculous mirth. Walt Drummond was drawn ineluctably into the circle of laughter.

All three of them were still hooting with incongruous delight when there was a knock on the door. A uniformed policeman came in and walked across to Corbin. When the newcomer whispered in his ear, the detective's quivering jowls froze. He pulled himself to his feet.

"Take over, Walt," he said. "Back in a minute."

The two men left the room, and Drummond quickly resumed the interrogation. His sense of humor had now completely vanished.

"You had nothing to lose, did you?"

"Lose?"

"Bumping that girl off. You picked the ideal spot, I gotta hand you that. Enough light to see what you were doing and enough noise to drown out any scream. You might have got away with it if those two guards hadn't happened along."

"You're determined to hang this one on me, aren't you?"

"You were caught in the act," said Drummond. "What other reason would you have to be where you were at that time of night? Smoking gun. We got you. Cold."

"Don't bank on that."

"We'll break you down in time. We always do." He sat back and stroked his mustache. "Maybe we oughta toss you into the Phoenix jail for a night. That's enough to loosen anyone's tongue. Twenty restless cons, all crushed together in the same stinking cage. They'd sure be pleased to see *you*. By the time they'd finished, you'd be ready to confess to every unsolved crime in the records. Just to get out of there and call your ass your own again."

"You can't punish an innocent man."

"We can if we want to remind him he's guilty."

"In my country, the police don't use these methods."

"You're not *in* your country, mister! I wish you were, believe me; then we wouldn't have this piece of shit to wipe off the floor. Back home, you may be someone. Here, you got a long way to go up to reach zero."

Merlin could not believe the two of them had just been laughing together. Walt Drummond had moved from amusement to vindictiveness in one chilling leap.

The door opened, and Noah Corbin came waddling back in with a piece of paper flapping in his hand. He stood beside his colleague and set the paper on the table. Drummond read it with patent disgust. He glowered up at his superior. Corbin gave a shrug and turned to Merlin.

"You're being released, son."

Merlin was thrilled. "You know that I didn't do it?"

"We don't know that at all. Let's just say that there are some doubts to be cleared up. You're still very much under suspicion, but we don't need to hold you here."

"I can leave?"

"See the guy at the desk. He'll take care of you."

"That's marvelous," said Merlin, standing up. "I thought this ordeal was never going to end. Thank you, Lieutenant."

"You're not out of the fire yet," warned Corbin, darkly. "We may well need to bring you in again for questioning. In the meantime, stick around. Got it?"

"Here in Phoenix?"

"Try to leave the area, you'll be arrested." He turned his back on Merlin. "Now take your portfolio and get the hell out of here!"

10

MERLIN'S MEAGER POSSESSIONS were returned to him by the desk sergeant. Putting on his watch, he was surprised to see that it was almost noon. The brutal impersonality of the police station was troubling, and he did not linger. With his portfolio under his arm, he went swiftly out through the main door, only to discover that he had changed one form of imprisonment for another.

Three cameras flashed in his face, and he was surrounded by a ring of reporters. They barked their questions at him in quick succession.

"What happened in there, Merlin?"

"Why did they let you go?"

"Who beat you up?"

"You gonna sue for wrongful arrest?"

"How well did you know Rosa Lustig?"

"Is it true you shared a tent with her?"

"What did you feel when you saw her lying there?"

"Tell us about her, Merlin."

"What sort of a girl was Rosa?"

"How did you meet her?"

"Tell us about yourself."

"Come on, Merlin. Give us a break."

Taken aback at first, he recovered quickly. He was less

annoyed by their inquiries than by the arm-tugging familiarity with which they were put. His experience with the detectives had toughened him; he was not going to allow himself to be badgered for intimate details by a group of complete strangers.

"No comment!" he said firmly.

"Why did the cops arrest you?" demanded a voice.

"Ask them."

"Give us *something* to print, Merl. Our readers got a right to know."

But Merlin was more concerned with his own rights. He pushed his way unceremoniously through the little cordon and strode off down the street. They pursued him for a block or two, then their questions gradually turned into protests and abuse. He kept walking until the last of them fell away.

As he marched on, he collected the kinds of looks and glances that made him very self-conscious. He paused to study his reflection in the window of a barber's shop and gulped. The combination of bruise, bandaging, and unshaven face made him look like a fugitive once again. He ducked down an alley to make one cosmetic improvement. Unwinding the bandage, he removed the pad that covered the stitches. It gave him marginally more confidence.

Food was now a priority. He decided to invest some of his money in a frugal lunch and give himself time to work out a plan of action. He went into the first restaurant that he found, taking care to choose a table in a corner and sitting with his back to the rest of the diners. While he studied the menu, a waitress arrived with a jug of water and poured him a glass. He placed his modest order. His glass was drained immediately.

"You must have been thirsty."

Merlin looked up to see a short, neat, middle-aged man in a white suit and a straw boater. He carried an attaché case and had a newspaper tucked under his arm.

"Sorry you had to run the gauntlet just now," he continued

with a polite smile. "Country hick reporters are like that. They'll hassle you rotten just to get some big headline. I'm ashamed to be in the same profession as most of them."

Merlin became defensive. "You're a reporter?"

"A feature writer," corrected the quiet-spoken stranger. "Clyde Willard. *Los Angeles Times*. Biggest circulation in the entire West. But don't worry," he added when he saw Merlin tense, "I haven't come to bother you. I'll just put my proposition and skedaddle. Unlike those sharks who tried to take a bite out of you, I'm prepared to pay for an interview." He took a ten-dollar bill from his wallet and put it on the table. "That's a deposit. Why don't you enjoy your lunch in private, then go back to that barber shop you walked past just now? I'm sure you'll feel a lot better after a shave."

"Then what?" asked Merlin, warily.

"That's up to you, sir. Go your own way, if you wish. I won't come after you. On the other hand, you might feel ready to talk. I'll be sitting on the other side of the restaurant having my lunch. I've been on the road all night, and I'm famished. Thank you for your time, sir."

He offered his hand, and Merlin shook it cautiously.

"What did you say your name was?" he asked.

"Willard. Clyde Willard." The man handed him the newspaper. "Today's edition. You'll find me in there."

He turned on his heel and walked smartly away.

TOM VERNON HAD an expression of blank dismay on his face.

"What's been going on out here, Joe?"

"Chaos!"

"We heard the news on the radio."

"I guess just about everybody knows by now."

"We were devastated," said Vernon. "Rosa! Of all people!

Great kid. She was such fun to be around. I just couldn't believe it at first."

"No," murmured Santana. "Nor me."

"Mr. Wright is terribly upset. He liked Rosa a lot. He sent me back here to find out what I could. Is it true that the cops have arrested someone?"

"Yeah."

"They didn't give his name on the news broadcast."

"It was that architect Rosa brought out here."

Vernon was nonplussed. "Merlin Richards?"

"That's the guy."

"They arrested *him*?"

"Coupla site guards caught him near the body."

"But he's the last person in the world who'd want to kill Rosa. They were friends. She helped him. Somehow, they just clicked. Merlin and Rosa looked good together."

"Not any more," said the other, sourly.

Tom Vernon was standing close to the canal with the site manager. The Arizona Biltmore was its usual buzzing hive of activity, but the murder of Rosa Lustig had left highly visible marks. Patrolled by uniformed policemen, the scene of the crime was still roped off. Other policemen were checking the credentials of everyone who went to and from the site, while detectives were interviewing those who had spent the night in the camp. The prevailing tension could be seen and felt everywhere.

"Couldn't have come at a worse time," said Santana.

"That's true."

"We're sweating to get the place finished, and *this* has to happen. On top of all the other problems we've had. I sometimes think this hotel is jinxed."

"It's had its share of trouble." Vernon pursed his lips and shook his head. His tone was incredulous. "But Merlin! I'll bet anything they got the wrong man there. The cops just won't make it stick."

"You could be right, Tom."

"What do you mean?"

"Word is, they let him go earlier today."

"He's free?"

"That's the rumor around the site."

"Well, I hope it's true," said Vernon. "And I hope he hasn't been scared off by all this. I need to see Merlin again."

"Why?"

"He's a nice guy. I like him."

"We don't want him out here."

"Speak for yourself, Joe."

"I do," said the other, truculently.

Vernon became soulful. "Thing like this happens, you're reminded that Arizona is still only frontier country. Phoenix is a pretty town. Fine buildings, clean streets, nice residential property. Hospitals, schools, libraries, movie houses, a theater, a museum, and new development all the time." He gazed around. "Come out here, and the desert lore takes over. Bit scary."

"They'll get the guy who did it."

"Could be anybody, Joe. A stray Indian off one of the reservations. Some loner who lives out here. Anybody."

"My guess is it's someone on the site."

"Why do you say that?"

"I talked with Rosa a few times," said Santana, looking sadly at the factory. "She always struck me as being real independent, used to taking care of herself. Not the kind of girl who'd let anyone creep up on her. No, I reckon she must've known the bastard. Trusted him enough to let him get close. Then he—"

"Maybe, Joe. Maybe not."

"I got this feeling."

"Opens up a wide field, then."

"Field?"

"She was a popular girl," said Vernon with a sigh. "Being

one of only a few women out here made her even more popular. Rosa made lots of friends very quickly."

"I know," muttered Santana, ruefully.

"So where do you start?"

"No idea."

"You must've seen her around the site a lot."

"I had other things to do, Tom."

"Did you spot her with any particular guy?" Santana pondered. "I guess I did at that."

"Who was he?"

"Pete Bickley. One of the guards."

"Was he out here last night?"

"Sure was. He was the guy who caught Richards standing over Rosa's body. No wonder Pete slugged him."

"TO BE PERFECTLY honest, I never thought I'd see you again."

"There was a line at the barbershop."

"It was well worth the wait," said Willard. "You look ten times better, and I get my interview. Did you read my article?"

"Yes," said Merlin. "I enjoyed it."

"Then you know that I'm not some hack reporter from a two-bit paper. I'm a responsible journalist. What I write are feature articles with strong human interest. My instinct tells me I got a humdinger of a story right here."

The roadster swerved to avoid a quail that darted across its path. Clyde Willard was driving toward the site, Merlin sitting beside him with mixed feelings. Though he had agreed to give the journalist an interview, he had reservations about the deal.

Willard sensed his reluctance. "You can back out of this at any stage, you know."

"Oh. I see."

"What's more, I won't ask for my money back."

"That's very generous."

"I'll write it off as legitimate expenses," said the other with a smile. "Let me tell you the angle that appeals to me, Merlin. Girl Brutally Murdered, Man Held, Prime Suspect Released by Police—I've got no time for that kind of sensational stuff. I prefer to go below the surface to get to the heart of the matter. You see, what intrigues me about Rosa Lustig is that she was a designer."

"A brilliant one. She showed me her drawings. They were wonderful. She had a real talent."

"Cut down in her prime. That's my take on this, Merlin. The wanton destruction of an artist. This girl sounds like something rather special. Well, you're an architect. How many people have you got like Rosa back home in Wales?"

"None at all."

"I guess it's a male-dominated profession over there."

"Very much so," said Merlin. "I've never come across a female architect yet. We have a few women designers, but none of them are remotely like Rosa."

"Why not?"

"There was such a sense of freedom about her. Of bold independence. Welsh girls don't have anything like that. They'd have been green with envy if they'd met Rosa."

"It must've come as a bit of a shock to you, then."

"Shock?"

"When you first met Rosa yourself."

"It was, Mr. Willard. But a very pleasant one. Rosa was one of the most fascinating people I've ever met."

Merlin talked enthusiastically about her for some time. It was only when he remembered his last sighting of her that his voice tailed off. Willard seemed pleased with what he had heard.

"This is just what I need. The young artist. Touring the reservations to garner ideas. Drawn to the Biltmore project because Frank Lloyd Wright was involved. This is a story of artistic commitment."

"It certainly is."

"But then, so is yours."

"Mine?"

"Yes, my friend. Giving up everything to come in search of your hero. You can't get any more committed than that. Have you managed to meet Mr. Wright yet?"

"Not exactly."

"Hasn't he been out to the site?"

"He was . . . too busy to spare any time for me."

"That's a pity, but understandable. It's a huge commission, and he's the sort of man who likes to keep a close watch on his buildings. How typical of his work is the Biltmore?"

"Very typical in some ways. That's why I was amazed to learn that he didn't actually design it. The architect was Albert Chase McArthur."

"Do you believe that?"

"Of course."

"Why?"

"It's what everyone has told me."

"Does the Biltmore itself tell you that?"

"Well . . . no. I suppose that it doesn't."

Willard did not pursue the topic. He eased the car over to the right as a police car came toward them. Merlin was glad when the vehicle raced past.

"Where do you go from here?" asked Willard.

"Oh, I'm not leaving until they find Rosa's killer."

"But when they do?"

Merlin shrugged. "I'm not sure."

"Ever thought of going to California? Masses of good architects in L.A. I'm not part of that world myself, but I've got a few contacts. Would you like some introductions?"

"Yes, please!"

"Who knows? Someone may offer you a job."

"That would be fantastic!"

"Leave it to me."

"Thanks, Mr. Willard."

"Friendly cooperation. That's the way we do things in this country. You help me, I help you. We both profit."

WHEN THE CAR reached the site entrance, it was waved to a halt by two uniformed policemen. They asked the visitors to identify themselves and state their reason for being there. As soon as they heard Merlin's name, the two men became quite hostile, and they left him in no doubt that he was still high on the list of murder suspects. Clyde Willard stepped in to rescue him, talking to the policemen with such firmness and easy authority that they backed off immediately and let the car through.

"Thanks," said Merlin.

"You have to know how to speak to cops."

"Well, you've certainly got the knack."

"Don't let them push you around. That's the secret."

When the car was safely parked, they decided to split up and meet later on. Willard wanted to take a look at the murder scene, but Merlin's first call was to the tent he had shared with Rosa. He was stunned to find it cordoned off and guarded by a uniformed policeman.

"I need to get in there."

"Move along, sir."

"But my things are in that tent."

"Nobody crosses that rope."

"What about my belongings?"

Lieutenant Noah Corbin emerged from the tent.

"You can have them back in the fullness of time," he said. "Cosy little love nest you had in there, son. No wonder the rest of the guys out here were cursing you."

"Cursing me?"

"For getting what they all wanted. Rosa's favors."

"There *were* no favors!"

"You know that—but they don't."

Corbin cocked his leg over the rope to stand beside Merlin. He was wearing a loose-fitting jacket, which hung open to expose his ample paunch. Set at an angle, a gray fedora kept the sun out of his eyes.

"They may not be too glad to see you back, son."

"Who?"

"The site manager, for a start. Joe Santana."

"He hardly knows me."

"You'd be surprised. Anyway, you can find out for yourself when you speak to him about the tent."

"Why should I do that?"

"Because it belongs to him."

"It was Rosa's."

"Not according to Santana," said the detective. "When she rolled up at the site, she had nowhere to sleep. Spent the first night in her car. Santana rustled up this tent for her. When we're done here, you'll need his permission to reclaim your things. Talking of which—" He pulled a sheet of paper from his inside pocket and unfolded it. "Run your eye over this list. Rosa's possessions are on the left, yours on the right. You travel light, son."

"Not by choice."

"Let me know if anything's missing."

Merlin only needed a glance at his own belongings.

"Everything of mine is here," he confirmed, "but I'm not so sure about Rosa. I don't see her camera down here."

"We didn't find one."

"It was in the tent yesterday. I remember her taking it out of the boot of her car." Another memory surfaced. "Wait a minute. She may have had it with her when she went off to meet that friend. Rosa was carrying something in a large paper bag."

"Booze, maybe?"

"It could have been her camera."

"Well, it was nowhere near the body when we examined it. All she had with her was her purse, and that was empty."

"What happened to the camera?"

"Are you sure there *was* one?" said Corbin, levelly.

Merlin bit back a reply. There was no point in banging his head against a blank wall of cynicism. Instead he took the opportunity to solve a mystery that had been puzzling him since they last met.

"Why did you let me go?" he asked.

"Just be grateful that we did, son."

"I'm entitled to know, surely? You and Sergeant Drummond put me through the hoops in there. It was very unpleasant. And completely unnecessary. I think that I deserve some sort of explanation."

Corbin thought it over and eventually nodded.

"Well?"

"It's not conclusive, mind you."

"Go on."

"We got the precise time when you were caught beside the dead body," said Corbin. "The medical report puts the girl's death a couple of hours earlier. You'd have to be real dumb to stand over your victim that long."

"She was not my victim."

"That's how it's starting to look, but there's a margin for error here. The time of death is only approximate. It's all they could give me." He closed one eye and watched Merlin closely through the other. "And it doesn't rule out the possibility that you bumped her off somewhere else on the site and carried her across to the factory later."

"My clothes would have been covered in blood."

"Not if you'd wrapped her head in something."

"It would still have been there beside the body."

"Unless you'd already disposed of it."

"What about the block that smashed her skull in?"

Corbin gave a grudging sniff. "Oh, yes. That was your other piece of luck."

"Why?"

"We couldn't find your fingerprints on it. Or anybody else's, for that matter. Plenty of blood, of course. And several particles of Rosa's hair and scalp. She was hit real hard." He looked meaningfully at Merlin's physique. "By a strong guy."

"Then get after him," suggested Merlin.

"We will. In the meantime, just stay around. Within easy reach. We'll be in touch." He walked away then halted. "Oh, I forgot. That guard who gave you the shotgun anesthetic. Pete Bickley."

"What about him?"

"Keep out of his way."

"Is that an order?"

"It's a piece of friendly advice," said Corbin. "Pete thought he had something going with Rosa. And he's not the only one around here, it seems. But he was real sweet on her. Claims they were close friends. That's why he's so sore that we've released you."

"But you have no evidence against me."

Corbin grinned. "Try telling that to Pete Bickley. Then remember to duck."

Merlin ignored the advice. He waited until the detective walked off, then went in the opposite direction. On his earlier tour of the site, he had noticed the wooden cabin used by off-duty site guards. Somebody would know where he could find Bickley, and it was a meeting that could not be delayed. His jaw ached afresh, and his scalp wound had started to throb violently. They wanted revenge.

When he stormed into the cabin, six or seven guards were sitting at the table. Bickley leaped to his feet.

"You killed Rosa!" he yelled.

"The police don't think so. They released me."

"Only until they can get further proof."

"It doesn't exist," said Merlin. "I'm completely innocent. But that didn't stop you hitting me with your shotgun. There was no need to do that."

"I should've blown your brains out instead!"

"I've come for an apology."

Pete laughed coarsely. "Apology! Hear that, guys?"

"I'm asking you nicely," said Merlin.

"Kiss my ass!"

"Are you going to say you're sorry or not?"

Pete thrust his face inches away from his visitor.

"Fuck you!" he growled.

One punch was all it took. Pete did not even see it coming. The right hook was delivered with such speed and power that it knocked him off his feet. He hit the bare floor with a bang and rolled in agony.

Merlin looked across at Pete's stunned companions.

"Tell him I'll have that apology another time."

11

CLYDE WILLARD COULD imagine all too clearly how Rosa Lustig had met her death. The concrete blocks were still stacked in piles near the wall of the factory. Her blood was still staining the ground. Her spirit still hovered at the place of slaughter. As he ran his eye slowly along the decorative variations on display, he wondered which pattern had been on the piece of concrete that dashed out her brains. It was an important detail in the demise of an artist.

Walking sadly away from the factory clamor, he took up a vantage point so that he could survey the hotel itself. Work was continuing in earnest on every part of the site. Men were throwing themselves into their tasks with more fervor than usual, burning the grim memory of the murder from their minds.

There were still several weeks to go before the Arizona Biltmore was completed and ready for the grand opening ceremony, but the shape, character, intricacy, and texture of the building were already apparent. Willard appraised it all with close interest and was deeply impressed.

It was a remarkable piece of architecture in a place where none had the right to exist, an alliance with nature in which both parties were equally well served. The palm trees gave it an exotic quality, and the swimming pool had the shimmer of a mirage.

With the mystical haze of a dream, the Arizona Biltmore also had a sense of rock-solid permanence.

Concrete blocks were used in the most ingenious way to create a bewildering variety of effects, at once contrasting and complementary, but Willard did not have the perception to appreciate the multiple decorative subtleties. His vision was in any case blurred by the thought of a young woman whose life had been sacrificed in the cause of the hotel. Clyde Willard could never see the Biltmore in its true light until her killer had been caught and convicted. Rosa Lustig was a glaring design fault in an otherwise perfect structure.

Merlin Richards strolled briskly across to him. There was a new buoyancy about him and a quiet smile on his lips.

"Have you seen all you wanted to see?"

"Yes," said Willard. "The only thing left for me to take a peep at is Rosa's tent."

"It's in the camp. Follow me."

"What have you been doing with yourself, Merlin?"

"Settling an old score."

"It seems to have left you in good spirits."

"Yes, Mr. Willard. I must do that kind of thing more often."

"What kind of thing?"

"Restoring the balance."

"There speaks an architect!"

The policeman was still stationed outside the tent. Willard walked around it in a wide circle.

"Basic living. As befits an artist."

"Rosa had done a lot of camping. That was obvious."

"Wasn't it cold at nights?"

"Freezing," agreed Merlin.

"This is far too bohemian for me. I'm an urban animal. I need buildings all around me. And the comforts of civilized life. If I slept out here, I'd be terrified of snakes, scorpions, and poisonous insects. Not to mention Gila monsters. Weren't you scared that you might get bitten by something?"

"Not really. Rosa told me that pests are more of a problem in warmer weather. Besides," said Merlin, rubbing his bruised chin, "the really dangerous creatures in this camp walk on two legs. As Rosa found out."

"Do you have any idea who murdered her?"

"None at all, Mr. Willard. Yet."

"What exactly was Rosa Lustig doing out here?" Willard asked casually. "It's not as if she was actually employed on the project."

"She'd like to have been. I know she submitted designs for the concrete blocks, but they weren't accepted." He gave a shrug. "Rosa came here anyway. She just wanted to be around Frank Lloyd Wright's work. So do I. It's an education in itself. That's why I was so interested in that offer you put to me"

"Offer?"

"To introduce me to some architects in Los Angeles."

"Oh, yes. Of course."

"Mr. Wright built some of his most famous houses there."

"He doesn't let us forget it."

"The Hollyhock House, La Miniatura, the John Storer House, the Samuel Freeman House, and—my own favorite— the Charles Ennis House."

Willard smiled. "You know them better than I do."

"The Hollyhock House is stuccoed tile and frame," said Merlin, warming to his theme, "but the other four are daring experiments in the use of concrete block. Just like the Biltmore. I've only seen drawings and photographs of those houses, of course. I'd love to visit the real thing."

"Perhaps you will. One day. But tell me more about Rosa. And much more about yourself. I'm beginning to see a lot of parallels between the pair of you."

Merlin needed no further incentive. He talked volubly about Rosa's personality, her work, her aspirations, and their shared worship of America's leading architect. But the more he talked, the more he felt the poignancy of her loss. His eyes were moist when he finished.

"Could I possibly see her portfolio?"

"It's in the tent. Effectively under lock and key."

"Tomorrow, maybe."

"I'll see if I can arrange it."

"You'll find me more than grateful," said Willard as he took another ten-dollar bill from his wallet. "Have this."

"But I haven't really earned it."

"I can't pay enough for a good story."

He pushed the money into Merlin's top pocket, making him feel oddly uncomfortable. Desperately needing the cash, he had an impulse to refuse it. It seemed somehow tainted, as if he were exploiting Rosa's death for his own personal gain.

Tom Vernon's voice diverted him from his doubts.

"I was hoping to catch you out here, Merlin!"

"Hello, Tom."

"Joe Santana said the cops arrested you. Is it true?"

"I'm afraid so. But I'm not going to talk about that now. It's something I'd rather forget."

Merlin introduced the two men and noted their contrasting responses to each other. Hearing that Vernon worked with Frank Lloyd Wright, the journalist's curiosity was immediately ignited. It threw Vernon himself on the defensive.

"How much has Mr. Wright been involved in this project?" asked Willard.

"Very little," said Vernon with a dismissive gesture. "His role was purely consultative."

"I wondered if that might just be a cover story."

"For what?"

"A bootleg commission."

"It's nothing of the kind!"

"Are you sure?"

"Completely."

"It wouldn't be the first bootleg commission that Frank Lloyd Wright has undertaken," observed Willard, dryly.

Merlin was baffled. "Bootleg commission?"

"Designing a house and letting someone else put his name on the plans. He's done that before, hasn't he, Tom?"

"Only when he was young," conceded Vernon.

"Or short of money, perhaps."

"Why would he undertake such work?" asked Merlin.

"In this case, he didn't," asserted Vernon. "Mr. Wright is only one of a number of consultants on this project. He was in at the start. Others have come along and made a lot of unwelcome changes to Mr. Wright's ideas. It's the thing that annoys him most of all. To have no overriding control."

"All the same, it does seem strange," mused Willard. "I can't imagine that Merlin would design a luxury hotel on this scale and take his father on as a mere consultant."

"He'd be insulted," agreed Merlin.

"So why isn't Mr. Wright? Why is he working for a man with considerably less talent and reputation than himself? I'd say it was demeaning. It just doesn't make sense."

"That isn't quite the situation," insisted Vernon.

"It looks like it to me. A master working for a servant. A sorcerer keeping the pot boiling for the apprentice."

"I never thought of it that way," said Merlin.

"What about you, Tom?"

Vernon lapsed into a watchful silence. Seeing his discomfort, Willard readily apologized for any offense he might have caused.

"Just idle speculation on my part," he said. "What do I know about architecture? Still, I need to get back to Phoenix. To work on my story at the hotel." He turned to Merlin. "Can I offer you a lift?"

"I'm staying here."

"After all that's happened?"

"That's exactly why, Mr. Willard."

"Brave man. Well, let's meet again tomorrow."

"I'll be around. And I'd value those names."

"Names? Ah, yes. My contacts. You'll get them, Merlin."

They exchanged farewells and Willard went off to his car. Vernon waited until the man was well out of earshot.

"Where did you find him?"

"He found me."

"What was that about a story?"

"He's been asking me a lot of questions about Rosa. For an article he's writing. I was out of my depth, really. I mean, we only met two days ago. I know nothing at all about her background. Except that she was born and brought up in Indiana."

"Kokomo."

"Where?"

"Kokomo. It's a small town in Indiana."

"She didn't seem to have very happy memories of it."

"So I understand. She talked about it to Norm Kozelsky. It sort of drew them together." Vernon brightened. "But let me tell you why I was so keen to track you down. Mr. Wright wants to meet you."

"He does?"

"I managed to put in that good word for you."

"Thanks, Tom."

"Any chance of borrowing your portfolio?"

"Of course." Merlin surrendered it at once.

"It will show him what you can do." He shifted his feet. "If I'm honest, this other business has helped. I told Mr. Wright about you and Rosa. He wants to ask you a few things about her. This has shaken him badly. He was very fond of her."

"He didn't show any affection toward her earlier. In fact, he was rather abrupt with her when she tried to introduce me to him."

"He's abrupt with everybody at times. Take no notice."

"What time is he coming?"

"When it suits him." His face darkened. "I just hope that your friend Willard isn't around the site when he arrives. I don't think that Mr. Wright would take to him at all. I certainly didn't." A note of concern sounded. "Do you really want to spend another night at the site?"

"Yes, Tom."

"I wouldn't, in your place. Sure it's possible?"

"Who's to stop me?"

"Lots of people. The cops, for a start. They might have other plans for you. And Joe Santana won't be pleased."

"It's not up to him, surely."

"Joe calls a lot of shots around here," said Vernon. "If he wants you off the site, out you'll go. Listen, let me have a chat with him. Maybe I can fix it." He pushed his glasses up the bridge of his nose as he pondered. "I've got it. I'll tell Joe that you're tied in with us. Ask him to let you stay as a favor to Mr. Wright. Okay?"

"You're a real friend, Tom."

"I'll need to find him first. Could take time."

"I want to do a little scouting round myself."

"Meet us at the site office."

"Right."

"Oh, and Merlin—"

"Yes?"

"Be careful. Very careful."

LIEUTENANT NOAH CORBIN chewed on an unlit cigar and looked despondently at the sheets of paper before him on the desk.

"Nothing!" he grumbled. "Next to goddamn nothing!"

"That's not true, Noah."

"All we got is a few skimpy leads."

"We're closer than we think," said Walt Drummond as he leaned against the filing cabinet. "The evidence is there, we just haven't sorted it all out yet. We may have witnesses. Quite a few of the statements taken at the camp mention sightings of a man and a woman last night."

"What does that prove?"

"Wait and see."

"I don't hold out much hope," said Corbin, gloomily. "The man and the woman will probably turn out to be some poor guy with one of those hookers we caught. We can't arrest a man simply because he has a hard-on. Start doing that and we'd put half the camp behind bars."

"That friend of Rosa's is the one we're after."

An envious cackle. "Lucky devil, whoever he is!"

"Yeah," agreed Drummond. "She sounds like an obliging lady. The two of them obviously whooped it up. But where? In a tent? A cabin? A car? Find that friend, and we're halfway there."

"Twelve hours ago, we were all the way there."

They were in Corbin's office, its air of neglect matching his forlorn mood. He needed three desultory attempts to light a match. His cigar glowed without conviction. He glanced at the information on his desk again, then swept the sheets of paper roughly aside.

"I got 'em all on my neck, Walt. Big Bill Ramsay, the chief, the mayor, the Biltmore people, the fucking newspapers, and even my wife. Why don't we catch him? How long will it take? Do I know how much damage this is doing to the image of the hotel?" He let out a snort of contempt. "Jesus! What about the damage it's doing to my innards?"

There was a long pause. Corbin puffed strenuously away on his cigar, trying to hide himself in a cloud of comforting smoke. The sergeant drummed his fingers reflectively on the cabinet. It was he who finally came up with a positive suggestion.

"Why don't we haul that Richards guy back in?"

"What use would that be, Walt?"

"He knows a lot more than he told us."

"That doesn't make him the killer."

"He's holding out on us, Noah. I'm certain of it."

"You could be right. Tough kid."

"And stubborn. Let's squeeze him a bit harder; it could help."

Corbin shook his head. "Leave him right where he is."

"On site?"

"He's far more use to us out at the Biltmore."

"How come?"

"Think it through. Old Merlin may not have bumped that girl off, but someone sure did. And that someone is probably still out there. With that Welsh madman on his tail."

"Richards?"

"I saw it in his eyes, Walt. He's in the hunt. He wants the guy who battered Rosa as much as we do. Funny thing is, he's in a much better position to find him."

"That's true."

"Now, then. Imagine you're the killer. You think you got away with it when suddenly you got this amateur dick blundering around after you. He starts to get close. What would *you* do if you had Merlin breathing down your neck?"

"Get rid of the bastard."

"Exactly," said Corbin with a wheeze of satisfaction. "When we let Merlin go, we may have done ourselves a real favor. We baited the hook. With a helluva big worm." He grinned broadly. "My guess is we'll get a bite before too long."

MERLIN WAS COMING around the corner of the main block when it happened. Light was fading fast, and most of the workers had downed tools for the day. They were either drifting across to the camp or climbing into lorries to be driven back into Phoenix. Only the men in the factory labored on to turn out the endless river of concrete.

Merlin had been conducting his own painstaking search of the site, looking for any clue that might have a bearing on Rosa's death, trying to retrace her steps, and hoping against hope that the missing camera might turn up. He was convinced that it held real significance. He was wondering what that could be as he came around the angle of the building.

There was a shuffling noise above his head. Merlin looked up to see a piece of concrete falling toward him. Reflexes sharpened by years on a rugby field came to his rescue. He put his hands up instinctively and caught the missile as if he were fielding a high kick, moving his arms at the exact moment of contact to take the sting out of the object's descent. What he was holding was a jagged section of one of the decorated blocks.

Flinging it to the ground, he ran out from the shadow of the building to give himself an angle to look up. He saw nobody. By the time he found a ladder, it was far too late. The area was completely deserted, and there were too many avenues of escape. Merlin climbed down to the ground to take another look at the missile.

It was roughly triangular in shape, a discarded remnant from a faulty block. Though not large, it would have caused him serious injury, at the very least, dropped from that height. Merlin was chastened. He would not walk that close to a building again.

TOM VERNON WAS coming out of the site office when he approached. When he saw Merlin, he gave a smile of relief.

"I was just about to send out a search party."

"Sorry."

"It's all set up."

"Thanks, Tom."

"It wasn't easy, mind you. I've been in there for half an hour with Joe. He took a lot of persuading. Joe doesn't want you anywhere near the site."

"Where will I sleep?"

"He'll tell you. But ask him nicely."

"I will."

"He's feeling very prickly just now. The murder has made his job ten times harder. Make allowances for that. Just be polite. Argue back, Joe may change his mind about letting you stay."

They shook hands, and Vernon walked in the direction of the parking area, the portfolio under his arm. Watching him go, Merlin was apprehensive about how his drawings would be viewed by Frank Lloyd Wright. He felt like a raw schoolboy, offering his first clumsy sketches to a critical art master.

Merlin knocked on the door of the site office. In response to a growl of welcome, he let himself in. Joe Santana had his back to the door. By the light of a lamp, he was bending over his desk to make notes on a pad. Merlin cleared his throat.

"Tom Vernon told me to see you, Mr. Santana."

"Oh, it's you, is it?"

"I'd like to stay around here, if at all possible."

"That's not what I want."

"So I understand."

"You're bad news, mister. Everything was fine out here until you turned up. With Rosa." He swung around. "You didn't come, she might still be alive."

"I had nothing to do with her murder."

"I think you did. Indirectly."

There was such contempt in his tone and such resentment in his gaze that Merlin wanted to speak out angrily in his own defense. But he remembered Vernon's warning and fought hard to control his temper. Santana glared at him as if waiting for an excuse to attack. He turned away again before he trusted himself with words.

"Use the same tent," he hissed.

"It was roped off."

"The cops have finished with it now."

"Did they leave Rosa's things in it?"

"Everything of hers has gone into Phoenix. But they left your gear. I was going to burn it. Now get lost."

"Right. Thanks, Mr. Santana."

"And keep out of my way."

Merlin was about to leave when a memory tugged at him.

"What was Ingrid doing out here last night?" he said.

"Who?"

"Ingrid Hansa. I saw you talking to her."

Santana was taut. "You did nothing of the kind."

"Oh? I could have sworn it was you. The pair of you were right outside this office. Ingrid was nodding, and you were pointing toward the factory."

"What the hell are you talking about?" shouted the other, rounding fiercely on him. "Ingrid wasn't even out here yesterday. You make accusations like that, I'll have you kicked off-site before your feet touch the ground. Watch what you say, mister. I did not talk to her, so you couldn't possibly have seen us. Got it?"

Merlin wanted to call him a liar, but his chance of staying at the site depended completely on his reply. Joe Santana was in a position to set the rules; Merlin had to abide by them. Taking a deep breath, Merlin contrived a penitent smile.

"I made a mistake," he said. "Sorry about that."

12

F R A N K   L L O Y D   W R I G H T sat in the lobby of the Hotel San
Marcos in Chandler, Arizona, and looked through the drawings
in Merlin's portfolio. Tom Vernon watched him carefully. He
could see that Wright was not impressed; some of the drawings
were given only a cursory glance.

"Merlin is full of real insights about architecture."

"Then why has he picked up so many bad habits?" grunted
Wright as he studied the design for a house. "Look here, Tom.
Would any human being want to *live* in a place like this?"

"I guess so."

"They must have a lot of blind clients in Wales."

"He's had to work within strict guidelines."

"There's no spark."

"His father keeps him on a tight rein," said Vernon. "It's
not easy to be creative when someone is looking over your shoulder all the time."

Wright smiled. "You manage."

"That's because you don't hassle us."

"Some of the boys think I do." He perused a design for a
warehouse, then sat back. "I'm doing my best to like his work,
but he's making it difficult for me. This friend of yours has got
a good eye and a steady hand, but where's the vision? Where's
the originality? Take this, for example. He even turns a ware-

house into a neoclassical box." He set the portfolio aside. "Merlin? Is that what he's called? I don't see any evidence of a
magician so far, Tom."

Wright stretched himself, gearing up for one of his familiar
monologues. He was wearing a long, loose-fitting coat over a
shirt with a high, starched collar. His green tie was large and
limp. His white hair shone in the light from the chandelier.

"Did I ever tell you about the Chicago Fair of 1893?"

"I believe you may have mentioned it," Tom said with a
tolerant smile. "I've forgotten most of what you said."

He remembered the story with great clarity, but would never
dare say so. To work harmoniously with Frank Lloyd Wright,
he'd learned, meant enduring a certain amount of booming repe-
tition. Wright himself delivered the lecture as if it were the first
time he had ever given it.

"The Chicago Fair," he mused, sitting back. "The World's
Columbian Exposition, officially. Why in Chicago? Because
that was the city showing the rest of America how beautiful
commercial architecture could be. Most of the credit for that
goes to Louis Sullivan. As you know, I worked for the Adler-Sul-
livan partnership in its best years. We broke new ground. We
opened people's eyes. And where Chicago led, other key cities
began to follow. Buffalo, St. Louis, and so on. And do you know
what was so wonderful about it, Tom?"

"What, Mr. Wright?" Vernon prompted, dutifully.

"It was *American* architecture. I had my differences with
Louis Sullivan, but there's one thing he did better than anyone
else at the time. He understood the American mind." He gave
a throaty cough. "That made him the odd man out at the Chicago
Fair. It was a chance to show the world what we could do, but
they lost their nerve. The decision came down that all the main
buildings would have a Renaissance design. Renaissance!" he
said bitterly. "If ever a word was mistranslated, that was it. The
Renaissance was not so much a rebirth as an exhumation. Imag-

ine the kind of stink you get when you dig up ideas that have been rotting in the earth for thousands of years! The whole fair was a travesty."

"It certainly sounds like a missed opportunity."

"When you first walked in there, it was like standing on the set of a movie about the Roman Empire. Columns, arches, and domes wherever you looked. Arcades built around this lagoon. Classical statues. Fake architecture of the worst kind, Tom. The marble was all made of plaster!"

"What did Mr. Sullivan do?"

"Stand out against them all," said Wright, proudly. "None of that Renaissance sell-out for him. He showed some individuality, some belief in America. Louis designed the only thing worth looking at—the Transportation Building." He took up the portfolio again. "That's what worries me about this boy. His mind is addled by classical ideas. Give him a ball park to design, you end up with another Colosseum. Ask him for a garden shed, he gives you a Roman temple."

"That's unfair," said Vernon. "He's still learning. And he's been working within a certain tradition. You can't blame Merlin for that. I think he's got promise."

"Of a sort," conceded Wright, flicking through the last few drawings. "It's neat, it's clever, it's in proportion. But it doesn't jump up at you, Tom. There's no bite here."

He came to the final sheet of paper and blinked in astonishment. It was Merlin's rough sketch of the Biltmore hotel. Wright devoured every detail of it hungrily before speaking.

"When did he draw this?" he asked.

"I don't know, Mr. Wright," said Vernon, looking over his shoulder. "Since he's been here, I guess. How else?"

"You didn't coach him or anything?"

"Of course not. It's all his own work. I never set eyes on that drawing until today. It's pure Merlin Richards."

Wright spent more time looking at the freehand sketch than

at any of the meticulous architectural designs in the collection. At length, with a quiet murmur of endorsement, he replaced the sketch, tied the ribbons carefully, and handed the portfolio back to Vernon.

"I want to meet this boy," he said.

MERLIN NEEDED A weapon. That was very clear. If he was to spend another night inside the flimsy protection of canvas, he had to have a means of defending himself. Bare hands were not enough. He was up against something far more threatening than the boisterous rough-and-tumble of the rugby pitch. Merlin could hold his own in weekly physical encounters against other fit young Welshmen, but he was facing more than muscle and guile here.

A concrete block had already claimed one victim. A discarded fragment might have sent Merlin off to join her. Some of the construction workers wore sheath knives, and every implement on site was a potential murder weapon. Then there was the alarming presence of guns. Every policemen left on site was armed, and the site guards carried revolvers and shotguns.

That thought made his wounds smart anew. Pete Bickley had enjoyed inflicting them. It had already crossed Merlin's mind that the guard might have been the attacker on the roof of the main building. A man who used the butt of a shotgun so maliciously would not scruple to drop a piece of concrete onto someone's head. It might not be his first experiment in the use of a building material against a human skull.

Merlin was brought to a dead stop by the notion. He had been picking his way through the camp in the gloom, but he forgot all about his search for a weapon. Pete Bickley had just moved from the role of a brutal guard to that of a potential murderer. Some sort of relationship had clearly existed between him and Rosa Lustig. But for her intervention, Merlin would have been thrown off the site by the guard. What influence did she have over him, and how had it come about?

There was supporting evidence of their friendship. Noah Corbin had talked about Bickley's affection for the girl. It explained why the guard was so vengeful toward the person he suspected of her murder, but it also gave him a motive for killing her himself. Bickley exuded jealousy. The idea that Merlin might be enjoying favors that he felt were due to him clearly rankled. Electricity had crackled between him and Rosa.

One thing was certain. Bickley was not the anonymous friend whom Rosa went off to meet on her last night alive. If the guard had found out about that tryst, his jealousy would have been stoked up to boiling point. Had he realized what actually took place between Rosa and her lover—Merlin himself had been shocked to hear the medical report's details—Pete Bickley might well have exploded with rage.

Merlin thought about the guard's fortuitous arrival at the scene of a crime. Was he really on a routine patrol with a colleague? Or was it his second visit to the spot, timed to coincide with the discovery of the body by someone else? There was no better way to throw suspicion off himself than by incriminating someone else. Bickley had been surprisingly eager to nominate Merlin as the killer; he had been given no chance to explain what he was doing there.

Felling the site guard with a punch had given him a warm glow of satisfaction, but it might have repercussions. Bickley would want revenge. If he had already killed once, he would not hesitate to do so again. This idea galvanized Merlin into action, and he continued his search for a weapon with increased urgency.

He soon found it. The broken pick handle had been tossed onto a pile of rubbish. It had snapped off near the business end, so Merlin had almost three feet of stout hickory with which to defend himself. Hefted in his palm, it gave him a strong feeling of security. It was both a club and a rudimentary spear, for the wood came to a sharp point at the end where it had parted company with the pick itself.

Merlin's stroll back to his tent was almost jaunty. The pick handle might be a poor defense against a firearm, but it would help to fend off other weapons. Its very presence in his grasp might deter an attacker. The long night ahead was a lot less fearful now.

It was dark when he got to the tent, with just enough spill of light from the factory area to allow him to see where he was going. Without Rosa, the tent seemed cold and empty. When he first entered it, happy memories of her washed over him, soon replaced by a choking grief. The image of the smashed skull and the gouting blood was so vivid in his mind that he had to shake his head violently to get rid of it. His resolve to avenge her was steeled even more.

A new idea dawned on him with such force that it made him reach for his weapon. Merlin would not have to hunt for the killer at all. The man might come to him.

THE ORDEAL OF the previous night had taken its toll, and it was not long before fatigue began to lick seductively at Merlin. He tried to stay awake, but it was a vain battle. When he dozed off into a light sleep, there were no dreams to haunt him, no faces from the past to arouse his guilt. An hour passed. He was just on the verge of yielding to a deeper slumber when he heard the distant scrunch of footsteps.

Awake in a flash, he grabbed his pick handle and crawled to the entrance, parting the tent flaps just above the point where he had retied the canvas strips. A figure was heading slowly toward him, guided by the beam of a torch. Inside the tent, Merlin would have little room to maneuver, forced into a defensive position. His survival depended on a surprise attack.

Flinging himself to the other end of the tent, he tore up the pegs that held its rear panel to the ground and wriggled out on his stomach. The footsteps got closer. Merlin knelt furtively with the weapon in his hand. When he peered around the edge of the tent, he saw the dark silhouette of a man. His visitor paused at the entrance to the tent, plucked gently at the flap, and shone in the torch.

Merlin did not hesitate. Launching himself at the man with furious power, he knocked him to the ground, sat astride his back, and pressed the pick handle down hard across his neck to force his face into the ground. His victim squirmed with fear and spluttered with pain.

"Lemme go! Lemme go, will you! For Chrissake!"

"What are you doing here?" demanded Merlin.

"Looking for someone."

"Who?"

"Guy by the name of Merlin Richards."

"Why?"

"I need to speak to him about Rosa."

Merlin relaxed the downward pressure. There was such a note of pleading in the man's voice that he took pity on him. His visitor seemed to have no weapon. Merlin slowly rose to his feet, pick handle at the ready.

"Who are you?" he asked.

The man rolled over and cowered away from him.

"I'm Norm Kozelsky."

FIVE MINUTES TRANSFORMED their relationship. Handing Kozelsky back his torch, Merlin led him to the lighted area near the site office so that they could see each other while they talked. Norm Kozelsky was inches shorter than him and of much slighter build. Dark, curly hair was slicked with brilliantine above a face with an almost flashy handsomeness. Merlin put his age around thirty.

Kozelsky regained his composure at once. He talked at high speed with dazzling confidence, using both hands in graphic gestures.

"What a welcome!" he said, brushing the dust off what had been a spotless white jacket. "I didn't expect the strong-arm treatment. I mean, is that what they teach you architects over in Wales? Pound your clients into submission, then demand your fees? Not a bad idea. I must try it. Let's start again, shall we?" He pumped Merlin's hand. "Hi, there. I'm Norm Kozelsky. This is the way I like to meet people."

"Why did you come here?"

"In search of you. I was in Tucson when I heard the news about Rosa. It made me weep buckets. That beautiful girl! That beautiful talent! Why *her*? And to go the way she did. It's grotesque. Nobody deserves to die like that. Except the heartless bastard who did this to her. I hope they get him soon. Rosa! A gorgeous kid like that!"

Merlin let him run on for a few more minutes before trying to extract any information out of him. Norm Kozelsky was patently shocked by the murder, but there was a limit to Merlin's tolerance. He held up a hand to slow Kozelsky down.

"Why search for me?"

"Because you were Rosa's friend. Probably one of the last people to see her alive."

"How do you know that?"

"I went to the cops. They told me. Yeah, they also said you'd been arrested on suspicion of the homicide at first. That must have been tough."

"It was."

"You don't look like a killer to me, Merlin." He gave a nervous laugh. "Though I had my doubts when you jumped me back there just now."

"I explained that. I have to be on my guard."

"So will I, from now on. But I'm so glad I found you." He

squeezed Merlin's shoulders. "I want to know everything you can tell me about Rosa. I need to know. She and I were very close at one time. Maybe she mentioned my name to you?"

"No, she didn't."

"Oh."

"But Tom Vernon did."

"Have you met Tom? Haven't seen him for ages. I lost touch with him when I split up with Daddy Frank. Tom's a swell guy. Loyal as a dog. I could never manage that kind of loyalty, but then I never had the same blind adoration of Daddy Frank."

"Mr. Wright?"

"Yeah—though even I wouldn't have dared to call him that to his face. The guy's unique. Head and shoulders above any architect in the world, I think, but that doesn't mean you have to follow him slavishly in every particular. Like Tom."

"Is that what he does?"

"Afraid so. He carries an invisible prayer mat around with him. Every time Daddy Frank delivered one of his lectures, Tom and the others used to get down on their knees. Ingrid was the same. Ingrid Hansa."

"Yes, I met her as well."

"She was worse in some ways. Left to herself, she'd have strewn flowers in his path when he walked. You've never seen hero-worship quite like it, Merlin. I should know. Oh boy!"

"What do you mean?"

"I caught the overflow."

"Overflow?"

"This is all boring old stuff," said Kozelsky with a grimace. "You don't want to listen to it. All over and done with. Ingrid's probably forgotten all about me by now."

"I don't think she's the type who forgets anything," said Merlin, levelly. "Tell me about this overflow. I'm interested."

Kozelsky paused for a second, as if weighing up the wisdom of taking Merlin into his confidence. Although he had come in search of the Welshman, he had given him very little chance to speak on his own behalf. He had to work on intuition. It came down on Merlin's side. When Kozelsky plunged on, his narrative picked up even more pace.

"What can I say?" he began with palms open. "You met Ingrid. Wonderful lady in many ways, but she's never going to win any prizes for beauty. That slabby face on her. Those big shoulders. Not that I have anything against her. She'd have made somebody a great wife. Solid, dependable, a swell mother, good at remembering people's birthdays. They give out awards for that kind of stuff, Ingrid would've won them all. As it was, she tried to run in the wrong race and got left behind by the rest of the field."

"I don't quite follow, Norm."

"Romance."

"Ingrid Hansa?"

"The two things don't exactly click immediately together in the mind, do they? But don't be fooled by that ice-cool Nordic appearance. Ingrid is all bonfire and fireworks underneath. When she finds a man who sets her alight, she roars like a furnace. I've seen it happen. Twice."

"What was this about an overflow?"

"That's what I became." He ran a hand through his hair. "And it was scary for a time. Let me cut this short. Ingrid fell for Daddy Frank. I mean, *really* fell. Dozens of women have. He's over sixty, and he can still have them drooling. Well, Ingrid did rather more than drool. You should've seen some of the letters she wrote to him. Thank goodness she didn't actually send them. It would've been a disaster. Anyway, Daddy Frank had problems enough without her. Miriam Noel—that's his second wife—was doing everything in her power to stop him marrying for the third time. She even had them arrested for violation of the Mann Act. Now, there's a misnomer for you. The Mann Act is really a Woman Act. Was supposed to stop white slave traffic, but it stopped the fun for a lot of other people as well. If a guy takes an unmarried woman across a state line, he violates the act."

"Tom mentioned that Miriam Noel was vindictive."

"You don't know the half of it," said Kozelsky. "But back to Ingrid. She finally accepts that she'll get nowhere with Daddy Frank, so she looks for a shoulder to cry on. I felt sorry for her. Who wouldn't? Out it all poured. And because I'm kind and sympathetic, she starts to shift her affections to me. See what I mean about an overflow? It was never the gush that Daddy Frank got out of her, but it was bad enough. I mean, I don't want to be anyone's escape valve."

"I think I can guess what happened next."

"Take a shot."

"She found out that you preferred Rosa."

Kozelsky nodded, eyes glistening. "I loved Rosa."

"Ingrid was deeply hurt."

"It's one of the reasons I had to pull out of there."

"What about Rosa?"

"She strung along for a while, then we split up. I had to go back to New York to sort out some family business, and Rosa had this crazy idea about touring Indian reservations."

"Did you never meet up again?"

Kozelsky's face paled for a second, as if the question was a knife through his heart. Tears threatened again. He began to gesticulate then his arms fell limp by his sides.

"No, Merlin," he said quietly. "We always planned to, but we never quite made it. With me in Tucson and Rosa coming to Phoenix, it looked like it might happen at last. Instead—this! Gone forever! If only I'd come a couple of days ago! To have her snatched away from right under my nose." He grasped Merlin by the shoulders again. "Do you understand why I'm here?"

"I think so."

"I want to know everything I can find out about Rosa. What

you did together, what she said. Everything. Hell, I loved the girl! I still do. I have a right."

"I'll tell you all I can," said Merlin. "But you knew her far better than me. You've already filled in a lot of gaps for me. About her. About Ingrid. And about Tom."

Kozelsky sighed. "We had such good times together. For the sake of those, I've got to keep my vigil."

"Vigil?"

"Here in Phoenix. I'm not leaving this town until they catch that guy. If it was my decision, I'd stick the bastard in an electric chair and pull the lever myself. That's the way I feel about this," he said grimly. "I need to watch him fry!"

13

MERLIN WAS EXHAUSTED. Two hours with Norm Kozelsky were a revelation in every way, but there was so much information being fired at him about people, events, and architecture that Merlin could not assimilate it all. His visitor had unquenchable vitality. Words come out of him like showers of sparks. And yet he was capable of listening as well. When Merlin began to describe how he met Rosa, the other man heard him out with rapt attention. He was patently touched by the innocence of the friendship. The description of how her dead body was found made him turn away in anguish.

It was a full minute before he was able to speak.

"That's been a great help to me," he said softly. "A great help. But I'd better leave you alone now. You look as if you're going to keel over if I keep you out here much longer."

"I am fading."

"One last favor."

"Of course."

"Show me where it happened."

"Are you sure you want to see it?"

"I have to. Painful as it's bound to be. You don't have to hold my hand. Just point me in the right direction and leave me alone for a few minutes to come to terms with it all. Is that too much to ask?"

"No."

"Let's go."

Merlin led him to the site then walked some distance away to wait. The area was still cordoned off, and Kozelsky held one of the ropes tightly in his hands while he stared at the spot where Rosa Lustig had fallen. Merlin saw his shoulders sag and his head fall onto his chest. It was a long wait. When the American finally rejoined him, he was much more subdued. Merlin escorted him to the parking area.

"Where will you spend the night?" he asked.

"I'm booked into a hotel in Phoenix."

"Will you be back out here again tomorrow?"

"Oh, yes. I'm sure there are lots of things I forgot to ask you. Besides, if I arrive in daylight, you won't ambush me with the pick handle." He offered his hand once more, but there was no strength in its grasp now. "Thanks, Merlin."

"If you come tomorrow, you may meet Mr. Wright."

"Will Daddy Frank be here?"

"Hopefully. So will Tom Vernon."

"I'd like to see both of them. Even in such lousy circumstances as these." A doubt festered. "Hold on a minute. Ingrid Hansa isn't in the party as well, is she?"

"She may be."

"Her, I can do without. She hated Rosa. I can't handle that sort of thing just now. I only want to be around people who loved and appreciated her. As you obviously did."

"Yes," agreed Merlin. "I thought she was marvelous."

"Let's hope Ingrid has the decency to stay away."

Kozelsky climbed behind the steering wheel of his Packard. He was clearly a person of some wealth. His car, his clothing, his manner, and his account of his architectural career since leaving Frank Lloyd Wright all spoke of success. Merlin was not at all surprised that his visitor had been closely involved with Rosa Lustig and that he had aroused the unwelcome attentions of Ingrid Hansa. Kozelsky had the striking looks and nervous charm that had doubtless attracted a lot of other women as well.

"Cherokee red!" said Kozelsky, slapping the side of the car. "You can't see the color in the dark, but it's Cherokee red. A touch of Daddy Frank. His favorite color for an automobile."

Merlin remembered a conversation with Clyde Willard.

"Is it true that Mr. Wright once did bootleg commissions?"

"He'd prefer to call it freelance work."

"But why did he take on the work?"

"Clients asked him."

"Couldn't he put his own name to the designs?"

"No, Merlin," explained Kozelsky. "He was working in Chicago for Louis Sullivan at the time. He was only allowed to handle set projects for them. But he was ambitious. And always in need of money. So he designed the houses and passed them off as someone else's." He laughed. "For a time, he got away with it. Then Mr. Sullivan drove past one of the houses, and that was that. He recognized the architect at once, and his Irish temper flared up."

"What did he do?"

"That depends whose version you believe."

"Give me the truthful one."

"Mr. Sullivan went straight to the office and fired him. He refused to have anyone in the practice doing work behind his back. The young Frank Lloyd Wright was the victim of his own brilliance."

"In what way?"

"He was too good an architect. Too bold, too clever, too distinctive. You can't hide that kind of talent. Louis Sullivan spotted the deception at once. That design had one architect's name on it, but he saw a much more flamboyant signature written in large letters across the house."

Merlin turned instinctively toward the hotel.

WITHIN MINUTES OF lying down again, Merlin was asleep. The firm hold on the pick handle relaxed, and it rolled away from his grasp. Though he told himself to remain vigilant, he could not obey his own instruction. The past twenty-four hours had left him mentally and physically sapped; the questing urgency of Norm Kozelsky had tired him beyond recall. His sleep, deep and untroubled, left him completely vulnerable. But nobody came.

What woke him at dawn was not the rowdy bustle of activity on site, but an eerie silence. At first he thought he had gone deaf, but he could hear the rustle of his blanket when he moved, and the song of a bird soon broke in. As he left the tent, he saw why the tumult had ceased. The factory had suspended operations. He was now so used to its rumbling monologue that its absence was almost uncanny.

With the production of the concrete blocks now ahead of schedule, the factory had reverted to two ten-hour shifts a day. Pandemonium was once more hyphenated. Merlin, unaware of the work schedule, preferred to believe that the silence was a mark of respect for Rosa Lustig.

By the time he walked across to the communal washroom to shave, the machines had started up again. He invested some of his money in a hearty breakfast at the site canteen. He felt less guilty about the twenty dollars he had been given by Clyde Willard now. Seen as compensation for the indignities, it took on a different character, and it gave him a temporary respite from his financial straits.

Back at the tent, he had a first opportunity to reflect on Norm Kozelsky's visit. It had given him a new insight into the world of Frank Lloyd Wright and his acolytes. Kozelsky's dynamism and sense of prosperity were rather wearing, and Merlin felt much more relaxed in the company of the laid-back Tom Vernon. It was as if Norm were trying too hard to make an impression. Merlin could not understand why he needed to do so.

In retrospect, he was peeved at some of Kozelsky's sweeping strictures. Loyalty was not a vice. Merlin had learned the value of a prayer mat on more than one occasion in his life. Humility had practical advantages of a kind that Kozelsky would never experience. And yet the man's abiding love for Rosa Lustig was sincere and moving. That was one thing in his favor.

The impending arrival of Frank Lloyd Wright was the major priority in Merlin's day. It might not actually occur for several hours yet, but it felt imminent. Merlin was determined not to make the mistakes that had bedeviled their first encounter. Lack of confidence would not handicap him this time. He was ready to fight back on his own behalf now, even if it meant contradicting a man whom he revered.

A walk around the site reminded him that he had few friends there. Joe Santana ignored him, Pete Bickley spat into the sand as he passed, and several of the workers just stared. Merlin was an outsider, interfering with the steady rhythm of the project. They were disappointed at his release from police custody. They wanted him to be the killer.

The car arrived at ten. Wright himself was driving, helmet and goggles in place. Tom Vernon was his only passenger, holding down his hat with his hand as they cruised in through the main entrance. The policemen on duty there did not hinder the sleek automobile in any way.

Merlin watched with trepidation when he saw his portfolio once again, tucked under Vernon's arm as he accompanied Wright to the site office. Merlin waited outside with growing impatience, succumbing to morbid speculations about Wright's opinion of his drawings.

It was an eternity before Vernon emerged from the office with Joe Santana. There was a heated discussion. When Santana went off toward the factory, Vernon beckoned his friend over.

"Hi, Merlin!"

"Good morning, Tom."

"Joe has kindly loaned his office for a while."

"I see."

"Come on in and meet Mr. Wright. Properly."

When they went into the office, the architect was poring over the drawing on the table. He straightened to his full height and shook hands with Merlin as the introductions were made. Waving him to a chair, he sat on the edge of the desk to look down at him. Vernon took a seat in the corner and gave Merlin a surreptitious wink of encouragement.

Wright's manner was friendly, but detached.

"Merlin, eh?" he said. "Who gave you that name?"

"My father."

"Merlin was a Welsh wizard. Is that what you are?"

"Not exactly, Mr. Wright."

"Don't you believe in wizards?"

"Oh, yes. I'm looking at one."

A first smile. "I have Welsh blood in my veins," he said, "and I am proud to acknowledge it. That's why I called my house Taliesin. After the great Welsh bard. Taliesin, as I am sure you know, means 'shining brow,' and that is an exact description of the site on which my home dwells. I have known great happiness at Taliesin, though it has been the scene of great tragedies as well. Tom may have spoken of them."

"A little, Mr. Wright."

"We all have to suffer for our art. Personal sacrifice is a necessary condition of all artistic endeavor. But I think you've found that out already. How are you feeling now?"

"Much better, thanks."

"Tom tells me that you got knocked about a bit."

"I survived."

"Merlin is made of granite," said Vernon.

"He'll need to be," observed Wright. "To make it as an

architect, you have to be able to take a lot of blows. Your critics may not use the butt of a shotgun, but they can hurt you just as much. If you let them." A sadness came into his eyes. "Tell me about Rosa Lustig."

"What would you like to know, Mr. Wright?"

"How you met her. How you found the poor girl dead."

Merlin was succinct. He did not want to dwell on details he had already recounted a number of times. Wright did not require the fuller version given to the police, to Clyde Willard, and to Norm Kozelsky. The bare structure of the story was enough for him. His quick mind filled in all that was left out.

"Rosa was sweet," said Wright with a nostalgic sigh. "A good sculptor and designer. I liked her. It saddens me that she came to take a more jaundiced view of me."

"But that's not true, Mr. Wright. She idolized you."

"Not at the end. Did she, Tom?"

"I'm afraid not."

"Explain it to Merlin."

Vernon nodded. "When the Biltmore project took off, they needed designs for the concrete blocks. Some sculptors were asked to submit ideas. Mr. Wright was kind enough to suggest Rosa's name, and she was considered along with the rest." He gave a shrug. "Well, you saw her work. It was excellent. But not quite what was wanted, so she was turned down."

"Not by me," said Wright.

"She blamed you for it all the same."

"It was Albert's doing."

"That's Mr. McArthur," explained Vernon. "He liked her work, but not enough. Rosa didn't take rejection easily."

"I wasn't the one who rejected her," insisted Wright. "I'd have asked her to come up with some more designs before making a final decision. But Albert wouldn't have it that way. What could I do? I'm only the consultant. I can scream and shout at Albert, but he makes all the decisions." Deep regret came back.

"I just wish I'd parted on better terms with her. We used to be friends."

"Rosa spoke very highly of you," said Merlin.

"I'll miss her."

"So did Norm Kozelsky. He was full of praise."

Wright was surprised. "Norm? You've met him?"

"When was this?" said Vernon, rising to his feet.

"Last night."

"He came out here?"

"Yes, Tom. Looking for me."

"Why?"

"To hear about what happened to Rosa."

The other men exchanged a meaningful glance.

"Did he say where he'd come from?" asked Vernon.

"Tucson."

"I thought he was working back East," said Wright.

Vernon nodded. "He was. Maybe he was down here on vacation. Or on a delayed honeymoon."

"Is he *married*?" said Merlin.

"So I heard."

"It took me by surprise as well," said Wright with a wry smile. "Norm has immense talent, but it was always a little too promiscuous for my liking. He wanted to jump straight into bed with every new idea on the architectural horizon. A dangerous philosophy. Never pursue novelty for its own sake." His eye dropped to the portfolio. "It's almost as bad as being fettered by the distant past."

Vernon took his cue. "Mr. Wright was only able to glance at your drawings, Merlin," he said, easily. "He could see that you're a very competent draftsman, but he felt your work was derivative."

"Fair comment," said Merlin. Sensing that Wright himself would have been far more critical of his portfolio, he was grateful that Vernon had delivered the verdict, protecting him from the full force of Wright's disapproval. But the danger was not completely averted. Reaching for the portfolio, Wright undid the ribbons and took out one of the drawings. Merlin tried to shore up his confidence by telling himself he would learn from the other's condemnation.

The sketch of the Arizona Biltmore was held out.

"When did you do this?" asked Wright.

"A couple of days ago."

"Why?"

"I wanted to, Mr. Wright. I borrowed a pencil and a sheet of cartridge paper from Rosa, and—that's the result."

"And is this what you actually *saw*?"

"In my mind's eye."

"This is not the way that the hotel is being built."

"It's the way I think it should be."

Merlin saw anger flicker in the old man's eyes, quickly replaced by a glint of curiosity. There was a long pause. Merlin felt the true, intimidating power of Wright's personality. He seemed to grow bigger before Merlin's eyes. Putting the drawing away, Wright handed the portfolio to its owner before walking out of the office. Tom Vernon indicated that they should follow him.

Wright had taken up his stance to view the hotel.

"Draw it for me again," said Mr. Wright. "Properly."

"Properly?" repeated Merlin.

"Take more time. Put in more detail. Redesign the Arizona Biltmore for me. We've brought materials for you, including a ruler and set-square. Tom will get them from the car." He turned to Merlin. "Will you do that for me?"

"Gladly."

"Start right away."

MERLIN WAS SO excited that the pencil trembled in his hand at first. The honor of meeting Frank Lloyd Wright and of giving a better account of himself had been sufficient reward in themselves for all the setbacks he had endured. To be given an impromptu commission by the architect was a wholly unexpected bounty. No money was involved, and nothing might result from his work, but Merlin did not care in the least. He had just been engaged by the most important client he could ever possibly meet. Wright took him seriously. That was inspiration enough.

He set about his task with great care. Tom Vernon furnished him with all the materials he needed, including a drawing board and a box of drawing pins. Merlin salvaged a large packing case for use as his drafting table, at which he could work in his preferred standing position. It was like being back home in the office.

What Merthyr could not offer was the Arizona winter sunshine, now so warm it obliged him to strip down to his shirtsleeves. As he basked in its glow, it was difficult to believe that Christmas was not far away. That thought brought a lump to his throat. It would be the first time in his life that he had not spent the festive season with his family. He would sorely miss the annual celebrations. That profound loss would be offset by one huge gain. Albeit briefly, he was working for Frank Lloyd Wright. It would be something to put on the Christmas cards he sent home.

Merlin had been sketching steadily for an hour before he was interrupted. His visitor approached quietly from behind.

"What are you doing?" asked a polite voice.

Merlin, startled, turned to see Clyde Willard. The journalist wore the same suit and straw boater, but his shirt and tie had been changed. The attaché case was in his hand.

"Hello, Mr. Willard."

"Why are you sketching the hotel?"

"It was Mr. Wright's idea."

"Have I missed him?" said the other in irritation.

"I'm afraid so. They left some time ago."

"Why didn't you tell me he was coming?"

"I didn't know myself until after you went yesterday."

"Is Mr. Wright coming back here?"

"I'm not sure."

"Where has he gone now?"

"Back to Chandler. He's designing a hotel there. You might catch him in Chandler, if it's that important."

"I needed to see him on *this* site." Willard relaxed and gave a bland smile. "Well, I guess I can't have everything. Though I would have liked to put a few questions to him about Rosa." He indicated the drawing board. "What's the point of this?"

"It's an exercise, Mr. Willard."

"In what?"

"Architectural technique," said Merlin. "Tom Vernon told me that it's the way Mr. Wright sometimes works. He takes buildings that he designed in the past and gets his apprentices to work on the plans for them."

"Sounds crazy to me."

"Not at all. Tom remembers doing perspectives of the Imperial Hotel in Tokyo, and that was completed in 1922. One of Mr. Wright's greatest achievements. It's astonishing."

"Why design buildings that already exist?"

"To learn from a master."

"Can't you do that just by studying his own plans?"

"No, Mr. Willard. You have to start—as he did—with a blank sheet of paper and confront all the same problems. It gets you right inside the mind of a genius."

"But according to Vernon, the genius didn't actually design the Biltmore. He only advised. What can you learn by sketching this hotel?"

"How different it would have looked if Frank Lloyd Wright had been the architect."

Willard gazed down at the sketch with fresh interest.

"I won't hold you up any more," he said, patting him on the back. "We'll speak later. I need to talk to a guy called Joe Santana. They said I might find him in the site office."

Merlin pointed. "It's that building over there."

"Thanks. Sorry to interrupt."

When the journalist had glided away, Merlin stared after him. Clyde Willard's manner had changed slightly. He was no longer as glib and affable as he had been. Merlin began to wonder if the offer of introductions to architects in Los Angeles had been a serious one or simply a carrot held in front of a donkey. He dismissed the thought. Frank Lloyd Wright had banished every other architect from his mind.

Soon absorbed in his task once again, he lost all purchase on time. It was only when he stopped to sharpen a pencil with the knife that Vernon had so considerately supplied that he saw Clyde Willard again. The journalist was crouching with Joe Santana beside a pile of rubble on the site.

They were reclaiming pieces of concrete from the pile and trying to fit them together again. It took them a long time to find the correct pieces, but their persistence was at last rewarded. Willard was so pleased that he took out his wallet.

Merlin was nonplussed. Why was Clyde Willard so keen to buy the fragments of a decorated concrete block?

14

PETE BICKLEY WAS not pleased to be interviewed by the police again. Told to sit down, he did so with a muted truculence. Lieutenant Noah Corbin and Sergeant Walt Drummond sat opposite him behind a trestle table covered with piles of documents. The detectives had commandeered the largest cabin on the site for their own use, but it fell short of the comforts they took for granted.

Corbin read through the statement in front of him. When he looked up, he gave Bickley a bleak smile.

"Take your hat off, Pete. Make yourself at home."

"How long is this gonna take?" asked the other, slowly removing his battered fedora to lay it across his knee. "I'm supposed to be on duty out there, Lieutenant."

"We fixed that with your boss," said Drummond.

"Yes," added Corbin, hands behind his head. "He was only too willing to release you for further questioning. You're our star witness. At least, you were."

"What do you mean?" grunted the guard.

"Well, you were the one who caught Merlin Richards."

"I still think he did it."

"Evidence is pointing another way, Pete."

"It was him," argued Bickley. "Why else would he go near

the factory? He had no right to be there. We found him standing over the body. What more do you want?"

"Motive, means, and opportunity," said Corbin dryly.

"He had the means," agreed Drummond. "There's enough of those concrete blocks around here to crack open every head in Maricopa County. And Richards had the opportunity. Sleep with a woman, you got all the opportunity you need. Not only to bump her off, either. But where's his motive? Sharing a tent with a lovely young woman is not a motive. Not for murder, anyway."

Bickley glowered. They gauged his reaction carefully.

"The way we look at it is this," said Corbin, taking up the lead again. "Richards is clean. He may be a greenhorn, but even he is not dumb enough to bump off a woman under the noses of a couple of site guards. Pity. Because it rather takes the shine off your halo, Pete."

"What halo?"

"Oh, come on. Two nights ago you were the big hero around here. A homicide is committed, and Pete Bickley catches the guy red-handed. You knocked him out cold and had him trussed up like a Thanksgiving turkey by the time we showed. I bet the boys all gave you a big slap on the back." He sat forward and rested his arms on the table. "Now, of course, they know that you were a bit quick on the draw."

"The guy was there. Beside Rosa's body."

"Spewing up like crazy. Explain that."

"Maybe he killed her in a rage," said Bickley.

"Somebody certainly did."

"When he realizes what he's done, he can't take it. Throws up. It figures, Lieutenant. I saw Rosa lying there like that, it made *my* stomach turn. It was all I could do to hang on to my supper, I can tell you."

"That was because you knew the girl," said Drummond.

"Eh?"

"You wouldn't have responded like that if she'd been a complete stranger. Or one of the guys from the construction gang, say. No, you *knew* Rosa Lustig. As a friend. Isn't that what made you slug Richards? You lost control."

"That's not true."

"He thinks it is. And he wasn't pleased about it."

"No," said Corbin with a grin. "I understand that old Merlin mentioned his displeasure to you. They say he packs quite a punch." A note of false sympathy sounded. "That's the way it goes, I'm afraid. One day you're the hero who catches a brutal killer. Next day, you're knocked flat on your back."

"Why are you two trying to rile me?"

"You look riled up enough as it is, Pete."

"I told you exactly what happened, Lieutenant. And I got nothing to add. So what am I doing in here?"

"Fleshing out our information. Walt?"

"We're trying to build up a fuller picture of Rosa Lustig," explained the sergeant. "We need to construct her movements in the days leading up to her death. That's where you can help us. By all accounts, you got pretty close to Rosa."

"Not really."

"The two of you were seen talking together a lot."

"Nothing wrong in a friendly chat."

"You were hoping it would lead to something else."

"That a crime, Sergeant?"

"No, Pete."

"So why call me in here again?"

"We want to hear how far you got with her. What Rosa promised, what she delivered. You may as well know that she gave someone the full works that night. But no," he added as he saw Bickley's sudden ire, "it wasn't Merlin Richards. He made no headway at all. Question is—did you?"

"Tell us," coaxed Corbin. "It could help."

Bickley shifted uneasily in his seat. The detectives were

probing into a sensitive area, and it unsettled him. He would do anything to avoid being made to look like a fool.

"Well?" prompted Drummond.

"I got nothing else to say."

"We think you have."

"That's your problem, Sergeant."

"Don't clam up on us," sighed Corbin, taking up a handful of documents. "We got a dozen or more statements here from guys who heard you boasting about what you were going to do with Rosa. You were the prize bull of the herd, Pete. That's why she chose you. So stop wasting our time and acting like a vestal fucking virgin." He beamed at the guard. "Tell us all about them."

"Them?"

"The secrets of the human heart."

MERLIN WAS UNHAPPY to see him coming. He knew that Norm Kozelsky could probably give him some valuable advice about his sketch, but he did not want to discuss it with him at all. That was why it was slipped quickly away inside the portfolio before Kozelsky could even see it. Other doubts had arisen about the man as well. Merlin hid them behind a token smile as the visitor came strutting across to him.

"Hi, Merl!"

"Hello."

"What we got here? The Richards studio? You're setting up a branch office right here on-site? Why not? I like a guy with enterprise. Go for it." He gave Merlin a playful punch on the arm. "So—what's happened since we last met?"

"Nothing much."

"Any sign of Daddy Frank yet?"

"He's been and gone."

"Oh, no!"

"Said to give you his regards. So did Tom Vernon."

"That was nice. I take it that Ingrid didn't show?"

"No."

"Let's be grateful for small mercies. Except that poor Ingrid is not exactly small, is she? How was Daddy Frank?"

"Amazed to hear that you'd been here."

"I like to amaze people."

"They wondered what you were doing in Tucson," said Merlin. "Tom Vernon thought you might be on holiday down here. Or on a second honeymoon."

Kozelsky's mouth twitched. "Told you about me getting married, did they? Well, it had to come one day, Merl. And I'd had a pretty good run so what the hell? My wife's got family down in Tucson. We were just visiting with them, that's all. End of the week, I go back to New York to keep the pennies rolling in." He became confidential. "By the way, if you need a loan to keep you going, say the word. Any friend of Rosa's can call on me for help. We've got a bond here, Merl. Use it."

Merlin was both grateful for the offer and slightly offended by the way it was put. There was a brashness about Norm Kozelsky that he found unappealing. Seeing him for the first time in daylight, Merlin noticed how handsome he really was. The cream suit was immaculate, the straw hat set at a rakish angle. A gold watch gleamed on one wrist. The silver tiepin had a deep luster. Even when he was visiting the scene of a cruel murder, Kozelsky liked to dress with ostentation.

"What I could really use is some more information about Rosa," said Merlin. "I'm still very hazy about some things."

"Show me the blanks. I'll fill them."

"Well, it really concerns those men."

"What men?"

"The ones she met in Phoenix."

"Tell me about them."

When Merlin described the way that the man in the café had

stared at her, Kozelsky held up a hand to stop him. There was no need to say any more. A note of bitter resignation took over.

"Rosa had a tough time as a kid," he said. "She grew up in a town in Indiana called Kokomo, and that was not the best place to be if your father happens to be a rabbi. They're not too fond of Jews in Kokomo."

"Why not?"

"Do I really have to explain?"

Merlin regretted his interruption. "Go on."

"You ever hear of the Ku Klux Klan?"

"Vaguely."

"They were pretty big in central Indiana. Rosa had them in her face all the time. Then came that Konklave."

"That what?"

"Konklave. A huge tristate meeting. Klan members from Ohio, Illinois, and Indiana, all gathered together in this park not far from Rosa's house. She was terrified. You see, the trouble is this. The Klan is an organization of rabid so-called true Americans. That means they don't like Jews, Catholics, foreigners, or Negroes." He gave a self-effacing laugh. "Now, me. I saw nothing of this. I grew up in Manhattan. We got more Jews there than in Warsaw. And those are the official figures. See what I mean? We're integrated. We blend in. Rosa and her family stuck out. The few among the many."

"What happened?"

"Kokomo had a population of about thirty thousand. Rosa reckons that the convention attracted six or seven times that number. Imagine that, Merl. Two hundred thousand of those bastards, wearing their white robes and their pointed hoods, going past your front door on their way to meet the Grand Dragon and the Imperial Wizard and all that other shit they go in for. Makes a big impression on you."

"When was this, Norm?"

"Five years ago. Rosa was eighteen."

"Was she attacked or something?"

"Not physically," said Kozelsky. "She just woke up at midnight to find this big burning cross on her lawn with a couple of hundred people yelling at the top of their voices. And the worst of it was, Rosa *knew* many of them. They were neighbors. Some of them even had their hoods off so they could see what was going on more clearly. That was the final straw for Rosa." He made a vivid gesture. "Next day, she was out of there. Left home for good." A rueful grin. "One thing about the world of art, Merlin. Toleration. All you need to make it is enough talent. It doesn't matter whether you're white, black, green, red, or yellow. We even allow the Welsh in."

"That explains a lot about Rosa," said Merlin. "What you're telling me is that this Ku Klux Klan is quite strong down here as well. Those men who looked at her—"

"Klansmen, in all probability. Arizona has had a fair bit of activity. You looked at Rosa, you saw a gorgeous, sexy woman with a real flair for design. Those men saw a kike." A dismissive wave. "Still, what are a few disapproving stares on the street in Phoenix? There are real atrocities in other states. Lynchings, whippings, beatings. They mean business, those madmen. Luckily, Rosa missed out on all that." A despairing chuckle. "Only to come up against *this*. Who said there was any justice in this lousy world?"

"Do you think there could be any connection?"

"Connection?"

"Between Rosa's death and those men in Phoenix?"

"No," said Kozelsky firmly. "They're cowards—they only hunt in packs. Besides, the Klan like to dress up in all that laundry when they pounce on a victim. What we're after here is one man, Merl. I just hope the cops get him before I do."

Merlin had his own hopes on that subject, but he did not confide in Kozelsky. The American reverted to his normal ebullience. He made a quick appraisal of the site.

148 / KEITH MILES

"Well, it sure looks better in the daylight!" he said with a smile. "You're going to stick around?"

"Yes."

"See you later, then."

"Right."

"First off, I want to take a closer look at the Arizona Biltmore. After what it's done to Rosa, I can never bring myself to like the place, but that doesn't mean I can't appreciate its finer points. Call it professional nosiness."

"I think you'll be impressed."

"That's my fear." He delivered another mock punch. "When I see you again, I'll tell you some stories about Daddy Frank that'll make your hair stand on end."

He did not pause to ask if Merlin wanted to hear them.

THE FIRST THING Tom Vernon did when he was dropped off in Phoenix was buy a copy of the daily paper, the *Arizona Republican*. He was still reading it carefully when Ingrid Hansa joined him in the restaurant for lunch. He folded the paper away.

"The cops don't seem to be making much progress," he said, sadly. "According to the report, they've drafted in more men."

"It must be hell out there."

"It is. I was there this morning."

She was hurt. "You never told me that you were going out to the Biltmore site."

"It sort of came up at the last moment."

"What took you out there?"

"Mr. Wright wanted to go. Asked me along."

"I'd have come myself if I'd known," she said, feeling slighted. "I think you made a point of not telling me."

"It wasn't like that, Ingrid."

"Wasn't it? This is not the first time, Tom."

"For what?"

"That little game you keep playing."

"Game?"

"Keeping Mr. Wright to yourself," she said, tartly. "We all know you're his favorite, but that doesn't mean you're entitled to monopolize him. The other guys are always grumbling about it, but they're too polite to tell you to your face. I don't have that handicap."

Vernon grinned. "That's why we all love you."

"And don't turn on the charm. I'm serious, Tom."

"Then you deserve a big apology," he said, removing his glasses to clean them with a handkerchief. "I really am sorry, Ingrid. Honestly. If I'd known you were that keen to go out there again, I'd have got Mr. Wright to pick you up as well. Truth is, it was only a flying visit. Less than half an hour on site."

"What was the point of going?"

"To see Merlin Richards."

"Why?"

"For one thing, Mr. Wright wanted to talk to him about Rosa. Don't forget, Merlin was the person who actually found the body."

"I wish I had!" she muttered.

"Ingrid!"

"Well, there's no point in being hypocritical. I loathed her. With cause. And you know why, Tom. So don't ask *me* to join in the weeping and wailing for Rosa Lustig."

"I'd hoped that even you might show a spark of human decency on this occasion," he chided with unexpected sharpness. "Rosa was murdered, for heaven's sake! Bludgeoned to death with a concrete block. Can't you find one ounce of sympathy for her?"

Coming as it did from someone who was usually so cool and easygoing, his rebuke wounded her to the quick. Ingrid could not rise to a verbal apology, but her lowered head was a faint indication of penitence. Both were glad when the waitress came to take their order, giving them a breathing space. When the girl had gone, Ingrid made an effort to be less spiteful.

"What will happen to her?" she said.

"Her father's coming to collect the body tomorrow. The cops have agreed to release it so that he can bring her back to Indiana. If you can't manage a kind word for Rosa herself, at least have some pity for her family."

"I do, Tom."

"How would *your* parents feel?"

It was a sobering thought.

"The other reason we went," said Vernon, moving away from a delicate subject, "was for Mr. Wright to have a chat with Merlin about his work."

"He doesn't know anything about it."

"I showed him his portfolio."

"Whatever for?"

"As a favor to Merlin."

"Well, it was no favor to the rest of us," she snapped. "There's not enough work to go around as it is. We don't want somebody else horning in on the action."

"Merlin isn't doing that."

"Then why are you giving him all this help?"

"I like the guy."

"There's no room for one more snout in the trough!"

He laughed. "You've got it all wrong, as usual. If you want the truth, Mr. Wright didn't have much time for Merlin's work. Apart from one drawing. So he's not a rival for you. He won't get anywhere near the trough."

She was mollified. "What it's like out there?"

"Spooky. I was glad to get away."

"Spooky?"

"Everyone pretending that nothing happened the other night. Averting their gaze whenever they walk past the spot where it actually happened. It was weird, Ingrid. And the site is still three feet deep in cops."

"Maybe it's as well I didn't go out there, then."

"It is." He replaced his glasses and pushed them up the bridge of his nose. "You might have bumped into him."

"Who?"

"Norm."

She sat back as if he had just slapped her across the face.

"Norm Kozelsky?" she gasped.

"Turned up out of the blue, apparently," he said. "I can't imagine that you'd have enjoyed seeing him again."

MERLIN WORKED STEADILY at the drawing board in the sunshine. A new Arizona Biltmore came to life on the white paper. It had most of the elements in the version that he glanced up at from time to time, but they were subtly rearranged or replaced altogether. Nothing was omitted. Every eucalyptus and palm tree was put in its place. He even sketched in some of the cars in the parking lot at the front of the main building. What ate up the most time was the fine detail of the decorated concrete blocks.

He was at once designing something far bigger than he had ever undertaken before and walking through the mind of his idol. Whenever he faltered, the voice of Frank Lloyd Wright seemed to whisper in his ear, and his pencil resumed its elegant pirouettes.

Clyde Willard was amazed by how much progress Merlin had made while he was away. He perused the result with meticulous interest.

"It's remarkable," he said.

"It will be when it's finished."

"What will happen to it then?"

"I don't know. I imagine that Tom Vernon will take it across to Chandler to show to Mr. Wright. It would be nice if he liked *something* I did."

"Good luck, anyway," Willard said, touching Merlin's arm.

"Look, why don't you come and have dinner with me this evening?"

"Dinner?"

"At my hotel in Phoenix. It would give you a chance to get away from here, and that might be a bonus. I've still got things to ask you about Rosa Lustig, but I can't stay here any longer. I'm at the Hotel Westcourt."

"How would I get there?"

Willard chuckled. "That's a strange question for someone who traveled thousands of miles to reach Arizona. Hitch a lift or hire a taxi. I'll happily pay."

"Thanks."

"Will you join me, then?"

Merlin hesitated. "Could I think about it, please?"

"Of course. I won't be offended if you don't make it. Listen, why don't we leave it like this? I'll be in the hotel restaurant at six. Find me there if you're hungry." He gave Merlin a farewell handshake. "Keep up the good work."

"I'll try. Oh, before you go, Mr. Willard—"

"Yes?"

"I noticed you earlier with Joe Santana."

"Yes. Helpful guy."

"Was that one of the concrete blocks he gave you?"

Willard's smile looked a trifle less plausible as he considered his reply. He finally opted for another chuckle.

"We didn't realize that anyone was watching," said the journalist with mock horror. "I'll have to let you in on the secret. Mr. Santana bent the rules for me."

"Rules?"

"Nothing is supposed to leave the site except by some authorized means. No materials, no tools, no equipment, and most important of all, no plans. They don't want somebody ripping off their ideas."

"What you took was from a pile of rubble."

"Even that is, technically, governed by the rules. But I was so keen to have one of the blocks as a memento that I persuaded Mr. Santana to find me a dud. Who's going to miss a concrete block that cracked into five separate pieces?"

"I saw money change hands."

"No, Merlin. You couldn't have."

"You took out your wallet."

"I was giving him my business card."

"My eyesight is very reliable, Mr. Willard.

A pause. "Well, he deserved something for being so obliging," said the other, conceding the point. "It was a tip, not a bribe. You know how generous I can be."

Merlin would not be shaken off so easily.

"You wanted it as a memento, you say?"

"Yes."

"Of what?"

"My visit to the Arizona Biltmore."

"Fragments of a decorated concrete block?"

"I'll stick them together again."

"Why?"

The plausible smile suffered another minor crisis.

"Have dinner with me, and I'll tell you."

But Merlin had lost all interest in the invitation now.

15

"YOU'VE GOT TO take your hat off to the old goat," said Norm Kozelsky. "He can still scramble up the mountainside faster than any of them."

"What do you think of the hotel?" asked Merlin.

"It works as a piece of architecture. What else is there to say? Daddy Frank has waved his magic wand, and another building suddenly blooms."

"But it wasn't designed by Mr. Wright."

"Enough of him is there to save it from mediocrity."

"He doesn't believe that."

"He wouldn't."

"Mr. Wright called it an architectural disaster."

Kozelsky laughed. "Then he must be mellowing. In my day, he would have used much more colorful language. Daddy Frank is a perfectionist. He's never satisfied. After all these years at the game, he still hasn't learned to strike a harmonious balance."

"Between what?"

"Art and finance, the beautiful vision and the problem of paying for it. Building is all about compromise. You can only create a masterpiece within the limits of your client's budget."

"Mr. Wright has always done that, hasn't he?"

Kozelsky laughed hysterically. It was minutes before he controlled himself enough to speak.

"Sorry, Merl," he said, "but that's the best joke I've heard in ages. Frank Lloyd Wright couldn't keep within a budget if he tried. His ideas always cost much more money than there is on the table. And the bigger the project, the wilder the cost overrun. Take this place," he said with a sweep of his arm. "Do you know what the initial budget was?"

"No idea."

"One million dollars."

"Good God!"

"You ever design anything in Merthyr for that amount?"

"We could rebuild the whole town."

"Not if you have to cope with the desert conditions they face out here. They had to create an entire water system. That meant drilling wells, building a reservoir in the foothills, and putting in a treatment plant on site. Then there's the electricity supply. You see any ugly pylons? Any unsightly cables? No. And why? Because the Biltmore has got the first underground electrical facilities in the state. How much do you think all that cost?"

"Thousands."

"And some!"

"Tom Vernon said the labor is very cheap here."

"What use is that if the materials are so costly? There's over thirty thousand pounds of prime copper in that roof. That's one hell of an expensive tribute to the Arizona mining industry."

"It looks superb."

"At that price, we should have a Taj Mahal."

"How do you know all this?"

"By reading the chitchat in the local papers. And by snooping around the place and talking to the right people. Did you know, for instance, that the ceiling in the main building will be covered entirely in gold leaf?"

Tom Vernon had only talked about the architectural facets of the Biltmore. There had been no mention of finance, still less of the commercial politics that lay behind it. With a combination of fact and informed supposition, Kozelsky gave him a crash course in the realities of the Biltmore project. Not for the first time, Merlin was made to feel like a novice in the school of American architecture.

They were standing beside the packing case that was doing duty as Merlin's drafting table. Before Kozelsky rejoined him, Merlin had hidden the sketch away in his portfolio once more. Kozelsky was now redesigning it for him with an invisible pencil.

"So there it is. The McArthur brothers set the ball rolling. Budget of one million. Now they've had to take on additional stockholders to raise more money. Budget is running at more than double the estimate."

"You can't blame all that on Mr. Wright."

"Not all, perhaps. But some."

"Tom says he wanted it smaller in scale."

"He'd still have found ways to overspend. Force of habit." Kozelsky shook his head in wonderment. "All that money tied up in this venture. Yet the irony is that Daddy Frank is only getting a consultant's fee. Plus a payment for a license to use his concrete block system. Add them together, and they're still peanuts compared to what he should be getting out of this deal."

"I don't follow."

"This looks, feels, tastes, and smells like a Frank Lloyd Wright building. As the architect, he'd have been entitled to a ten percent fee. Of two million plus. Work that out."

"It makes you ask why he took it on in the first place."

"Same old reason."

"What's that?"

"A chronic shortage of money."

"Tom Vernon didn't mention that."

"He wouldn't. Blind loyalty at work again. Protecting his master from any embarrassment." He tightened the knot on his tie. "Put it this way, Merl. Frank Lloyd Wright will never be the patron saint of bank managers."

Merlin felt uneasy. He quickly diverted Kozelsky from any more disclosures about Wright's private affairs. He was finding his chirpy iconoclasm both annoying and inappropriate.

"I thought you came to talk about Rosa."

"I did, I did."

"Why don't we stick to that?"

"Sure. Sorry. I was only firing off that shit to keep myself from thinking about her. Every time I caught a glimpse of that factory, I nearly lost it." Kozelsky became pensive. "What was the last thing Rosa said to you?"

"I can't remember the exact words."

"Give me the gist."

"She was rushing off. Didn't want to be late."

"For what?"

"The meeting I told you about."

"With a friend."

"Yes."

"And she gave you no hint who he might be?"

"Only in her manner, Norm."

"Her manner?"

"He was obviously special to her. Very special."

"Lucky guy!" he murmured.

"The police are very anxious to trace him."

"So am I. He'd have seen Rosa after you."

"Yes, and he'll be dreadfully shocked by what happened to her. Unless he was responsible for it, that is."

The idea shook Norm Kozelsky. It had clearly never occurred to him. His exuberance vanished completely as he brooded in silence. When he came out of his reverie, he spoke to himself.

"Nobody who loved Rosa could do that to her." He became aware of Merlin. "I need to get back to the hotel to phone my wife," he said, brusquely.

"Right."

"Unless you got anything else you want to ask."

"Nothing," said Merlin, glad to see the back of him.

"Need a lift into Phoenix?"

"No thanks."

"My car is yours while I'm around."

"That's very kind of you."

"I'll be back before too long, I imagine."

Kozelsky walked off. A sudden thought flashed into Merlin's mind. Much as he resented the man in some ways, there was no reason why he should not make use of him.

"Could I ask a favor of you, Norm?" he called.

Kozelsky stopped and turned. "Fire away."

"There was a journalist out here earlier. From the *Los Angeles Times*. His name is Clyde Willard."

"What does he want?"

"A story about Rosa."

"I hope you didn't tell him the things you told me," said Kozelsky with alarm. "Newspapers distort everything. I don't want them printing lies about Rosa. Safest thing is to keep clear of reporters altogether."

"This man is not like other reporters."

"He probably gets paid more, that's all."

"There's something odd about him. It set me thinking. I just wanted to check up on him, if possible."

"Is that the favor?"

"Yes. Mr. Willard is staying at the Hotel Westcourt."

"First name, Clyde. *L.A.Times*."

"That's it," said Merlin. "Just find out if he really is registered there."

"Have you any reason to doubt him?"

"Yes and no."

Kozelsky was brisk. "Leave him to me. If someone is that interested in Rosa, I want to know why on my own account.

Thanks for the tip-off. This is not a favor to you, Merl. It's a duty to Rosa. Let's find out what this guy is really up to."

CLYDE WILLARD OPENED the newspaper and laid it on the carpet. The pieces of concrete were heavy, but the effort of carrying them up to his hotel room had been more than worth it. He took all five of them carefully out of the sack and put them on the paper. Kneeling down, he fitted the fragments together. The decoration on the block's face—a series of wavy lines—stood out in bold relief. It was not a difficult jigsaw, but the resulting picture made him smile with almost childish glee. If the pieces were cemented together again, the block would be almost perfect.

He went to the bathroom to wash the dust from his hands, then came back to take a second look at his memento. This time, he laughed quietly. He crossed to the telephone and picked up the receiver. After cranking the instrument, he got through to the hotel switchboard.

"Can I help you?" said a female voice.

"Yes," he said. "I want to place a call to Los Angeles—"

HE NEVER EXPECTED the attack in broad daylight. Merlin was walking toward his tent when it occurred. Hours of working at his makeshift drafting table had produced a detailed perspective of the Arizona Biltmore. Refinements could be added later. They needed a lot of consideration.

Portfolio and drawing board under his arm, he strolled happily along. The camp was deserted. Everyone was working on the building, in the factory, or out in the grounds. Merlin felt no sense of danger. He did not have to negotiate any dark corners or pass any high buildings from which missiles could be dropped on him. He was safe.

The ambush took place behind a storage hut. He was completely off guard when someone jumped on him from behind, threw a powerful arm across his throat, and began to squeeze the breath out of him. Dropping the portfolio and the drawing board, he tried to rip away the bare arm around his neck, but it was locked too securely. As more pressure was applied, Merlin felt his veins pulse and his head start to pound. He did not even have the strength to call for help.

He pummeled with his elbows but still could not dislodge his assailant. One last tactic remained. Feinting to bend forward, Merlin instead hurled himself backward with full force, and the two fell heavily to the ground. Merlin's weight saved his life. As he landed on top of his assailant, he heard a grunt of pain and felt the arm loosen. He wrenched himself free at once, rolling over and leaping to his feet.

But a new hazard faced him. The man was drawing a long knife from its sheath. Merlin ignored the social niceties and jumped straight in. The first kick hit the man in the ribs, the second caught him full in the face. Merlin was onto him in a flash, twisting the knife from his grasp and pounding his face until all resistance ceased. Panting from his exertions and covered with the blood gushing from the man's nose, Merlin got up. He retrieved the knife before he took a proper look at his adversary.

It was an Indian, a short, muscular young man with long black hair and weathered skin. He wore torn denim pants with an old scarf tied around the waist like a sash, and moccasins and a leather waistcoat completed the outfit. But it was the face that interested Merlin.

As the man began to revive, Merlin waved the knife threateningly. He held the advantage now. Site guards were within call, and he was no longer deprived of his voice. Seeing that he was cornered, the Indian used an arm to wipe some of the blood from under his nose. Malevolent eyes glared up.

"Who are you?" demanded Merlin. "Why did you attack me?" A resentful silence. He brandished the knife. "Why?"

The man's voice was a deep grunt. His grasp on the language was poor. "You. Rosa. Tent."

"Yes," said Merlin. "I shared her tent. Go on."

"You. Rosa."

He twisted his two index fingers together in such an obscene gesture that Merlin's cheeks colored. Merlin shook his head.

"No," he insisted. "Nothing like that."

"You. Rosa." The Indian pointed to his eyes. "See."

Merlin understood. The Indian had come into the tent while he and Rosa had been sleeping on his first night there. The man bending over him in the darkness had not been part of Merlin's nightmare. A reason for the attack was now emerging. The man thought that Merlin and Rosa were lovers.

"No," repeated Merlin, firmly. "What you saw was this."

He used the point of the knife to draw a rectangle on the ground then drew two bodies side by side. He made sure that there was a gap between them.

"The tent," he explained, using the knife as a pointer. "Me, here. Rosa, there. That is what you saw. Nothing else. Friends. We were friends. Do you understand? Nothing more."

The man remained hostile, but some of the smoldering intensity had gone from his gaze. He pointed to his chest.

"Me. Rosa. Friends."

"Were you?"

"Me. Rosa."

He put his hand into his pocket to take out a piece of paper, unfolded it, and held it out. Merlin recognized the drawing at once. Inspired by Navajo weaving art, it was one of the designs he had admired in Rosa's collection. The man put the drawing on the ground, then splayed out his scarf beside it. Made of some rough, thick-woven material, it bore a motif very similar to the one used by Rosa.

"Me. Rosa. Help."

"You helped Rosa?"

"Friend. Help."

Merlin was touched. The Navajo was offering him a crumpled piece of paper by way of credentials. He had clearly known Rosa and was deeply attached to the memory. Merlin looked at the blood still streaming down the other's face. As a gesture of faith, he took out his handkerchief and offered it to the man.

"Take it," he said. "Go on."

After a long pause, the Indian put the handkerchief to his nose to stem the flow. Merlin felt that it might be time for introductions.

"My name is Merlin," he said.

"Mlin? Mlin?"

"No. Merlin. M-*errrrrr*-lin."

"Mullin."

It was close enough. "What's your name?" said Merlin.

"Yazzie."

"Hello, Yazzie."

Merlin offered his hand, then realized he was still holding the knife. Another gesture of faith was required. The man had attacked him, but Merlin saw no virtue in simply handing him over to the police. Yazzie might have valuable information about Rosa if it could be drawn out of him.

Turning the handle, he proffered the knife.

There was an even longer pause this time as Yazzie weighed all the implications. He looked down at the sketch in the sand, then back up at Merlin. A nod confirmed the armistice. He took the knife and slipped it back into its sheath.

Merlin helped him back to his feet. Another mystery could now be solved. He pointed toward the main building of the hotel.

"Was it you who dropped that piece of concrete?" He repeated the question in mime and Yazzie understood. "You?"

"Yazzie," admitted the other.

"No more attacks, please," said Merlin with a smile. "Or I'll run out of luck. We're friends now. Okay? Friends."

"Friends."

He offered the bloodstained handkerchief, but Merlin shook his head and indicated that he could keep it. Yazzie picked up Rosa's drawing and folded it with care before putting it away. Merlin was puzzled.

"How did you get it from Rosa's portfolio?"

"Mine," said Yazzie with fierce pride.

"Did Rosa give it to you?"

"Mine. Keep."

"Or did you take it?"

Yazzie displayed his scarf once more. He tapped his chest. Merlin realized what he was trying to say. Yazzie had designed the motif himself. He had not just been a friend of Rosa's. He was a fellow artist.

Merlin suddenly thought of a dozen things to ask him, but Yazzie was in no mood to linger. With an abrupt nod of farewell, he turned away and loped off toward the main building. Merlin was disappointed to see him go, but the encounter had left him greatly relieved. Some light had been thrown on puzzling events, and there was a decided bonus.

He had made a friend.

AT THE END of the working day, Joe Santana sauntered wearily back to the site office and locked himself inside. He poured himself a glass of bootleg whiskey from the bottle that he kept hidden behind the filing cabinet. It tasted good. The worst of the dust had been washed out of his mouth. He was about to pour himself a second glass when there was a knock on the door. He put the bottle out of sight at once.

"Who is it?" he called.

"Merlin Richards!"

"Scram!"

"I need to speak to you, Mr. Santana."

"I'm busy."

"Then I'll wait."

Santana had paperwork to attend to and letters to write. There was also a second glass of whiskey to savor. It was half an hour before he finally unlocked the door of his office. Having forgotten all about Merlin, he was surprised to see him sitting on the step.

"What the hell do you want?"

"Some help, please." Merlin got up. "It's important."

"Well?"

"I notice you employ a number of Indians."

Santana nodded. "Most of them were used to clear the trails up to the mountains. They can do that kind of thing. We only got a handful on site. They have no building skills. Basic labor is all they're good for, and some of the lazy bastards can't manage that sometimes."

"Do you keep a list of them?"

"A list?"

"I'd appreciate a glance at it, if you do."

"All employment records are confidential."

"I'm trying to track down a Navajo Indian."

"Then drive to the nearest reservation, they got hundreds to choose from out there."

"All I want to know is which part of the site this man is working on. I need to speak to him."

"Not while he's doing his job. Stay well clear."

Merlin was up against the man's black resentment again. It was time to confront it, to see what was causing it.

"You don't like me very much, do you, Mr. Santana?"

"I don't like you at all."

"What have I ever done to you?"

"Got in my way. We don't need you around here."

"It was Rosa, wasn't it?" said Merlin. "Because I turned up with her, I was doomed from the start. Was she on your hate list as well? If you disliked her that much, why on earth did you loan her a tent?"

Santana winced. He hid his discomfort by turning to lock the door of the office. When he faced Merlin again, a more rueful look had taken over.

"You want an Indian, search the camp," he said.

"I just did that. There was no sign of him."

"Then he's probably wandered off."

"Where?"

"Who knows? Those guys make up their own rules. Sometimes they vanish and you never see them again. I got no time for them. Tell them to do some hard work, they act dumb and pretend they don't understand. Come payday, they can speak our lingo as well as they want. That's Indians for you."

"I need to talk to this particular one. A Navajo."

"Why?"

"It's personal."

"Well, don't expect me to help you. The Navajo keep to themselves. Some of them don't even sleep on-site at all. They wander off into the desert night and bed down with the rest of the wildlife. Maybe that's where your boy is. Why not search out there?" He brushed past Merlin. "And forget to come back."

"How much did he pay you?" asked Merlin pointedly.

Santana halted. "What are you on about?"

"Clyde Willard. That journalist."

"That's none of your damn business, mister."

"I didn't think you'd be allowed to sell off one of those concrete blocks," said Merlin, ambling up to him. "One of your jobs is to stop that kind of thing happening, isn't it? Pilfering on-site."

"It wasn't pilfering."

"Oh, I see," said Merlin with light sarcasm. "Mr. Willard was just helping you to clear away the rubble, was he? And paying handsomely for the privilege?"

Santana contained his anger and spoke with icy calm.

"How long were you thinking of staying around here?"

"A few days yet. At least."

"Maybe you should leave right now, Mr. Richards."

"Now?"

"Yes," said Santana, softly. "While you still can."

A new friend had vanished, but an old enemy was still there.

16

A UNIFORMED POLICEMAN was waiting impatiently
for Merlin outside his tent. He braced himself against the prospect of further torment.

"The lieutenant wants to see you," said the man.

"Why?"

"Try asking him."

He led the way to the large cabin, rapped on the door, then
sent Merlin inside on his own. Corbin was seated behind the
desk, rolling an unlit stub of a cigar in his mouth as if trying to
decide whether to swallow it or spit it out. Standing nearby,
Sergeant Drummond was fingering his mustache while reading
through his notes. He gave the newcomer a scowl, but his colleague offered a flabby smile of welcome and struggled to his
feet.

"Come on in, Merlin," he said, shaking his hand. "Good to
see you again. Take a seat."

"What's this all about?"

"Park your ass, and we'll tell you."

He and Merlin sat down. Drummond remained standing.

"So what's been happening since we last saw you?" asked
Corbin. "Apart from the Big Fight, that is."

"Big Fight?"

"You and Pete Bickley. We heard it was the next best thing

to Dempsey versus Tunney. You had him on the canvas with one
punch. Is that true?"

"He deserved it."

"That's not the way Bickley sees it," noted Drummond. "He
may come calling for a rematch."

"I'll be waiting."

Corbin chuckled. "You got more spunk in you than when we
saw you last, son. That's good. You'll need it round here. So what
else have you been doing with yourself?"

"Nothing."

"Gone into hibernation, eh?"

Merlin looked from one to the other, trying to work out what
they actually wanted. Drummond's face was expressionless, but
Corbin's false bonhomie suggested that he was trying to wheedle
something out of his visitor. Merlin got in first.

"Have you found the killer yet?" he said.

"We're still working on it, son."

"That means you've got nowhere."

"That means we've been working twenty-four hours a day
on it, and that we've been over this site with a fine-toothed
comb."

"But there's been no arrest."

"Not since you."

"Do you have any suspects?"

Corbin tossed a glance at Drummond, then leaned forward
to spit his cigar butt into the large metal bin that served as a
wastepaper basket. There was a loud ping.

"We think maybe it's time to trade," he said.

"Trade?"

"Yes, Merlin. Your information for ours."

"But I haven't got any information."

"Horseshit!"

"I've been keeping my head down since I got back here."

"Slugging Pete Bickley? Is that keeping your head down?"

"I was owed a crack at him, Lieutenant."

"You had it. Now give us the rest."

"There is no rest."

"Of course there is," said Corbin irritably. "What have you done, who have you talked to, where did you sleep, how many times have you taken a piss, when did you decide you could do our job better than we can? There's enough material for a whole novel there. All we're asking for is a page or two." Merlin was stubbornly silent. "Okay, let's take it one step at a time. Why have you got that weapon in your tent?"

"Weapon?"

"The pick handle."

"I thought it might come in useful in case I had a sudden urge to do some digging."

"A handle without a pick?" said Drummond. "That's like a woman without a twat. No fucking use at all."

"Not true, Walt," corrected his colleague. "A woman without a twat has still got a mouth. Think of Rosa."

Corbin smiled, Drummond sniggered, and Merlin looked at both of them with disgust. The detectives became more businesslike, firing questions at him alternately.

"Why did you find a weapon?" asked Corbin.

"Have you had to use it yet?" added Drummond.

"Who was the guy who drove you back here?"

"Where did he pick you up?"

"What did he want from you?"

"How much money was that he put in your top pocket?"

"Who was the guy who came after dark?"

"Why was he back here again today?"

"What happened in the site office with Mr. Wright?"

"Why did Tom Vernon give you that drawing board?"

"There you are," said Corbin, hands clasped across the Moby Dick midriff. "Plenty to choose from, Merlin. Which question are you going to take first?"

Merlin felt a slight tremor at the thought that his movements had been watched and recorded. The irony was that the tussle with Yazzie had gone unremarked. At the one time when he would have welcomed police intervention, it was nowhere to be seen.

"Start at the end and go backward," suggested Corbin. "What was it you said to upset Joe Santana just now?"

Merlin struck back. "You first, Lieutenant," he said. "If you want to trade, let me see what you have to offer. I'm not interested in the kind of one-sided deals I've been getting around here so far. What have *you* found out?"

"Fucking cheek!" said Drummond.

"Now, now, Walt," soothed his superior. "It's a fair point. Merlin is afraid that we'll take all he's got and give him nothing in return. He wants a sign of good faith."

"I'll be happy to give him one!"

"Let me handle this." He turned to Merlin. "We've taken statements from every man, woman, and beast on this site. Lots of them are plumb useless, but a lot of interesting facts have been thrown up. One—he came in a car."

"Who?"

"Rosa's friend. Parked a distance from the site."

"How do you know?"

"The car was heard. She was seen flitting off there. All their billing and cooing was done on four wheels. Then the car went off into the night, though I'm amazed the guy had enough strength to drive it. Rosa—or at least a female fitting her description—came back into the camp. It was dark, remember, so we can't be one hundred percent certain."

"How many witnesses were there?"

"Two. And not overreliable."

"What do you mean?"

"They were otherwise engaged, Merlin," said the detective with a grin. "It seems that Rosa was not the only willing woman that night. There were three hookers out here. One of them was doing it alfresco with this guy in the moonlight against the back of a delivery van. And get this, will you? They were standing up. Jesus! *How?* Imagine me trying to hump a hooker in a vertical position," he said as he patted his stomach. "My dick would be at least a foot off target. Anyway, these two are at it out there when Rosa goes tripping right past. Scared the guy so much, he shot his wad straight away, then complained to the hooker that he didn't get his money's worth. Rosa probably ruined a lovely romance there. Still, it gives us a fairly precise time. We can place Rosa at that spot around eleven o'clock. Alive and well."

"It rules out one theory," observed Merlin.

"Theory?"

"That the friend was also the killer."

"No chance of that."

"Unless he doubled back in the car."

"It was spotted five miles down the road, heading for Phoenix. How do we know? Investigate one crime, you find a lot of others hinging on it. It wasn't just the hookers we latched on to. Someone's been running bootleg liquor out here. The guy was on his way to make another delivery that night when this car comes screaming at him."

"Did he see who was in it?"

"No, all he saw were the headlights and a cloud of dust. The car was going like a bat out of hell. Rosa's friend was a long way away when she was murdered."

"So the killer was already on site."

"We believe he still is."

"Who are your suspects?"

"That's enough from us to be going on with," said Corbin, cagily. "Now it's your turn. Who are *your* suspects?"

"I've only got one or two so far."

"Who's the first one?"

"Pete Bickley."

"He's on our list as well. Though he doesn't know it. Security guards are usually guys who like to pack a gun and throw their weight around. Bogus cops, we call them. Lip enough to wear a uniform, but not the balls to do it for real. Pete fits the bill perfectly. And he did sort of happen along at exactly the right time to catch you."

"What's your other name?" asked Drummond.

"Joe Santana."

The detectives exchanged another look but said nothing.

TOM VERNON WAS doing his best to talk her out of it. He stood with his back to the car so that she could not get in.

"I really don't think this is a good idea, Ingrid."

"That's up to me to decide."

"It's madness, driving out to the site now."

"I have to go, Tom."

"But it will be dark in an hour or so."

"Then the sooner I leave, the better," she held out her hand. "Now give me the key, please." Vernon was reluctant. "Come on, Tom. I need to borrow your car."

"Maybe I ought to come with you."

"I'd rather handle this on my own, if you don't mind."

"Ingrid—"

"Give me the key."

After more hesitation, Vernon put his hand in his pocket to dig out the ignition key. When he gave it to Ingrid, she eased him aside and climbed into the car. They had spent most of the afternoon together. Hour after hour, Ingrid had shuttled between hope and recrimination before reaching her decision. Vernon was wishing that he had never told her that Norm Kozelsky was in Arizona.

"He may not even be out there," he reminded her.

"I'll take that chance."

"It could turn out to be a wild goose chase."

"I must see him, Tom. Don't you understand?"

"Frankly, no."

"Norm was special to me."

"That was a long time ago. Why open old wounds?"

"This may be the way to heal them," she said, gunning the motor. "I know you think I'm crazy, but I may never get an opportunity like this again. Okay, he's not out at the site or he doesn't want to see me or he tells me to go to hell. But at least I'll have tried. Besides," she added as a new determination came, "what's past is past. We can start afresh. Rosa is dead now. Everything is different."

"Listen, Ingrid—"

"You're holding me up."

"There's something you ought to know about Norm."

Her words came in a torrent. "Don't you run him down in front of me again, Tom. I know you still hate him for walking out on Mr. Wright. Though I still say that was Rosa's fault and not his. You keep your opinions to yourself. I won't hear a word against Norm."

Vernon stood back with a sigh and waved her off.

"Then I guess you'd better go," he said, sadly. "And if it's that important for you to meet Norm Kozelsky, I hope he's out there waiting for you."

Ingrid drove off with a manic glint. Vernon felt sorry for her. He had not told her that Norm Kozelsky was married. It was only the latest insurmountable barrier between her and any real happiness.

NORM KOZELSKY'S RETURN was both unexpected and unwanted. Merlin had only just gotten to his tent after his interview with the detectives when he saw the Cherokee-red Packard draw into the parking area. He noted the curious mixture of arrogance and absurdity in Kozelsky's strutting gait as he walked toward the tent. He was wearing two-tone brogues.

Kozelsky used both palms in an effusive handshake.

"Hi, Merl. Glad I caught you."

"Why?"

"I had to come straight back to tell you. You remember that guy you asked me to check up on in Phoenix?"

"Clyde Willard?"

"He's a phony. To start with, that's not his name."

"How do you know?"

"I called at the Hotel Westcourt and asked for him. They had nobody by the name of Willard on the register."

"Had anybody checked in from Los Angeles in the last couple of days?"

"Several people. But the desk clerk wouldn't give me their names. He said it was more than his job was worth. And of course I didn't know who I was looking for, so there was no point in hanging around the lobby for him."

"I wonder if 'Clyde Willard' is just a pen name."

"I thought of that, Merl. He wouldn't be the first journalist to use a pseudonym. So I chased that ball down as well. All the way to L.A. I sent a wire to the newspaper. Asking for Clyde Willard to get in touch with me as a matter of urgency."

"What happened?"

"Here's the reply."

He took a flimsy sheet of paper from his pocket and held it in front of Merlin's eyes. The letters were printed in a slightly uneven line.

REGRET WILLARD ON VACATION CHICAGO.

"What the hell is going on here, Merl?"

"I wish I knew."

"Why is he trying to pass himself off as someone else?"

"To win my confidence, I suppose," said Merlin as he searched for an explanation. "I must have something that he desperately wants. And yet all I did was to talk to him endlessly about Rosa."

"What was the link between them?"

"He said he was writing an article."

"Article, my ass!"

"God!" said Merlin. "I've been so bloody gullible!"

"It wasn't your fault."

"I was completely taken in, Norm."

"He's obviously a smooth operator. But who is he working for? And why has he taken such an interest in Rosa?" He slammed a fist into the other palm. "Jump in the car."

"What?"

"I'll drive you straight back to Phoenix right now, and we'll corner him at his hotel. I want the truth."

"We've got no guarantee that he's still there."

"It's worth a try," urged Kozelsky. "Come on, Merl. This guy's a fraud. He took you for a ride. Let's go."

"We can't go anywhere," said Merlin, looking over Kozelsky's shoulder. "Not yet, anyway. You've got company."

"Where?"

Norm Kozelsky turned to see Ingrid Hansa bearing down on him. Her face lit up at the sight of him, but Merlin saw a shudder pass through Kozelsky's frame. The man recovered with remarkable speed, opening his arms wide to greet her.

"Ingrid! Come to me, baby!"

"Hi, Norm!" she said, flinging herself into his arms.

There was a long embrace, tearful on her part, before Kozelsky broke away to turn back to the watching Merlin.

"I believe you two have already met."

"Yes," said Merlin. "Nice to see you again, Ingrid."

She gave a tepid smile. "Hello."

"You and Norm must have a lot to talk about. I'll leave you to it." He backed away. "See you later, Norm."

"Yeah. Right. Won't be long—"

But Ingrid Hansa clearly was not going to be satisfied with a brief reunion. As they strolled hand in hand toward the main building of the hotel, Merlin could see him soothing and reassuring her. His arm was soon around her shoulders.

Using the last of the light, Merlin sat outside the tent with the drawing board across his knee and worked on his perspective. Half an hour or more must have passed before he looked up again. Kozelsky and Ingrid had moved across to the factory; standing by the rope, he was indicating the exact spot where Rosa fell. He mimed the picking up of a concrete block.

Ingrid wanted a more realistic reconstruction. She moved across to a pile of concrete blocks farther along the wall and took hold of the top one. Merlin knew from experience how heavy they were, yet Ingrid swung the block up into the air with comparative ease as if she were about to dash it down on someone's head.

HE KNEW IT would be a wasted journey, but he was swept along by Norm Kozelsky's urgency. Finally detached from Ingrid Hansa, Kozelsky drove Merlin toward Phoenix on the trail of the man posing as Clyde Willard.

"Oh boy!" he said. "What an ordeal!"

"You seemed to get on very well together."

"Well, I tried. I mean, Ingrid deserves a break of some kind. After today, I may never see the poor girl again. So I patted her ass and kissed her cheek and told her what she wanted to hear. At times like this, it's all you can do. Ingrid was overwrought. I had to talk her down. That kind of thing can't be rushed. She was eating out of my hand by the time I finished."

"So I noticed."

"How can I help it if the girl is still crazy for me?"

"Does she know that you're married?"

That stopped the monologue at once. Instead, Kozelsky

talked himself into a rage against the fraudulent journalist; by the time his car pulled up outside the Hotel Westcourt, he was pulsing with fury.

The man was not there. They searched the restaurant and loitered for an hour in the lobby, but the man calling himself Clyde Willard did not appear. Merlin announced that he would take a taxi back to the site, but Kozelsky insisted on driving him, racing along the empty road at top speed as if trying to prove something to himself. It was alarming. Merlin was glad to arrive safely back at the site entrance.

THEY WERE WAITING for him near his tent as soon as he got back. Two of them came out of the shadows, Pete Bickley carrying his shotgun. Merlin recognized the other man who had accosted him on the night of the murder. He was only wearing a handgun. Both were in the standard uniform of the site guards.

"Let's take a walk," suggested Bickley.

Merlin stood his ground. "Why?"

"We got unsettled business."

"I've got no quarrel with you any more."

"Turned yellow, have you?"

"No!" said Merlin, hotly.

"Then shift. I brought Dave along to make sure it's a fair fight. Just you and me. No weapons."

When Merlin looked at the shotgun, Bickley tossed it to his colleague, then handed over his revolver. The three of them walked casually through the camp until they reached the adobe hut on the edge of the golf course. Their venue gave them a degree of privacy, and the moon shed enough light for them to see each other clearly.

Bickley removed his hat and tossed it away, bunching his fists and circling his man. Merlin was not afraid. He had not sought the fight, but he would certainly not run away from it.

Putting up his guard, he too moved around as he looked for an opening. Bickley struck first with a relay of punches to the body. Merlin took most of them on his arms, then spun on his heel to leave his opponent hitting the air.

Before he could congratulate himself on his nifty footwork, he convulsed with pain as the butt of the shotgun jabbed him in the kidney. Merlin realized that he was fighting the two of them. Seeing him weaken, Bickley lumbered in, arms flailing. A sense of injustice fired Merlin up again. Though he took some solid punches, he landed even more and sent Bickley reeling backward with blood seeping from a gash above his eye.

Once again the shotgun came into play, thudding so hard into Merlin's left shoulder that it was numbed. Hardly able to raise that hand, he backed away from both men. The two of them advanced on him together. Bickley held a menacing fist out while his colleague brandished the shotgun like a baseball bat. They were coming in for the kill. There was no way that Merlin could survive against the two of them.

"Arghhhhh!"

Dave was suddenly felled from behind, struck across the head with the flat of a spade. Yazzie gave a smile of encouragement to Merlin. Bickley began to lose his nerve, but Merlin gave him no chance to withdraw.

With his left arm restored to full strength, he used it to jab into his opponent's face before delivering a piston of a right into his solar plexus. Bickley was strong and fought back hard, but he no longer had confidence that he could win. Merlin punched away until he saw the glassy stare and the buckling legs. One last uppercut sent Bickley to join his colleague in oblivion.

Gasping for air, Merlin shook Yazzie warmly by the hand. His friend had saved him from a terrible beating. Merlin wanted to leave the prostrate guards there, but Yazzie insisted that they deserved a final humiliation. His mime was graphic. Both guards were tossed headfirst into the canal.

17

SIDNEY LUSTIG WAS a short, stout old man with a roly-poly face and a tonsure more suited to a Benedictine monk than a rabbi from Indiana. Robbed of what little strength he still possessed by the murder of his only daughter, he was a frail and pathetic figure. Only his faith sustained him. The journey from Kokomo had been an ordeal, involving a bus and a train and taking him from a windswept winterland into the blazing sun of Arizona. There was an even greater shift between extremes when he reached the police morgue.

His daughter's body had to be formally identified, yet the mutilated face bore no resemblance to the beautiful girl who had fled from her home. Rosa had been a beloved daughter in Indiana, but a five-year absence had wrought the most hideous change in her. Sidney was shocked and bewildered. How could he claim as his own a disfigured corpse? Only the supporting evidence of her papers and her few possessions convinced him that he was looking at Rosa Judith Lustig.

Conscious of his suffering, the police handled him with tact and compassion. Tom Vernon turned up to lend his sympathy to the grieving father. Sidney was glad to meet someone from the world into which Rosa had escaped, and he quizzed Vernon carefully about his daughter, as if trying to rebuild her face in his mind to convince himself that he had not sired the monster in the coffin. Vernon was considerate, presenting only the attractive aspects of Rosa's career to her father.

When it was time to leave, Sidney Lustig shed tears on Vernon's lapel. With his heavy cargo in tow, the journey back to Indiana would be even more distressing and onerous.

"I am so grateful to you, Mr. Vernon," he said.

"Rosa was loved and valued, sir. We will miss her."

"She was such an ambitious girl. It worried us deeply. Rosa would drive herself on and on. She would never settle for second best. Only the top would satisfy her." He sobbed quietly. "That kind of attitude leads to success or tragedy. We always feared she might end up on a slab somewhere."

Vernon escorted him out of the building, then took his leave. The coffin had already been discreetly loaded into the hearse, and all the papers had been signed to eliminate any kind of delay. Until the murder was solved, however, Rosa would never be entirely free of trailing paperwork.

Sidney Lustig was just about to step into the vehicle when a middle-aged man in a white suit and a straw boater eased himself politely forward.

"Excuse me, sir," he said. "You must be Rosa's father."

"That is so. Did you know my daughter?"

"I had that pleasure."

"Rosa was a wonderful daughter."

"We are devastated by her loss," said the man, taking an envelope from his inside pocket, "and we offer you heartfelt condolences at this sad time. As a small token of our appreciation of her, please accept this," he said, slipping the envelope into the old man's hand. "Use it to buy something by which Rosa can be most suitably remembered."

"Thank you, thank you."

"It is the least we can do, sir."

"But I don't even know your name—"

"Willard. Clyde Willard."

The man withdrew as courteously as he had come, and Sidney Lustig was driven on to the station behind his daughter. It was only when he was a hundred miles from Arizona that he recalled the soft-spoken man outside the morgue. Fumbling with clumsy fingers, he brought the envelope out of his pocket to examine it.

Inside was a white card bearing a tiny picture of some red roses tied up in pink ribbon. Two hundred-dollar bills slipped out of the card, simply inscribed to Rosa. It was unsigned.

DRAWN TOGETHER BY common love of art and by a mutual affection for Rosa Lustig, they were hopelessly separated by language. Conversation with Yazzie was slow and laborious. Merlin learned simply to enjoy the pleasure of his company.

Merlin slept with his weapon beside him again that night, but it was not required. A restful sleep put him in good spirits the next morning though his ribs still ached from Bickley's punches, his shoulder was sore from being pounded by the shotgun, and a bruise was darkening his temple—small prices to pay for the feeling of quiet triumph.

After breakfast, he took the sketch pad he had been given and made a leisurely tour of the site in search of the influence of Frank Lloyd Wright. At first glance it was everywhere, yet it sometimes shrank dramatically or mysteriously vanished altogether under close scrutiny. The Arizona Biltmore was not simply a fabulous architectural concept; it was an optical illusion.

Coming around one of the wings at the rear of the main building, Merlin came to a sharp halt. Yazzie was on the other side of the patio, moving a pile of rubble in a large wheelbarrow. Merlin waved cheerfully, but the Indian did not respond, pretending not to recognize him. He was clearly embarrassed to be seen by his friend doing such menial work. A respected artist in his own community, he was no more than a hired slave in the world of the white man.

Within seconds, Yazzie ceased to be even that. Joe Santana came striding toward him and yelled something at him. Out of earshot, Merlin nevertheless understood exactly what was going on. Yazzie was roundly reprimanded, given a pay packet with contempt, and summarily ejected from the site.

Merlin first ran to intercept the site manager.

"What was that all about?" he demanded.

"I fired him."

"Why?"

"Because he was a lazy, stinking, no-good Indian."

"He works hard."

"How do you know?"

"I was watching him."

"Do I need your say-so before I can get rid of him? Since when were you put in charge around here?"

"Give him another chance, Mr. Santana."

"What's it to you if he stays or goes?"

"I know him. I can vouch for him."

"Well, the foreman says otherwise," said Santana. "That Indian was surly and disobedient. Yesterday, he disappeared for an hour and came back with his nose split open. Obviously been in a fight." His eye flicked up at Merlin's bruised temple. "There's too much of that kind of thing round here. Yazzie is trouble we can do without."

Merlin simmered. "You *knew*, didn't you?"

"What are you on about?"

"When I asked you about the Indians employed on the site, you knew that Yazzie was the one I was after. So you fire him next morning. Why, Mr. Santana? Just to get back at me? Or is there some other reason?"

"He's not up to the job."

"Then why was he hired in the first place?"

Santana looked away for a second. "It was a mistake."

"Is there no way you can let him stay here?"

"What is this?" exploded the other. "I got hundreds of men to worry about here. Skilled craftsmen from every trade. Why should I bother about some dumb Navajo who can't even push a barrow around when he's told? He's just one more piece of rubble to toss on the pile. Now out of my way."

He pushed roughly past Merlin and went off to talk to one of the foremen on the site. Yazzie had now vanished. Merlin broke into a trot and went after him. He caught up with him walking toward the factory. Merlin's shout made Yazzie stop and turn.

"I tried to get him to keep you on," said Merlin with explanatory gestures. "But it was no use, I'm afraid. He just wouldn't listen to me."

Yazzie shrugged. "I go."

"Where?"

"My people."

"At least let me say a proper good-bye."

He offered his hand, and Yazzie shook it clumsily. He was neither hurt by his dismissal nor nursing any resentment. There was an air of dignified resignation about him, matched with a sense of relief. He was glad to be leaving.

Yazzie gazed in silence toward the place where Rosa had been struck down and paid his last respects, then looked back at Merlin.

"Man. Car."

"What man?" asked Merlin. "What car?"

"Man. Rosa."

"You saw a man with Rosa?"

"Car."

"I'm sorry, Yazzie. I need more than that."

"Man. You. Car."

His sign language became more frantic, but it was beyond

Merlin's powers of translation. Yazzie indicated the sketch pad, and Merlin handed it over with a pencil. The Indian sat cross-legged on the ground and drew a picture with the utmost concentration. When he showed it to Merlin, the latter was none the wiser. The drawing of a car had an endearing childlike simplicity, but it was impossible to tell from the naive sketch which model it was supposed to be.

Yazzie became increasingly annoyed by Merlin's failure to understand. He jabbed a finger at his drawing, then pointed toward the parking area. Merlin shook his head in bafflement. Taking his knife from its sheath, Yazzie drew the blade across his palm to open up a wound. Blood seeped out. He wiped his hand across the paper.

Merlin looked down at the blood-covered automobile. He was more confused than ever. It was only after long consideration that the message began to get through to him. The blood denoted Rosa's murder. The car had brought the friend whom she had met that night outside the perimeter of the site. Yazzie had seen it. He was a witness.

Merlin raised his head to speak, but Yazzie was gone.

TOM VERNON WAS visibly discomfited by the appearance of an old colleague. While Norm Kozelsky was staying at a luxury hotel near the center of the town, Vernon could only afford a rooming house in the suburbs.

"How did you know where to find me?" he asked.

"Ingrid gave me the address."

"I wish she'd told me that."

"Her head was full of other things, I expect," said Kozelsky with grinning complacence. "We had a long talk together out at the site. Kicked our way through the ashes of past times together. She's still the same Ingrid. I daresay she was bubbling with excitement by the time she got back with that jalopy of yours."

"Ingrid was happy," conceded Vernon.

"That's the way I like to leave 'em!"

"I remember it differently, Norm."

Kozelsky laughed. "Oh, come on!" he said, slapping the other man on the shoulder. "You've broken a few hearts in your time. That's life, Tom. You have to accept it. Now, why don't we go and find somewhere to have a cup of coffee and talk properly? We got lots to catch up on."

Vernon agreed. He felt at a disadvantage talking to Kozelsky outside a modest rooming house while the other was leaning against a superb new car. It brought two opposing worlds into a painful collision. When they drove to a restaurant several blocks away, Vernon was able to relax and even take a genuine interest in his companion's life.

"I hear that things have really worked out for you, Norm."

"Yes. Going back to New York was a wise move."

"You're a big-city kind of guy."

"There's nothing quite like New York. Makes every other place in America look so provincial. When I come to a town like Phoenix, I feel I'm in some kind of village."

"Not many villages with a population of over fifty thousand," said Vernon defensively. "Phoenix is a fast-developing city. Building permits topped the five-million-dollar mark this year. Things are buzzing, Norm."

"All I hear is the drone of boredom."

"Each to his own."

He stirred his coffee. "So how is he?"

"Mr. Wright?"

"I lavished all that time on Ingrid last night, and she never even mentioned Daddy Frank. How is the old wizard, Tom?"

"Still weaving his spells."

"So I saw. Out at the Biltmore."

"His interest in that project has effectively ceased," said Vernon easily. "Mr. Wright only stepped in to help out an old friend. McArthur bit off more than he could chew."

"I heard a slightly different story."

"Then I'm glad to be able to correct it. Our main reason for being down here is San Marcos in the Desert, the new resort hotel near Chandler. That will really remind people what Mr. Wright can do when he's given a free hand. Not as big as the Biltmore complex, but far more interesting in many ways. And making a more imaginative use of the nature of the site."

Kozelsky chuckled. "Your impersonation of Daddy Frank gets better all the time, Tom. Ever have an idea of your own?"

"Every architect needs someone to inspire him."

"Oh, sure. But that doesn't mean you have to sit on his knee like a ventriloquist's dummy. Don't you ever get fed up with having his hand stuck up the back of your shirt?"

Vernon smiled. "I've learned to live with it."

"You should have outgrown him by now, Tom."

"Is that what you've done?"

"I think so."

"Then tell me what *you're* working on, Norm. All we have on the stocks is this luxury hotel with a budget of half a million," he said with gentle sarcasm. "Now that you've outgrown Mr. Wright, you must have moved on to something much more prestigious than that. What is it? A new skyscraper? A museum and art gallery? A hotel? What exactly has Norm Kozelsky got on his drawing board at the moment?"

It was the other man's turn to go on the defensive.

"A house in Brooklyn Heights."

"A house? Is that all?"

"It's a six-bedroom residence with a half-acre garden. And I design lots like it. Quick turnover."

"I'm sure."

"The bucks roll in."

"But those commissions will never make you the kind of international reputation that Frank Lloyd Wright has."

"At least I won't reach the age of sixty and still be scratching around for money."

"No, Norm. You'll still be designing houses."

"Everybody needs one."

"Even if they all look the same."

"Even then."

"Now you know why I prefer to stay with Mr. Wright."

"Okay," said Kozelsky, "he writes symphonies while I only build pianos. But my pianos sell like crazy, and Daddy Frank is running out of concert halls in which to conduct his music."

"Oh, I don't think so. He'll be up on the podium a long while yet. Those pianos you build, Norm, are they the kind with handles on the side?"

Kozelsky burst out laughing, and Vernon grinned. The tension between them eased, and they were able to talk in a more relaxed way, enjoying shared memories in which Rosa Lustig played an important role. When it was time for them to part, Kozelsky threw in a last question.

"This new hotel in Chandler. Is it going to have the same concrete block system as the Biltmore?"

"Yes," said Vernon with enthusiasm. "Only it will be used on a much larger scale. At the Biltmore its only function is decorative, and that's really upset Mr. Wright. At San Marcos in the Desert the block system will be used for structural purposes as well. Put your earplugs in, Norm. When that hotel is built, it will be his loudest symphony yet."

HE MISSED THE harp. Not just an instrument that could produce a unique sound, it was Merlin's form of relaxation. Seated at his harp, he could retreat from the workaday world and lose himself in beautiful music. But the harp yielded another benefit. It allowed him to think properly.

Like many things he had come to love, it had begun as an

188 / KEITH MILES

object of hate. Merlin was a reluctant musician. While the other boys were out playing in the street, he did not want to be chained to an instrument twice his size, producing sentimental Welsh melodies. He remembered all too well the blistered fingers, the aching back, the nagging voice of his tutor. But the rewards had finally come.

188 / KEITH MILES

object of hate. Merlin was a reluctant musician. While the other boys were out playing in the street, he did not want to be chained to an instrument twice his size, producing sentimental Welsh melodies. He remembered all too well the blistered fingers, the aching back, the nagging voice of his tutor. But the rewards had finally come.

Merlin could play so well that his mind was free to wander while his hands drew wondrous repeating patterns on the strings. He missed it. He needed to think. The harp would have helped.

He was back at his drafting table on the site, studying the hotel to sketch separate details of it, noting the way that the building yielded cunning new felicities of design every time he scrutinized it. Even a practiced eye like his could not take in every facet of its brilliance at one viewing. The Arizona Biltmore was a hotel of shifting perspectives and changing colors.

It was there, Merlin was convinced of it. Somewhere in the stirring spectacle before him was the vital clue to the murder of Rosa Lustig. The beauty of the project had lured her even though she was not professionally involved with it. Her interest in it had been obsessional. Yet the hotel had rewarded her devotion by killing her. It had smashed Rosa's head to a pulp with its most innovative design feature. In every sense, it had been an architectural death.

Yet Merlin could still not explain it. No harp. No plangent harmonies to unlock his mind. No inspiration. His stomach was more eloquent than his head, rumbling in discontent and telling him that it was time for lunch. Merlin abandoned his meditations.

His attention was instantly engaged elsewhere. A familiar scene was being played out beside the site office. Joe Santana was talking to Ingrid Hansa and pointing toward the factory. She shook his hand before hurrying off. Santana went straight into his office.

Picking up his sketch pad, Merlin jogged across to the

site office and opened the door without bothering to knock. Santana, in the act of eating a sandwich, spat out a mouthful of crumbs.

"What the fuck are you doing here!"

"I came so that you could tell me you hadn't been talking to Ingrid Hansa again. That wasn't her I just saw walking away. It was the woman I didn't actually see the last time."

"Get out!"

"Not until we've had a chat, Mr. Santana."

"I've got nothing to say."

"Well, I have," said Merlin firmly, "so you can do the listening. And before you have me thrown off the site," he added as Santana made as if to rise, "remember one thing. Lieutenant Corbin ordered me to stay around. Get rid of me, and you'll have to answer to him. Somehow I don't think that you enjoy talking to policemen, do you?"

Santana looked at him with a mixture of anger and curiosity. He took a bite out of his sandwich while he was deciding what to do.

Merlin's tone became more reasonable. "All I want is some information, that's all."

"What about?"

"Yazzie, for a start."

"He's gone."

"But why did you employ him in the first place?"

"Cheap labor."

"Who brought him here?"

They both knew the answer. Santana's eyes blazed, but his anger was muffled by the grudging curiosity. A distant respect seeped into his manner.

"Shut the door," he said.

"What?"

"Shut the door and lock it." He tossed the key to Merlin. "Go on. Afraid to be trapped in here with me?"

Merlin locked the door and handed the key back.

"Take a seat."

"I'll stand."

"Please yourself, mister. Like a drink?"

"A drink?"

Caught off balance by the sudden hospitality, Merlin looked around for signs of coffee or soft drinks. There were none. Santana took two glasses from the drawer of his desk, then retrieved the whiskey bottle from behind the cabinet. He held it up for inspection.

"The real stuff. Not that rotgut bourbon or bathtub gin they peddle to the construction gangs. This is good." He poured two glasses, then handed one to Merlin. "Enjoy it."

"Thanks." Merlin sipped it and coughed violently.

"Kicks like a mule till you get used to it," said Santana with a grin. He took a sip from his glass. "How much did she tell you?"

"Who?"

"Rosa."

"What about?"

"Me."

"Nothing at all."

"Then how do you know about Yazzie?"

"I guessed."

"What did you guess?"

"That Rosa asked you to give him a job as a favor to her. He was a friend of hers. She wanted him around."

"Go on."

"That's it, Mr. Santana," said Merlin. "Now that Rosa is gone, there was no reason to keep Yazzie. He was probably an unpleasant reminder. That's why you fired him."

"I was doing him another favor."

"Favor?"

"Getting the crazy fool out of here before the cops latched

on to him. It was only a matter of time before they did." He emptied his glass. "You see, the thing is that I'm glad that sweet little come-and-get-it Rosa was bumped off. That's why I was ready to help Yazzie."

"Yazzie?"

"I think he killed her."

18

MERLIN WAS SPEECHLESS. The idea had never even crossed his mind. And the casual way in which it was put to him gave the notion even greater force. Santana had time to pour himself a second shot of whiskey before his guest rediscovered his voice.

"Yazzie?"

"Why not?"

"But he worshiped Rosa. She was his friend."

"At first."

"She got him the job here. You admitted that."

"Yes. But what kind of a job was it? Fetching and carrying. Taking loads of blocks from the factory. Barrowing rubble. Shifting earth. They even had him digging a latrine trench at one point. What kind of a friend pushes you into a job like that?"

"There was nothing else he could do."

"Yazzie thought so."

"What?"

"Work alongside her."

"But Rosa wasn't employed on the project."

"She tried to be, but Mr. McArthur turned her stuff down. That really took the wind out of her sails. Rosa had staked everything on getting a huge commission here. She thought she had the edge on the others because she'd worked with Mr. Wright before."

"But he didn't make the final decision, did he?"

"No," said Santana, "but she believed that he would. Think of the status that would have given her. Think of the dough. This hotel could have made her name."

"What about Yazzie?"

"She'd have kept him around as her assistant. Some of the designs she submitted were based on ideas that he'd come up with back on the reservation."

"I know. I saw them. They were first-rate."

"Useless in their raw form," continued Santana with a dismissive shrug, "but worth something by the time Rosa had adapted them to her purpose. She and Yazzie were a team. He gave her the inspiration, but she came up with the commercial product."

"They needed each other."

"Until the deal fell through."

"Couldn't they market their ideas somewhere else?"

"Nobody wanted them."

"So the partnership collapsed."

"It was on the verge of doing that, anyway," Santana said. "Yazzie must have been very useful to her when she was touring the reservations in search of ideas. A girl needs protection up there. It's not all that long since those savages stopped taking scalps." A knowing leer. "But Yazzie kind of stuck out when she got back to civilization. I mean, he's not the kind of guy you take to a fancy restaurant in the middle of Phoenix."

Merlin began to see the logic. Spurred on by her promises, Yazzie had left his tribe in order to accompany her. It was a massive wrench for him to break away from the world he knew, and she must have used every method of persuasion. Yazzie's emotional commitment to her had been apparent.

"She led the poor guy by the dick," Santana said, bluntly. "And what happens? Instead of humping Rosa in some cozy little hogan, he's sleeping alone in the desert and shoveling dirt for eight hours a day. As attractions, the two don't really compare."

"Why did she lose interest in him?"

"He was no use to her any more."

"But they'd worked together on the designs."

"No one bought them."

"They could have come up with some fresh ideas."

"All Rosa was interested in coming up with was some fresh dick. And that meant giving Yazzie the cold shoulder. Proud man, your Navajo. Can't blame him for being jealous."

"I suppose not."

"He was ready to kill anyone who got near Rosa."

Merlin remembered the piece of concrete dropped from a roof and the daylight ambush behind a storage hut. He had been a victim of Yazzie's seething jealousy. If he was prepared to attack someone he mistook as her lover, what would he do to Rosa herself? Especially if he had witnessed her assignation with the man for whom she really cared. Merlin was horrified that something so obvious had never occurred to him. Now that it was forced upon him, however, he still found it hard to accept.

"You really think Yazzie did it, Mr. Santana?"

"He'd be my best bet."

"Why on earth did he stay around afterward?"

"Because he's not that dumb," said Santana. "If someone is killed and one person is missing from the site, who are the cops going to start looking for first? They'd have trailed him back to the reservation right away."

"They could still do that."

"Only if they find out. And I won't tell them."

"Why not?"

"Because there's an outside chance I may be wrong."

"In that case, there's no harm done."

Santana pulled a face. "Yes, there is. Tell the cops what I just told you, and they'd drag him all the way to Phoenix by his balls. Navajo Indian kills white woman because she wouldn't screw him? Yazzie wouldn't stand a chance."

"He would if he was innocent."

"And how is he supposed to defend himself when he can't speak the language? Innocent or guilty, they'd string him up inside a week. No," he continued as he drained the second glass, "I'd rather let him go. Let's face it. He did us all a big favor."

Merlin gaped. "Favor? Murdering someone is a *favor?*"

"Come on, Richards. You're in this with the rest of us."

"In what?"

"The club," he sneered. "She made a monkey out of all of us; You, me, Yazzie, Pete Bickley, and God knows who else. When Rosa gave you that special look of hers, you felt as if she was sucking your dick for you."

"She never gave *me* that look."

"Well, you were getting the real thing."

"I certainly wasn't!"

"According to Pete Bickley—"

"Nothing happened between us," insisted Merlin. "If it had, why did she go off to meet someone else the night she was killed? *He* was the only person she really wanted."

Santana ran a hand across his face as he pondered.

"It figures. Maybe I weighed you up wrong."

"Maybe you did."

"Who was that other guy?"

"The police haven't found him yet."

"What could he see in a little tramp like that?"

"Rosa was not a tramp!" said Merlin, vehemently. "Maybe that's what you wish she *had* been, Mr. Santana, but she wasn't. So stop running her down. She was battered to death not fifty yards from where we are now. Doesn't that mean anything to you?"

"Yes! It means she's not around to wave that ass of hers under our noses!" Repentance came quickly. He brought both hands up to his face for a moment. When he took them away, he was much calmer. "I take that back," he said, quietly. "It was our fault. We're all grown men. And in my case, it wasn't just what I thought she was dangling in front of me. I felt sorry for the kid. Not only because she hadn't landed the commission to design those blocks. It was personal."

Merlin sat down and sipped some more whiskey. It tasted much better this time. Santana flicked a glance at him.

"She ever talk about Indiana to you?"

"No," said Merlin. "But someone else did."

"Oh?"

"I know she had a brush with the Ku Klux Klan up there. It sounded dreadful. Would they really put a burning cross on her lawn?"

"Far more than that," said the other, bitterly. "I've had my own brushes with the Klan. It's what drew us together at the start. Common bond."

"Why were they interested in you?"

Santana smiled. "I can see you don't know much about their targets. My ancestors were all Mexican. With a name like Santana, it's no good pretending I'm not Catholic. And there's a lot of places in this country where that's not such a healthy religion to have."

"Why not?"

"Cast your mind back. Many of the settlers who came to America from Europe only did so to escape Catholic persecution. Those memories don't die. They're bred in the bone. The pope would never win a popularity contest in some states. I discovered that when I was a kid and we moved to Louisiana."

"What do you mean?"

"The Klan practically controls parts of the state," said Santana. "Of course, the Negroes got the worst of it. But they had plenty of bile and abuse left over for us." He crossed to look out of the window. "That's what we talked about. Rites of passage. Being made to suffer for something over which we had no control. It sort of brought us together. When Rosa said she'd like to stay around, I was dumb enough to think it was partly because of me. So I found her the tent and gave Yazzie a job to keep him occupied." He faced Merlin again. "I kept expecting her to invite me across to that tent one night, but she never did. Rosa dropped me and moved on to Pete Bickley."

"Why?"

"He's a good-looking guy."

"There's more to it than that, Mr. Santana. I was very fond of Rosa, and my memories of her are good ones. But she does seem to have manipulated you."

"I was in a position to do things for her."

"Pete Bickley wasn't. He's only a site guard."

"Maybe she wanted him to ride shotgun outside her tent at night. A lot of the guys here had their eye on her." He picked up his sandwich again. "What does it matter? Rosa's dead, and Yazzie is gone, and that's the end of it."

He bit into his sandwich and munched noisily.

"That still leaves Ingrid Hansa," reminded Merlin.

"What about her?"

"Why did she come?"

"Free country."

"She was here with you the night Rosa was killed. I saw you clearly. Why did you lie to me about that?"

A pause. "Close the door behind you when you leave."

"What's Ingrid doing on site today?"

"You'll need the key," said Santana, proffering it.

Merlin took the key from him, then finished his whiskey.

"Thanks for that," he said. "And for what you told me."

"I was the biggest sucker of them all," said Santana with a rueful shake of the head. "The others were single. Rosa was fair game to them. I'm a married man with a wife and

three kids, yet I still fall for *that*. I must have been mad."
He reached for the bottle. Merlin let himself out.

BAD PUBLICITY CONTINUED to dog the Arizona Biltmore. The unsolved murder brought in scores of irate telephone calls and indignant letters from those with vested interest in the hotel. The governor lent his weight to the general criticism of police activity. As long as the killer was still on the loose, there would be damaging headlines. Lieutenant Noah Corbin was constantly reminded of the fact by those in authority over him. Hounded from above, he was in no mood to accept comments from those with no authority.

That did not prevent Ingrid Hansa from accosting him.

"Have you seen this, Lieutenant?" she demanded, waving a copy of a newspaper in his face. "The *Arizona Republican*."

"Stopped reading it years ago," said Corbin.

"This front page is disgraceful!"

"Then you should stop reading it as well, lady."

"Something has got to be done."

"Yes," he agreed. "A homicide case has got to be wrapped up. You step out of my light, maybe I'll be able to get on with the investigation."

"Look at this first!"

They were standing outside the cabin where the detectives had set up their site headquarters. Ingrid was quivering with rage. With such an important issue at stake, she was not going to be brushed aside. She thrust the newspaper right under his nose.

"Well?" she said. "Do you see it?"

"Yes, lady. It's the *Arizona Republican* right enough."

"Read that article."

"I got better things to do."

"It's libelous."

"Does it libel me in any way?"

"No, of course not."

"Then I got no time even to look at it."

"Don't you care about the pain this can cause him?"

Ingrid spoke with such passion that the detective relented. He threw a weary glance at the headline. FRANK LLOYD WRIGHT LINKED TO MURDERED GIRL. Photographs of the architect and the designer were printed side by side.

"What's libelous about this?" asked Corbin. "From what we hear, Rosa Lustig did work for him up in Wisconsin once."

"The article is suggesting a closer relationship."

"So?"

"It never took place."

"How do you know?"

"I was there, Lieutenant."

"I wish you still were, lady," said Corbin with exasperation. "Who the Sam Hill are you?"

"Ingrid Hansa. I work with Mr. Wright."

"Ah, I get it! You want *your* picture in the paper."

"No!"

"I'll try to arrange it. FRANK LLOYD WRIGHT LINKED TO WOMAN HAMPERING MURDER INQUIRY. Will that get you off my back?"

"I'm sorry, Lieutenant. I know this must appear trivial to you, but it does have a bearing on this whole business. That article is full of cruel innuendoes about Mr. Wright and Rosa Lustig."

"You got a complaint, take it up with the editor."

"I did. He refused to speak to me."

"That figures."

"I want you to stamp on them at this end, Lieutenant."

"Who?"

"Reporters," she said. "I know that you're in charge of the press conferences because I asked. Next time you get them all together, make it clear that this kind of smear will not be allowed. Or we will take libel action."

"We?"

"Well—Mr. Wright, that is."

"Did he send you out here, Ingrid?"

"Not exactly."

"Does he even know what you're doing?"

"Probably not," she said. "But I'm sure he'd approve. He and Mrs. Wright are in Chandler. The last thing they need to see is this kind of filth in the morning paper."

Corbin took it from her and read a few paragraphs. He let out a throaty cackle and handed the newspaper back.

"Lady," he said, grinning, "if I was sixty-one and my name was linked to a gorgeous young woman of twenty-four, I'd be delighted. I wouldn't sue the paper, I'd have the article framed and set over my mantelpiece." He became serious. "*Was* Rosa Lustig involved with Mr. Wright in that way?"

"No, Lieutenant."

"Then it's not relevant to our enquiries."

Spotting the argument, Merlin came across to butt in.

"What seems to be the trouble, Lieutenant?"

"You know this lady, sir?"

"Yes," said Merlin. "Ingrid Hansa."

"Great! Take her off my hands, we drop all charges."

"You haven't heard me out."

"Let him do it," said Corbin, making his escape. "He's got more time on his hands than I have."

He went into the cabin and slammed the door after him. Merlin raised a quizzical eyebrow at Ingrid, and she handed him the newspaper. He read the front-page article with a mixture of interest and irritation.

"This can't be true, surely?" he said.

"It isn't."

"Then why did they print it?"

"Mr. Wright's name will always get attention."

"Where did they get all of this nonsense?"

"From her," she said, reclaiming the newspaper. "Miriam Noel. Mr. Wright's second wife. That's my guess, anyway."

"Would she invent scandal like this?"

"Miriam Noel would do anything to make Mr. Wright's life a misery. Before the divorce, she had private detectives on his tail for months. They helped to get Mr. Wright arrested."

"Tom mentioned that."

"Then you know the kind of woman she is."

"But Mr. Wright is married again now."

"That won't stop her. Miriam Noel would do anything to ruin his happiness. That's why he needs people like Tom and me to defend him. Miriam never lets go. She must have read the report of Rosa's death in the papers and seized the chance to throw some mud. It's disgusting!" She screwed up the newspaper and threw it away. "I feel like washing my hands after touching it."

"Is that what brought you out here, Ingrid?" he asked. "To complain about that article?"

"No," she said. "I picked up that copy when I arrived. I really came in the hope of seeing Norm again." She looked around. "Is he here, by any chance?"

"I'm afraid not."

"Did he say that he'd be back?"

"His plans are pretty fluid, from what I gather."

"Norm was staying in Phoenix, but he wouldn't tell me which hotel." She took a step closer. "Do you happen to know the name of it?"

"Sorry. Can't help you."

A sigh of disappointment. "If he does show up, say that I was looking for him."

"I will."

"He knows where I'm staying."

"I'll pass on the message. But before you go—"

"Yes?"

"I just wanted to check something with you. On the day that Rosa was murdered, you came out to the site, didn't you?"

"What makes you say that?"

"I saw you talking to Joe Santana."

"You couldn't have," she snapped. "I wasn't here."

"I could have sworn that it was you."

"Have you mentioned this to Mr. Santana himself?"

"Yes."

"What did he say?"

"He denies it as well."

"There's your answer, Merlin," she said crisply. "You were mistaken." Her eyes narrowed. "Oh, by the way, Tom says that you were doing some kind of little sketch for Mr. Wright."

"Yes. He asked me for it."

"I should forget all about it now."

"Why?"

"He won't have time to look at it, anyway. Work in Chandler starts in earnest tomorrow. Mr. Wright will be fully occupied with that. You'll probably never even see him again."

She walked away, leaving Merlin shattered.

THE AFTERNOON SUN was the hottest he had felt since he had been in Arizona, but he took no pleasure in its passionate embrace. And though the Arizona Biltmore turned to gold before his eyes, its copper roof glistening like a fairy-tale palace, he was not moved to capture any more of its magic on paper. His sketch pad lay unopened on the upturned packing crate. Still tucked away in his portfolio, the perspective of the hotel now seemed like a waste of his time and energy.

Even allowing for Ingrid Hansa's desire to hurt, he had to accept the truth of the situation. Frank Lloyd Wright was in Arizona to work on a major new commission. He had no reason to visit the Biltmore again, and every reason to stay away. Wright was angry at the way his advice had been ignored and furious at the misuse of his concrete block technique. The article in the morning newspaper would hardly encourage him to visit a place where a young woman with whom his name had been romantically linked was murdered.

Tom Vernon was a good friend, but his conversations with Norm Kozelsky had given Merlin a new slant on the man. Vernon now appeared as a loyal but rather ineffectual man, lacking the drive and ambition to strike on his own and happy to trail around after his idol. Once he was engaged in the Chandler project, Vernon would no longer be able to show much interest in the Welsh architect. Merlin would simply be one more discarded follower of Frank Lloyd Wright.

He tried to shake off his pessimism. Against the losses, he could set some very positive gains, and he tried to concentrate on these to avoid sliding into a morass of self-pity. Rosa Lustig deserved all the pity that was available. She could not be laid to rest until her killer had been caught and convicted. His search for the man had not so far yielded fruit, but he had to press on. He owed it to her.

Rosa was like the Biltmore itself, a beautiful vision that constantly changed its shape and color while retaining its essential mystique. Merlin had his Rosa. Tom Vernon and Ingrid Hansa each had another. Norm Kozelsky had offered the most fully realized portrait of her, but his tendency to use vivid oils was a distraction. Joe Santana's Rosa was a vulnerable yet calculating creature. Pete Bickley saw merely an easy conquest. Yazzie had been lured by her charms, then estranged by her cold indifference. Frank Lloyd Wright had fonder memories. So many differing versions of the same person, with Rosa's own perspective on herself to complicate the picture even more.

The wail of a police siren interrupted Merlin's train of thought. As the truck pulled in through the entrance with its light flashing, Noah Corbin and Walt Drummond came out of the cabin. The truck screeched to a halt beside them, and two uniformed policeman jumped out. Merlin found himself part of a small crowd that had converged on the scene.

"What's up, Charlie?" asked Corbin.

"We hit someone, Lieutenant."

"I've spent the whole day wanting to do that."

"This guy just stepped out in front of us a mile down the road," said the policeman, letting down the tailgate. "It was almost like he wanted to get killed. I hit the horn, but he wouldn't move."

"Why bring him here?"

"I figured he was from the site. He had a pay packet from here with a name on it. Unless he stole the money, the guy was employed on the site."

"Let's take a look at him," said Drummond.

The body lay under a tarpaulin in the rear of the truck. One tug exposed the rawboned face, bruised and lacerated yet bearing a strange look of contentment. Merlin felt a sharp pang as he recognized Yazzie, even more acute when he guessed what must have happened.

The Navajo had nowhere to go. Having deserted his people to follow Rosa Lustig along a false trail, he could not bring himself to return in ignominy. Death was the only option for a man with his wounded pride. He had loitered beside the road until the first vehicle offered him his release.

While the police speculated on the cause of the apparent suicide, Merlin turned away. Yazzie was one more casualty of the Biltmore, but his demise would cause only a tiny ripple. Appalled at the waste of a young life, Merlin flicked open his pad to look at the sketch that the Navajo had done for him.

The shapeless car was smeared with Yazzie's blood, now dried to a dark brown. When the globules had oozed from the cut on the Indian's palm, they had been a deep red. Merlin was jolted as he realized what the artist had been trying to tell him.

19

N O R M   K O Z E L S K Y   D R O V E at high speed along the desert road, leaving billowing dust clouds in his wake. When the Biltmore began to rise behind the cacti, he slowed the vehicle to make a more leisurely survey of the prospect rising before him. Frank Lloyd Wright was a master at choosing materials to match a particular site. His concrete block system might not be suitable for colder climates, where sharp frosts would crack and persistent rain infiltrate the porous surface, but it was ideal for the dry heat of Arizona.

But it was the scale and opulence of the project that impressed Kozelsky most: solid concrete turned into a stately home. When he thought of the brownstone he was designing in Brooklyn Heights, he felt a twinge of regret that he had severed his connection with Wright. It did not trouble him for long.

A policeman stopped him at the site entrance and asked him to identify himself before waving him through. The Packard rolled into the parking area and halted. Kozelsky was pleased to see Merlin Richards waiting for him.

"Merl!" he said. "Hi!"

"I was hoping that you'd come out here again."

"Only a flying visit. Got to get back to Tucson. My wife is complaining like crazy. I bring her all the way down to

Arizona, then vanish for a couple of days." He glanced around
with mild anxiety. "Ingrid's not here, is she?"

"She was earlier. Looking for you."

"Tell her I had to leave town on business."

"Shall I mention your wife?" said Merlin.

Kozelsky's annoyance soon faded into laughter.

"Why not?" he said. "Ingrid's got to know sooner or later.
I'm surprised Tom Vernon hasn't already told her. Though he
rather specializes in protecting his friends from learning things
that might upset them." He pointed to the newspaper on the
passenger seat. "Seen that article about Daddy Frank in today's
Republican?"

"Ingrid showed it to me."

"Well, you can bet your bottom dollar that Tom will somehow spare him the shock of seeing it. Not that there's one iota
of truth in all those sly hints and naughty nudges about him and
Rosa. Ridiculous!" he boasted. "Rosa was with me at the time."

"That's what I want to talk to you about."

"Eh?"

"Could you come across to the tent, please? I've got something to show you."

"What is it?"

"A drawing. To do with Rosa."

"One of her designs?"

"Come and see."

Merlin was polite and relaxed as he led the visitor to his
tent. When they reached it and had a measure of privacy, his
manner changed at once and he bristled with anger. Yazzie's
sketch was folded up in his shirt pocket. He took it out and
shoved it unceremoniously into Kozelsky's hand.

"What's this?" asked the other.

"Take a look."

Kozelsky unfolded the paper.

"This some kind of joke, Merl?"

"Don't you recognize it?"

"All I see is some doodle by a three-year old."

"It's your car, Norm."

"Well, you could have fooled me!"

"Why didn't you tell me?" demanded Merlin, snatching the sketch from him. "Why didn't you say that you were out here with Rosa on the night that she was murdered?"

"Are you crazy?"

"I wondered why you were so keen to pump me about her. You wanted to make sure she'd told me nothing that could possibly tie her to you. But you were too overeager, Norm. You're supposed to be in mourning for Rosa, but all you're really interested in is saving your own skin."

"I don't have to listen to this crap," said Kozelsky, moving away only to find himself grabbed by the lapels and held tight. "Take your hands off me!"

"Not till we've sorted this out."

"I'll call the cops."

"Go ahead," urged Merlin. "I'll tell them who you are. They've been trying to find you for days. Would you rather talk to me or to them?"

Kozelsky weighed up the situation and nodded.

"We'll talk, Merl. Only not like this. Let go. I'm not going to run off anywhere." Merlin released him. Kozelsky straightened his lapels. "That's better. I'm sure we can sort this out. We're friends, aren't we?"

"Tell me what really happened that night."

"No," countered the other, going on the attack. "Because there's nothing to tell. I was over a hundred miles away from here with my wife. You make accusations like that, you got to have something to back them up."

"The proof is right here," said Merlin, indicating the sketch.

"Some kid's drawing?"

"It was done by Yazzie."

"Who the hell is he?"

"A friend of Rosa's. An ex-friend, that is. Like you."

"Could you try talking sense for a change?"

"Yazzie was a Navajo Indian she met on her travels." A distant look of fear came into Kozelsky's eyes. "Yes, that's the one. I thought Rosa might have mentioned him to you. She took what she wanted from him, then cast him aside."

"So why is this Indian doing a sketch of a car?"

"It's the one he saw on the night of the murder. Long and shiny. Yours, Norm."

"He couldn't have seen mine. It wasn't here."

"Not on the site," agreed Merlin. "You parked a short distance away so that you wouldn't be disturbed when Rosa came out to you. Everybody else was in the camp. Except Yazzie. He slept out in the desert. And he saw your car arrive." Merlin jabbed the sketch. "It may not look like a Packard, but that dried blood tells me it was red."

"He saw the color at night?" said Kozelsky with disdain. "Come on, Merl. What kind of stunt are you trying to pull here?"

"The nights are not that dark out here," argued Merlin. "And Yazzie is used to finding his way around in them. He came into this tent when I was fast asleep, and I didn't even know he was there. You'd have to be able to see in the dark to do that. It's the one thing you didn't count on, isn't it?"

"What?"

"Being recognized."

"But I wasn't, Merl!"

"Yes, you were," reasoned Merlin, watching him intently. "It explained why you came to see me that first time after the sun had gone down. You told me you'd raced here as soon as you heard the news. It was on all the radio broadcasts the next morning. You couldn't have missed it."

"So?"

"Tucson is less than four hours away by car. I checked. The

way you drive that Packard, you could probably have been here
in three and a half. Yet somehow the journey took you most of
the day. We both know why."

"Do we?"

"You'd arrive in the dark again. Nobody would see you."

"I've never heard such a load of crazy nonsense!" said
Kozelsky with a laugh. "All you got is the word of some dumb
Indian and a scribble on a piece of paper."

"No," said Merlin, quietly. "I've got a man who is so anxious
to come back here to check everything out that he abandons his
wife for a couple of days in the middle of their holiday. Why not
bring her with you?"

"Be serious!"

Merlin grabbed him and hurled him against the tent so hard
that it collapsed to the ground under his weight. "Which is it
going to be?" he asked grimly. "Are you going to tell the truth,
or do I have to beat it out of you?"

"Calm down, Merl."

"How can I be calm when I see what you've done? Rosa was
killed out here by some brutal thug. And you've been holding
back vital information that could help the police to catch him.
That's almost as bad as being an accessory to murder." He
hauled Kozelsky up and lifted a fist. "I ought to kick seven
barrels of shit out of you."

"No, no," whimpered Kozelsky, arms up to cover his face.
"Don't, please. Okay, I'll come clean. There's no need to hit
me."

Merlin released him. "Let's have it."

"Maybe I *was* out here that night. But it was Rosa's idea.
She wrote me and begged. It was a sort of farewell get-together.
I didn't realize the farewell would be that final."

"Go on."

"That's it, Merl. Honest. We met, we talked, we ... got close
once again, and then I was off. Back to Tucson. When I left her,

Rosa was fine." He gave a shudder. "You can imagine how I felt when I heard the news first thing next morning."

Merlin was bitter. "First thing next morning, I was stuck in a police cell before they gave me another going-over. It was hell. When I told them about the friend Rosa went off to see, they didn't believe me. If you'd come forward straight away, you could have saved me a lot of aggravation."

"How could I come forward?"

"By jumping into that Cherokee-red Packard of yours and driving up here."

"And getting my picture plastered all over the papers? Have a heart. My wife thought I was visiting old business colleagues that night. What is she going to think if she learns that I was alone in a car with Rosa?"

"She'll think that she married the wrong man."

"I couldn't do that to her."

"You did far worse by coming here in the first place."

"Spare me the lectures on morality."

"Did Rosa know that you had a wife?"

"Of course."

"And she still agreed to meet you like that?"

"She loved me!" retorted Kozelsky. "Can't you get that into your thick Welsh skull? Rosa loved me. That girl would have done anything for me."

Merlin looked at him with absolute disgust. Rosa Lustig, as he had now discovered, was highly attractive to men of all kinds and very skilled at manipulating them to serve her own ends. Yet the person for whom she really cared was a mirror image of herself. She had put her trust in a man who toyed with her affections in order to get what he wanted out of her. Exploitative herself, she loved the man who was so adept at exploiting her.

Kozelsky read his thoughts.

"I loved her as well," he pleaded.

"Not enough."

"I took one hell of a risk for her that night."

"Where were you when she really needed you?"

"What do you mean?"

"After she was dead. If you'd helped the police right away, they might have caught her killer by now."

"How could I help them?"

"You're a crucial witness."

"I was miles away when she was killed."

"But you were the last person to speak to her before it happened. She might have said something to you that could give the police a valuable lead."

"She didn't, Merl," he said. "I can tell you that. There wasn't too much conversation in that car."

"Didn't she tell you where she was going when she left you? Back to the tent, maybe? Or to meet someone else?"

"No."

"She must have said something."

"Good-bye, that was all."

"There must have been more than that."

"There wasn't, I swear it!" said Kozelsky. "We had a pretty steamy time in that car. When you part after a farewell like that, you don't need words. Only a touch and a kiss." He saw the intensity of Merlin's gaze. "That's the truth, Merl. She just took the camera and went."

"Camera?"

"The one she brought with her."

Merlin thought long and hard before reaching a decision. He took Kozelsky by the arm to march him away.

"I want you to meet someone," he said.

LIEUTENANT NOAH CORBIN was more discontented than ever. The cabin was baking, the coffee was cold, and he had forgotten to bring any cigars with him. As he sat in his shirtsleeves behind the trestle table, circles of sweat had formed under his armpits, and his stomach had escaped from its moorings to float freely above his belt. His misery was compounded by the lack of progress they were making. He slapped the pile of documents in front of him.

"These are worse than useless!" he complained. "We been here two days, and all we got to show for it is a dead Indian."

"We're close, Noah," said Walt Drummond. "I feel it."

"Yeah, but close to what? Insanity?"

"The guy is *here*. All we got to do is dig him out."

"If we last that long."

"It's our case."

"Not indefinitely. The chief is threatening to bring someone in over us if we don't make an arrest soon. And why? So that the nasty smell will vanish from this perfumed garden we got out here. That's all we are, Walt. Sanitary engineers. Our job is to get rid of the stink of shit so that the guests can breathe in clean, wholesome air when the hotel opens." He scratched his chest. "We do the dirty work, and what happens? Do we get lavish rewards? Like hell we do! On police pay, we won't be able to afford to buy a postcard of the Biltmore, let alone stay out here."

"Would you want to stay, Noah?"

"Yes," said the other, wistfully. "As a matter of fact, I would. I really would. It's going to be a swell place when it's finished. I could just see myself sitting in that lobby with a Havana."

There was a tap on the door. "Who is it?"

The door opened, and Merlin Richards stepped in.

"Well, lookee here," said Drummond, sizing him up. "I do believe he's come to confess at last."

"Not exactly," said Merlin.

"So what do you want?" asked Corbin.

"To trade."

"Back in the heady world of commerce, are we?"

"I need one of your squad cars to drive me into Phoenix immediately," said Merlin.

"This is a police department, not a taxi service."

"I'm ready to trade, Lieutenant."

"What do we get?" asked Drummond. "The killer?"

"No," admitted Merlin, "but you may be able to take a giant step toward him. I've brought you the friend who was in the car with Rosa that night. The one you refused to believe even existed at first."

He stood aside and motioned forward a shamefaced Norm Kozelsky. The detectives looked at the newcomer in amazement. Drummond grabbed his pad, and Corbin rubbed his hands with glee.

"Well?" said Merlin. "Do I get my lift?"

"Choose any car you like, son," offered Corbin magnanimously. "Tell the driver to take you direct to Doc Osborne."

"Why?"

"He's the guy that put those stitches in your head for us. Might as well take 'em out now. They're police property." He waved a sweaty palm. "Now beat it. We need to talk to Mr.—?"

"Kozelsky. Norm Kozelsky."

"We read all about you in our medical report, sir—"

WHEN THE STITCHES had been removed, Merlin turned his attention to another injury. His pride was still deeply wounded by the way he had been used. There might yet be time to heal the gash.

The drugstore looked somehow different, but he was certain that it was here that he had met Rosa on their first visit to the city. The sign above the pharmacist's counter was all the confirmation he needed: Photographs Developed. He hurried across to speak to a portly woman in a white coat.

"May I help you, sir?"

"Yes," he said. "I came in here a few days ago with a friend. She picked up some photographs you developed for her. I wondered if you could tell me anything about them?"

"Why not ask her, sir?"

"That's rather difficult."

"We don't keep records of our customers' photographs," said the woman. "They're private items. We simply make a note of when they were collected and how much they cost."

"I hoped somebody might remember these."

"Why?"

"My friend's name was Rosa Lustig."

The woman's face turned pale. She mumbled an excuse and disappeared into a room behind the counter. Merlin heard agitated voices. When she came back, she was accompanied by a tall, spare old man in a white coat and wire-framed spectacles. He regarded Merlin with the utmost suspicion.

"What exactly do you want?" he asked.

"Information," said Merlin. "Three days ago, I came in here to meet Rosa. She was paying for some photographs. I remember seeing the little wallet in which you'd put them."

"And?"

"I don't need to tell you what happened to her."

The man nodded. "We read the papers."

"Those photographs have disappeared," explained Merlin. "Along with the camera that took them. It's vital that I find out something about them. Do you remember them?"

"Extremely well, sir. Such unusual subjects."

"Unusual?"

"Concrete blocks," said the man, simply. "They were photographs of a series of decorated concrete blocks."

WHILE THE MAN in the white suit was paying his bill, the porter wheeled his luggage out of the elevator. In addition to the suitcase, there was a heavy object wrapped up in thick brown paper and secured with strong twine. The porter hovered for instruction beside the guest.

"Did you enjoy your stay, sir?" asked the desk clerk.

"Very much," said the man. "Most satisfactory."

"Good." He handed the bill over. "You're all set, sir."

"Thank you. Bring that out to the car, if you would."

The two of them crossed the lobby and left by the main entrance. The car was parked at the curb, but the man could not get into it. Merlin Richards was sitting behind the steering wheel.

"I had a feeling you'd be out soon." he said.

"What are you doing in there?"

"Waiting for you, Mr. Willard." He hopped out of the car to confront the other. "Or whatever your real name is."

There was an awkward pause. The man decided that this conversation did not need the porter as a witness. He thrust some coins into the latter's hand.

"Just leave them on the sidewalk."

"Yessir!"

The porter tipped his cap and lifted the suitcase off his luggage trolley. Merlin noticed how heavy the object in the brown paper was. He could guess why. When the porter had gone back into the hotel, the man tried his plausible smile.

"I'm glad I bumped into you again, Merlin."

"Why?"

"Because I wanted to know where I could reach you," he said. "So that I could send you those names and addresses I mentioned. I always fulfill a promise, you know."

Merlin was blunt. "The only name and address I'm interested in is yours."

"Mine?"

"You told me that you were Clyde Willard."

"I am."

"Then show me your business card."

"I don't happen to have one on me at the moment."

"Let me see some other identification."

"Look, what is this?" said the other, impatiently. "I have a train to catch. I can't stand out here with you all afternoon."

"Why did you book into the hotel under another name?"

"Excuse me. I need to load up my car."

"Why did you pretend to be Clyde Willard?"

"Do I have to summon a policeman to remove you?"

"The real Clyde Willard is on holiday in Chicago," said Merlin. "I wonder what he'd think if he knew that someone was impersonating him down here."

"He need never know."

"Supposing I told him?"

"So that's it, eh?" said the man with a sigh. "A little gentle blackmail. Well, why not?" He took out his wallet. "I did mislead you slightly, Merlin. Sorry about that. But it was the only way I could win your confidence." Some bills appeared in his hand. "What shall we say—forty, fifty?"

"Keep your money. I want the truth."

"You know it. I'm not Clyde Willard."

"Then who are you?"

"Does it matter?"

"Yes."

"Why?"

"Because it may help to explain why Rosa was killed."

"I had nothing to do with that!"

"Not directly. But you're involved in some way."

The man folded his wallet and put it back into his pocket. He reached for his suitcase and swung it into the rumble seat. When he turned back for the rest of his luggage, however, it was no longer on the sidewalk. Merlin had hoisted the brown paper parcel up into his arms to cradle it.

"That belongs to me," said the man.

"It was stolen from the Biltmore site."

"It's worthless."

"Then why did you pay Mr. Santana for it?"

"Those pieces were lying on a pile of rubble."

"Somebody has put them back together again, by the feel of it," said Merlin, testing the weight of his cargo. "Why?"

"That's my business."

"And what about those photographs Rosa took? Were they your business as well? Did she know you as Clyde Willard?"

"I haven't a clue what you're talking about," said the man, smoothly. "You're flailing around in the dark."

"Then shed a bit of light for me," invited Merlin.

He lifted the parcel high, then dashed it on the curbstone, shattering its contents into a dozen pieces and splitting the brown paper in the process. The man gave a yell of protest. Merlin towered over him.

"Who *are* you?" he said.

20

FRANK LLOYD WRIGHT lifted a gnarled hand to shield his eyes against the late afternoon sun. Ahead of him was the looming magnificence of the Salt Range, and all around him was sparse, dry, unyielding and unforgiving desert, whipped into life by a chill wind so that it seemed to move and ripple. They were ten miles from Chandler beside a low, rocky mound that spread out across the great floor of the desert like an island in a vast ocean of red dust and nothingness. As the wind made his hair dance to its music, Wright let out a sigh of pure contentment.

"This is it, Tom!" he said proudly. "This is it!"

Vernon had misgivings. "We're going to live *here*?"

"Dr. Chandler brought me out here himself in that little gray Ford coupe he drives like a demon. When he offered me this, I accepted it at once. Dr. Chandler thought we'd like to be nearer the hotel site itself, but I stuck out for this. What do you think?"

"It's a beautiful location," agreed Vernon.

"Do you know what Victor Hugo said about the desert?"

"No, Mr. Wright."

"He said 'The desert is where God is and Man is not.' No better description for the Arizona desert."

"It's cold out here," said Vernon with a slight shiver. "Are you sure this is such a good idea, Mr. Wright?"

"We'll sing to keep warm."

"Why don't we all stay in Chandler?"

"Because there's nowhere else suitable, and it would cost too much. That's why I decided that we could build our own camp in the desert. Makes a lot of sense, Tom. It presents us with a great challenge, and we must respond to it vigorously. What better way to comprehend the mysteries of life than to make ourselves a home in a wilderness? Live in the desert, and you look over the rim of the world."

"Dr. Chandler says this is the coldest winter down here in ten years. If we camp out here, we'll start each morning by brushing the frost off our drafting tables."

"Would you rather be up in Wisconsin, freezing in the snow and watching the children skate on the ice?" said Wright with a twinkle in his eye. "This climate speaks more softly in my ear. Cool mornings, scorching afternoons, and long evenings with a painted sky to admire and a bracing wind to shave off our whiskers. Yes, Tom," he added with a sweep of his cane, "and with the desert flora all around for us to look at and learn from. A cactus is a work of architecture just as surely as a building. Even a prickly pear is worth studying for its structure. Nature is our greatest engineer."

"We'll have to come to terms with it out here," said Vernon, still unpersuaded. "Nature won't do us any favors. Building a camp from scratch in these conditions will be quite an undertaking."

"That's what appealed to me."

"How many cabins will we need?"

"Fifteen."

"Facing south?"

"No, Tom. Place any building out here on a north–south axis, and you have a permanently cold side to the north with a permanently hot side to the south. Like hot and cold faucets on a bathtub." He twisted an invisible building around at an angle. "Tilt the plans off the direct compass point, and you get sun and

shade in every part of the structure as each day unfolds." A
teasing grin. "That way, throughout the year, everyone gets a
fair chance to sweat and shiver."

"What about materials?"

"I've spoken to Dr. Chandler about all that. The lumber
arrives tomorrow. Boxboards and two-inch battens. Just as well
we have our trusty carpenter joining us."

"We'll *all* have to be trusty carpenters, Mr. Wright."

"That won't hurt us," said Wright, cheerfully. "Best way to
learn how to design a house is to build one. It gives you a respect
for materials." He stretched to his full height and inhaled
deeply. "Feel that keen air, Tom. Look at this eternity stretching
out before us. We'll have this whole huge piece of heaven as our
playground." He slapped his thigh. "Oh, it will be so good to
work on something big again! San Marcos in the Desert exhila-
rates me. I can rectify all the mistakes made at the Biltmore and
achieve something much nearer to perfection out here. Organic
architecture of the purest kind. A masterpiece in concrete." A
gust of wind lifted his hair vertically. He smoothed it down
again. "Breeze is getting up. Let's go back to town. Olgivanna
will think I've run off."

They strolled back to the car and got in. When Wright had
put on his helmet, he looked across at his companion.

"Still have doubts, Tom?"

"Not anymore. Where you lead, I follow."

"I need my boys around me. This is a massive project."

"We'll be with you all the way."

Wright started the engine, pulled up his goggles, and turned
the Packard slowly toward Chandler. As they picked up speed,
the powerful purr of the motor echoed across the desert landscape. Wright found new sights to excite him at every turn. His
enthusiasm was inexhaustible.

"Do you know what Victor Hugo said about the desert,
Tom?"

"Yes," replied Vernon. "'The desert is where Frank Lloyd Wright is and lesser architects are not.' Is that correct?" They laughed together happily.

JOE SANTANA STARED at the empty whiskey bottle with a mixture of disgust and despair, at once ashamed of himself for drinking so heavily at the end of his working day and distraught that there was no alcohol left to drown that sense of shame. He snatched the bottle from his desk and put it back in its hiding place, where it could neither accuse nor entice him. When he sat down again, he rested his elbows on the desk and put his head in his hands. He began to doze off.

The loud rapping on the door soon woke him. Hoping the caller would go away, he ignored the summons. The doorknob rattled, but the door was locked. There was a silence. Santana was about to drift off again when he heard a tapping on the glass directly in front of him. The face of Merlin Richards was framed in the window.

"Go away!" said Santana, waving a hand.

"I need to speak to you!" called Merlin.

"We've said all there is to be said between us."

"I want to tell you about Clyde Willard."

"Who?"

"You gave him those fragments of concrete."

Santana dimly remembered. He also recalled that Merlin was a persistent visitor. Unless he was dealt with and dispatched, he would camp on the doorstep until Santana finally emerged. With great reluctance, the site manager turned the key in the lock.

Merlin let himself in and smelled whiskey. Santana was swaying slightly; he put a hand out to steady himself.

"Perhaps you should sit down," suggested Merlin.

"I'm just fine where I am," insisted the other. "Now,

what is it you have to tell me about this Mr. Willard?"

"He fooled the pair of us."

"How do you mean?"

"His name was not Clyde Willard."

"He said it was. Told me he was a journalist with the *Los Angeles Times*. That's a big paper. Lot of readers."

"It was a good cover," conceded Merlin. "He took me in completely at first. Then I began to have doubts. I became so suspicious about him, I went into Phoenix in the hope of catching him at his hotel. I've just hitched a lift back from there now."

"And did you catch him?"

"Only just. He was about to leave for Los Angeles."

"What's his real name?"

"George Imbert."

"Never heard of the guy. Who is he?"

"A private detective."

"He reckoned he was writing an article about Rosa."

Merlin nodded. "Imbert was certainly linked with her in some way," he said, "but I still don't know how. All he'd admit was that he was acting for clients in Los Angeles."

"What sort of clients?"

"Wealthy ones, at a guess. George Imbert was good at his job. He probably charges highly for his services."

"But what exactly were those services?" said Santana in alarm. "I don't like the sound of this. A private eye snooping around here, and I was dumb enough to go along with it. What did that two-faced bastard want from us?"

"One of the decorated concrete blocks."

"Why?"

"As evidence."

"Of what?"

"I still haven't worked that out."

"He told me he was a great admirer of Mr. Wright's work. Begged me to let him have a few fragments to stick together again as a memento to put in his garden. He gave me twenty bucks," continued Santana. "Jesus! For that amount, he could have had a whole pile of rubble."

"That's all Imbert ended up with."

"Eh?"

"Someone had cemented that block together again for him," said Merlin. "But it was quite brittle. I dropped it on the ground and smashed it into little pieces."

"You did?" Santana burst out laughing and slapped his desk in appreciation. "That's great to hear!"

"He wasn't too pleased about it. And I don't think his clients will be, either. Anyway, I thought you ought to know all this, Mr. Santana."

"Yes, yes. Thanks for coming."

"I think I managed to turn the tables on him."

"This deserves a celebration."

Still swaying, he reached behind the filing cabinet for the whiskey bottle. It was only when he set it down on the table that he remembered that it was empty. Slumping into a chair, he stared morosely at the bottle as if he had just been betrayed by a close friend. He turned to Merlin.

"What do you do?" he asked.

"Do?"

"When things get tough. Reach for a bottle like me?"

"No."

"What do you reach for? A woman?"

"A harp."

"A *what*?"

"A Welsh harp," explained Merlin. "It wouldn't work for everyone, but it gives me a terrific lift. It sort of makes my blood tingle."

Santana grimaced. "I'll stick to whiskey," he said. He put the bottle under the desk. "So what are we going to do about this George Imbert?"

"Find out what his game really was."

"How can we do that?"

"I'm not sure, Mr. Santana. But I'd like to start by looking at the duty roster for the site guards."

"Whatever for?"

"Because they seem to have set shifts and patrols."

"They do," said Santana. "Security is vital out here. We'd be robbed blind if we didn't protect everything day and night. There's material out there worth hundreds of thousands of dollars. It needs guarding around the clock."

"Do you keep the duty roster in here?"

"It's in the security chief's office."

"Any chance of getting a look at it?"

"Why?"

"I want to see what Pete Bickley's patrols were."

"You think he's tied up in all this somehow?"

"I don't know."

Santana sat back in his seat and cocked his head to one side as he regarded Merlin. He surrendered a small smile.

"You're growing on me, Richards."

"Wait till you hear me play my harp."

"When you first showed up with Rosa, I thought you were a complete jerk. And when you actually bedded down with her in that tent—*my* tent, for Chrissake—I really took against you." He gave a mirthless laugh. "You might as well know that I thought you were the killer at first."

"I thought *you* were, Mr. Santana."

"Me? Well, why not? I won't say it didn't cross my mind to throttle that girl. I guess that makes us quits. We were both wrong about each other. And about Rosa." He rose to his feet and led the way out. "Let's go find that duty roster."

It was still light as they walked across the site. The fresh air seemed to revive Santana, and he walked steadily.

"You heard about Yazzie?" he said.

"I was there when they brought him in."

"They reckon it was suicide."

"It was."

"I still got Yazzie penciled in as the killer."

"No, Mr. Santana."

"Why not?"

"He would never have murdered Rosa," said Merlin. "His anger was directed at the other men she took an interest in. Like me. The person he'd really have wanted to kill was the man she saw on the night of the murder."

"Who was that?"

"Norm Kozelsky."

"That well-dressed guy with a lot of lip on him? I met him. He was strutting around the place like he designed it."

"He was Rosa's special friend."

"Do the cops know that?"

"They do now. I told them."

"I wondered why that guy was hanging around here."

"He's still telling the police that," said Merlin. "When I got back just now, I noticed his car still here. That red Pack ird."

"Smart automobile. A man who drives a piece of machinery like that wants to get himself noticed."

"He was."

They had reached the wooden hut used as an office by the security chief. Merlin stopped Santana from going in.

"What was she doing here?" asked the Welshman.

"Who?"

"Ingrid Hansa. On the night Rosa was murdered, Ingrid came to see you. I watched the pair of you talking together. Yet you denied she was even here, and she denied it just as strongly. Why, Mr. Santana? What did Ingrid want?"

There was a long pause. The warmth between them seemed to evaporate. Santana's manner grew surly and defensive once more.

"Let's look at that roster," he said.

PETE BICKLEY HELD the match until his colleague's cigarette was alight, then used it to light his own. The spent match was dropped to the ground. Darkness was starting to fall. Work had comprehensively stopped for another day. Bickley shared a coarse joke with the other man, then they walked off in opposite directions.

His patrol took him around the perimeter of the main building. He moved with his characteristic swagger. The revolver at his hip and the shotgun in his hands made him feel important. He still bore the bruises from the fight with Merlin, but they no longer hurt so much. On patrol at the Arizona Biltmore, he was a person of consequence.

The glow of the cigarette marked his approach, but Merlin expected it in any case. Having examined the schedule for the guards, he knew exactly which patrol Bickley would be on that evening. It enabled him to choose a suitable venue for the confrontation.

Bickley came around the angle of the building at the rear and drew on his cigarette. Merlin stepped out of the shadows that dappled the grass.

"Good evening," he said.

Bickley stopped. "What do you want?"

"A few minutes of your time."

"I'm on patrol."

"I know. And that's what I want to talk to you about. Your duties here as a site guard."

"You've got a lot of gall, mister."

He tossed away his cigarette and put both hands on the shotgun. They were in a secluded part of the site. Nobody could see or overhear them. In the distance, the rumble of the factory was unabated. Merlin was patently alone. Bickley sensed an opportunity for revenge. He tapped the butt of his shotgun.

"You come back for another dose of this?"

"Tell me about Rosa," asked Merlin, easily.

"Rosa?"

"You helped her on that last night, didn't you? You made it possible for Rosa to get what she wanted."

"What are you on about?"

"The duty rotation," said Merlin. "Joe Santana showed it to me. You weren't even supposed to be on patrol that night, were you? So you took over someone else's shift. That put you in a position to help Rosa."

"Shut up about her."

"There had to be something you could do for her. Rosa wouldn't have shown the slightest interest in you otherwise. That's what puzzled me at first. I couldn't see what she'd want from a site guard."

"I know what *you* want, mister!"

"Then I realized what it must be," continued Merlin. "Freedom to take those photographs. Uninterrupted access to the factory at night. If any other guard had seen her, she would have been reported and her camera confiscated. She needed some fool who'd turn a blind eye."

"You're the fool," said Bickley, pointing the shotgun at him. "What happened between me and Rosa is private."

"She had plenty of photographs of the blocks themselves," said Merlin. "Rosa took those in the day when nobody was looking. She had them developed at the drugstore in Phoenix, then posted them off to whoever it was employing her. But what she really needed was photographs of the process itself, and she wasn't allowed in the factory. That's where you came in, isn't it?"

"You got a big mouth, Richards."

"What did she ask you to do?"

"Nothing."

"Let her take those photographs through the window? The

lights were blazing inside the factory; she could have got some good shots, and nobody in there would have been any the wiser. What did she offer you, Bickley?"

"I told you to shut up about her."

"What did Rosa promise?"

Bickley brought the butt of the shotgun around toward his face, but Merlin was ready for it this time. Parrying it with one hand, he used the other to deliver a hard punch to the stomach. As Bickley gasped in pain, Merlin followed with a knee into the man's groin that sent him sprawling on the ground in agony. He dropped the shotgun, and Merlin kicked it well out of reach.

Howling with rage, Bickley reached for his revolver, but Merlin stamped on his hand, producing further yells of pain. The guard rubbed his fingers as if they had been burned. Merlin quickly grabbed the revolver from its holster and tossed it away into the gloom. Then he lifted Bickley up and pushed him back against the decorated concrete blocks.

"Now," said Merlin. "Let me ask you again—"

THE INTERROGATION OF Norm Kozelsky had been long and exhaustive. Noah Corbin probed for every detail, and Walt Drummond recorded it all in his notebook. Kozelsky shuttled between shame and bravado, embarrassed to be dragged out into the light yet confident that the police had no specific charge to bring against him. When their questions finally stopped, he had one of his own.

"Is that it, Lieutenant?"

Corbin picked his teeth. "For the moment, sir."

"Does that mean I can go?"

"No, Mr. Kozelsky. It means that you can come back to the station with us while Walt writes up your statement. It will then be read out for you to approve and sign."

"But that could take ages."

"We like to be thorough."

"My wife is waiting for me in Tucson."

"She's had plenty of practice at that recently."

Kozelsky looked from one to the other, observing their oleaginous grins. He spoke ingratiatingly.

"You're both men of the world," he said. "I can see that. I'm sure you appreciate my position here. There's no need for any publicity about this, is there? I mean, it will be kept out of the press." He leaned forward. "The thing is, guys, I'd hate my wife to open a paper and see my name in it."

"Oh, your name won't be in the papers," said Drummond.

"Thank goodness for that!"

"It will be all over the goddamn front page."

"With a big picture of you," added Corbin with sardonic amusement. "MYSTERY MAN IDENTIFIED AT LAST."

"But I helped you!"

"Only because you were forced to. Until then, you kept your head down so low, you were looking out of your ass." Corbin stood up from the desk. "That comes under the heading of hampering a police investigation. You're a material witness, and you refused to come forward."

"I didn't want my wife to know about this."

Corbin was scathing. "The sooner she finds out the kind of guy she married, the better. Your girlfriend is murdered in cold blood, and all you can think about is yourself. Take him down to the station, Walt. He makes me want to puke."

Still protesting, Kozelsky was hustled out by the sergeant. Corbin pulled on his jacket, gathered a pile of documents from the trestle table, and walked to the door. He saw Merlin approaching.

"You did us one big favor there, Merlin," he said.

"Did Norm tell you what you needed to know?"

"Eventually. First of all, he came on like the big city architect dealing with hick cops from the backwoods. But Walt and me soon straightened him out. We still owe you."

"Then I'll collect part of the debt, please."

"If you're asking for a squad car to drive you all the way back to Wales, forget it. That's beyond us."

"I'll settle for another lift into Phoenix, Lieutenant."

"Fine. Ride with me."

"Thanks."

Merlin had smartened himself up after his tussle with Bickley, and he was now wearing his jacket and tie as well. Corbin noted the way his hair had been combed for once.

"You look as if you got a hot date."

"I have, Lieutenant."

"A compliant lady?"

"I hope so."

Corbin beckoned him in. "Talking of compliant ladies, I got something of Rosa's that might interest you. We had the canal dragged, and one of the guys found this."

Merlin stepped into the cabin to see the object lying on a newspaper with a ticket attached to it.

"Why did she throw away a thing like that?" asked Corbin. "It's the most expensive camera on the market."

"Yes," agreed Merlin. "It cost Rosa her life."

21

THE HOTEL WAS a long, low adobe structure on the out-
skirts of the city. Three guests getting directions from the desk
clerk made the small lobby seem absurdly crowded. Ingrid
Hansa was sitting in the tiny alcove with her back to the window.
When the door swung open, she looked up hopefully, but the
sight of Merlin Richards turned a tentative smile into a disappointed frown. He walked across to her.

"Oh, it's you," she said dully.

"Were you expecting someone else?" he asked.

"Tom was going to put his head in when he got back from
Chandler. To tell me what the plans are for tomorrow. I have to
say, I won't be sorry to pull out of Phoenix."

She had obviously been hoping for a different face to come
in through the door, however. Merlin took his cue from that fact.

"I've got some news about Norm Kozelsky."

Her interest flared. "You have?"

"Do you mind if I sit down?"

"Please do."

She pulled herself upright, but his knees were still almost
brushing hers when he sat in the chair opposite. The three guests
departed, but the desk clerk was within earshot. Merlin dropped
his voice to a confidential whisper.

"You might as well hear this from me before you find out

another way," he said, trying to put it as gently as he could. "Norm is in a spot of bother at the moment."

"Bother?"

"He's being questioned by the police."

"What about?"

"Rosa's murder."

"But that had nothing to do with him," she said. "Norm hasn't seen Rosa for ages. They drifted apart completely. He only turned up now for old time's sake. Why should the police want to question him?"

"On the night she was killed, Rosa went off to meet a man at the Biltmore site."

"That doesn't surprise me."

"It was Norm Kozelsky."

"Never!" Her scorn changed to disbelief. "*Norm?*"

"His car was seen parked near the camp."

"It couldn't have been. I mean—why? He had no reason to see Rosa again. That was all over. He was telling me about it yesterday. Norm had put all that behind him."

"He's admitted it, Ingrid."

Her mouth continued to frame silent protests, but her mind was slowly processing the information. When she finally came to accept the possibility that she had heard the truth, she sat there in melancholy paralysis.

"Are you saying that he was responsible for—?"

"No," assured Merlin, "he was miles away from the site when she was killed. But Norm is implicated, and the police are very annoyed that he took so long to come forward."

"I can understand that."

"He needed a lot of persuading to do it."

"Why?"

An even quieter whisper. "Norm is married."

There was the same progression from incredulity to horror, but it was much faster this time, and it left Ingrid even more dazed as the full implications were borne in upon her.

"I felt I ought to mention it before you see tomorrow's newspaper," he explained, softly. "You suffered a blow from today's headline about Mr. Wright. The blow would have been a much harder one tomorrow."

She nodded. "You're very kind, Merlin."

"I was there when you and Norm met again."

"And what a false reunion that turned out to be!" she said bitterly. "He has a wife, and he was still seeing Rosa? I don't believe Norm Kozelsky has ever been faithful to another human being in his entire life!" Conscious that the desk clerk could hear her outburst, she sought to control her feelings. "I'm grateful to you," she said quietly. "Very grateful. It was considerate of you to come."

"You gave me the name of the hotel to pass on to him."

"I suppose I should be glad that he didn't turn up himself." She twisted the magazine between anxious fingers. "The police ought to arrest him for what he's done. It's wicked."

Merlin gave her time for at least a partial recovery.

"That wasn't the only reason I came here," he said at length. "I needed to speak to you."

"Oh?"

"It's about that first visit you paid to the site. On the day of the murder."

The coldness returned. "You've got me confused with someone else."

"I could never do that, Ingrid."

"I wasn't out at the Biltmore that day."

"You were talking with Joe Santana."

"No!"

"Then you walked toward the factory."

"You're making this up."

"I'm not the only witness. Pete Bickley saw you as well."

"Bickley?"

"One of the guards."

She was indignant. "A guard? You accept the word of a mere guard over mine?"

"In this case, yes. Bickley was in no position to lie to me. I'd have hit him again if he'd done that." He leaned in close. "You went into the factory with a sketch pad under your arm. When Bickley looked in through the window, he claims, you were showing some drawings to the foreman. What exactly were you doing in there."

"Nothing!"

"What's so important that you and Santana have to cover it up with lies? I know what I saw. So does Bickley. Why don't you try telling the truth for a change?" He looked her firmly in the eye. "I'm not going to be fobbed off again."

"This doesn't concern you at all."

"Oh yes, it does."

"It's private."

"I'm involved right up to my neck," he insisted. "It all comes back to those concrete blocks, doesn't it? Rosa was battered to death with one. Santana tried to keep me away from the factory where they were made. You went in there to discuss something with the foreman. Imbert tried to take a sample back to Los Angeles with him—"

"Who?"

"George Imbert. That isn't the name he was using when he was here. He was passing himself off as Clyde Willard, a journalist, to get what he wanted."

"And what did he want?"

"One of the blocks."

"Why?"

"That's what I'm trying to find out."

"Look, who was this man? I don't like the sound of this. Who was he?"

"A private detective."

"Are you sure?"

"I got it out of him in the end," said Merlin. "What I couldn't get was the name of his clients and their reason for sending him out to the Biltmore. Why could a man want to put together five fragments of a decorated concrete block?"

Ingrid looked furtive. She stood up abruptly.

"We can't talk here," she said.

"It's not exactly the most secluded place."

"Come to my room."

He was less surprised by the invitation than by the change in her manner. Ingrid had become soft, feminine, and trusting. Her lurking resentment of him had given way to a warm sympathy. He had broken through her defenses at last.

Merlin followed her down a passageway on the first floor and into her room. It was small but well-furnished and impeccably clean. A portfolio lay on the bedside table. Beside it was a signed photograph of Norm Kozelsky, angled so that it would be the first thing she saw when she awoke. Ingrid grabbed the frame and turned it facedown. She indicated the one easy chair.

"Sit down."

"Thanks," he said, lowering himself into the chair and looking around. "Nice room. It certainly beats sleeping in a tent at the Biltmore. You've got a lock on your door. I had to put up with midnight intruders."

"You've had a rocky time out there, haven't you?"

He grinned. "One way and another."

"You must wish you'd never heard of Frank Lloyd Wright."

"Oh no, not at all. Meeting him has been the most wonderful thing that's ever happened to me. For a young architect, it's a bit like shaking hands with God."

"I've known him for years, and I still feel that."

She sat on the bed and reached for the portfolio.

"Before I go on, I need a promise from you."

"Promise?"

"That what I tell you stays within these four walls."

"Is it that secret?"

"Yes," she said. "Even Mr. Wright doesn't know it all."

He shrugged. "You have my word of honor, Ingrid."

"I'm sure I can rely on it." She began to undo the ribbons on the portfolio. "Have you any idea how Mr. Wright came to be involved in the Biltmore project?"

"Yes. Tom Vernon explained it. Mr. McArthur wrote to him and asked Mr. Wright to act as a consultant architect."

"That isn't quite what happened. Initially, he just asked for permission to use the concrete block system that Mr. Wright had developed with his son in California. Mr. McArthur was ready to pay a handsome fee for the license. He liked the effect that could be achieved with decorated concrete, but there were financial considerations as well. It was cheap."

"How cheap?"

"The estimated cost per block was fifty-six cents."

"Is that all?"

"That was using Mexican labor, on a piecework basis. Anyway, the point is this. Mr. McArthur needed advice on how to make the system work, so Mr. Wright invited himself down to Arizona. He was here six months."

"That sounds like more than consultation, Ingrid."

"There were lots of problems to be ironed out," she said. "But the plans were eventually finished, and the contractor was engaged. You've seen the results so far."

"I'm impressed every time I look at it. What I love is the breathtaking simplicity of the concept."

"But it's not simple," she said, opening the portfolio to take out a drawing. She handed it to him. "Do you know what this is?"

"Yes," he said. "It's a perspective of the Samuel Freeman House in Los Angeles. I've seen photographs of it in our architectural journals."

"It's a perfect example of the concrete block system," she said. "Inexpensive concrete blocks, easy to manufacture, easy to assemble, easy to maintain. As you can see, they're made in varying patterns, sizes, and surfaces. And they're linked together with a series of horizontal and vertical rods that Mr. Wright and his son invented." She took the drawing back from him. "So much for the theory."

"What happened in practice?"

"We hit major problems," she admitted. "The Freeman House required over eleven thousand blocks, cast in a dry concrete. But the intricate patterns on them didn't usually come out cleanly in the first pass through the mold. In some cases there were as many as four stampings to get the block just right."

"There must have been a lot of wastage of concrete."

"Not to mention time and money. But there were other complications as well. We used over forty patterns in the Freeman House, and each block had to cure for twenty-eight days before it could be used."

"I've seen them drying out at the Biltmore."

"Did you notice how fragile some of them are?"

"Yes," he said, recalling the one he destroyed.

"Handle them roughly, and bits chip off," she said. "We lost quite a few that way. What I'm telling you is that it's not a simple system at all. It's highly complex. And the real truth of the matter is that Mr. Wright himself is not as well versed in the manufacturing techniques as he seems to be. His son, Lloyd, is the real expert. I picked up all my knowledge from him."

He blinked. "You?"

"Don't look so shocked," she said with a smile. "I come from an engineering family. While other girls were playing with dolls, I was building my first bridge across a pond in the garden. I love solving constructional problems. And I was involved in the block system from early on. That's why Tom Vernon sent for me. A slight emergency arose."

"Emergency?"

"One of the blocks would simply not come out right no matter how many stampings they tried," she explained. "It was a particularly tricky pattern. I was due down here tomorrow in any case with the rest of the team, but Tom begged me to come a few days earlier. To see if I could help them overcome the problem."

"Is that what you were doing on-site that day?"

"Yes, Merlin. Showing them what they were doing wrong."

"Why did it all have to be kept secret?"

"Because of Mr. Wright. This was his problem, really, but his patience with the Arizona Biltmore was exhausted a long time ago. His advice has been ignored time and again, not least over the size of the blocks. Tom was scared to tell him they'd hit a snag like that. Especially as Mr. Wright might not know how to sort out the problem."

"Now I see why Joe Santana was so brusque with me."

"He was in on the conspiracy. As far as Mr. Wright and everybody else was concerned, I wasn't there. That's why he denied it. Working with Mr. Wright sometimes means working around him to spare him the aggravation."

"I begin to understand now," said Merlin. "You and Tom are acting as buffers between Mr. Wright and the Biltmore."

"Exactly. We're like the two outward faces of a concrete block, linked together with steel rods. The space between us acts as an insulation. Against Mr. Wright."

"Why didn't you tell me all this earlier?"

"Because it was none of your business," she replied as she got up. "You're a complete stranger with no professional stake in the project." She smiled again. "Besides, I was frightened of you."

"Why?"

"I sensed competition."

TOM VERNON WAS glad that he had taken his hat and coat with him to Chandler. The weather was even cooler on the drive back to Phoenix. When he brought his car to a halt outside the hotel, he pushed his glasses up the bridge of his nose before jumping out of the vehicle. Vernon was just about to go in through the main entrance when Merlin Richards came out.

"What are *you* doing here?" Vernon asked in amazement.

"Hello, Tom. I just wanted to have a chat with Ingrid. She's been very illuminating."

"When she puts her mind to it, Ingrid can be. But this is a wonderful coincidence."

"Is it?"

"Yes," said Vernon. "I was only calling in here before I drove out to the Biltmore site to see you. Mr. Wright was asking after that drawing he asked you to do."

"I thought he'd forgotten all about that."

"He didn't, and neither did I." He indicated his car. "Why don't you hop in, and I'll drive you back? Unless you have a lift already lined up, that is."

"No, no. I was going to take a taxi."

"It's waiting for you right there." He moved off. "I just need a moment or two with Ingrid. Be back soon."

Merlin climbed into the passenger seat. The vehicle was stationary, but his mind was racing at top speed. The talk with Ingrid Hansa had been riveting, opening his eyes in ways he had not anticipated.

Vernon was gone for several minutes. When he got in behind the steering wheel, he seemed a little preoccupied. Starting the car up, he drove off. The conversation began less smoothly.

"Is it true about Norm Kozelsky?" he asked.

"Yes, Tom."

"I thought all that stuff with Rosa was over and done with long ago. Norm was actually out at the site?"

"The night she was murdered."

240 / KEITH MILES

"I'd never have believed it."

He lapsed into a long, brooding silence. When he came out of it, he sounded tetchy.

"Don't pay too much attention to what Ingrid says."

"About what?"

"Mr. Wright. She doesn't know him as well as I do."

"Ingrid never claimed that she did."

"So what *was* her angle?"

"She told me how well you shield Mr. Wright from things that are likely to depress or enrage him. It's a full-time job. Ingrid called you a brilliant stage manager."

"Is that all she thinks I am?"

"She meant it as a compliment, Tom."

Another lengthy pause. Vernon made an effort to brighten.

"Mr. Wright took me out to the hotel site today. San Marcos in the Desert. It's going to be magnificent." He gave a dry laugh. "Once we've built ourselves a camp."

"You're going to live out there?"

"That's the idea. Live and work in the desert."

"Just like being on the Biltmore site."

"No, we'll have everything our way this time."

The mordant edge to his voice made Merlin turn to look at him. Vernon gave him a strained smile and increased the speed of the car as they hit open country. His headlights raked the dusty road ahead of him. Norm Kozelsky remained at the forefront of his mind.

"I knew there was something funny going on," he said.

"Funny?"

"Yes. Norm came and rousted me out of my rooming house. Took me for a coffee. He was even more restless than usual. Norm has always been kind of high-strung, but today . . . I knew there was something funny going on. Why else was he in Phoenix? It was too great a coincidence."

"That's one of the things that put me on to him."

"Him and Rosa together? So soon before she . . . ? It's weird. I'm having a job getting my mind around it. What happened? Did Norm hang around the site? Or did he just cut and run? And why didn't he come forward before?"

"I'm sure that the police asked him exactly that."

"I DEEPLY REGRET not being able to cooperate with the homicide investigation at an earlier stage. This was due to a number of factors, one of which was the great pressure I have been under recently in my professional and personal life—"

Walt Drummond read the statement in a flat tone that concealed his contempt for much that it contained. When he had finished, he handed the statement to Norm Kozelsky.

"Is that a full and accurate statement of what you said, sir?" he asked.

"Give or take the odd grammatical error."

"Is that a criticism, sir?"

"It was a joke," said Kozelsky wearily.

"Just sign it, please."

Kozelsky glanced through the document, then scribbled his signature at the bottom of it. He had been in Noah Corbin's office for almost two hours, and the cigar smoke was making him feel queasy. He gave the statement back to Drummond.

"Can I go now?" he asked.

"Not just yet, Mr. Kozelsky," said Corbin, puffing away.

"But I've told you everything I know, Lieutenant."

"Not in the way we like to hear it. And that—first and foremost—is early. As in, the exact moment you hear the news. Got it? When you realize that the woman you had the fun of screwing the night before was killed, maybe minutes after she pulled her pants up again. Early. Immediately early."

"You made your point."

"Then let me make another one, sir," said Corbin as he sent up Apache war clouds. "We got Prohibition in this state. We prohibit sexual activity in a public place such as a Packard on a highway. We prohibit skunks like you from turning their backs on a dead girl just because your wife might get a little upset if she knew how you spend your time away from her. We prohibit gross deception of the police department, which you attempted when we first interviewed you. We prohibit threats about hotshot New York lawyers who are going to sue our asses off for harassing their client. And we prohibit shoot-their-mouth-off guys who treat us like we got fifteen letters missing when we say our alphabet. Understand?"

"Yes, Lieutenant," sighed Kozelsky.

"Because you violated those prohibitions, we're going to lock you up for the night so you can reflect on your wrongdoing and come out of that cell a better boy in the morning."

"You can't keep me here!" wailed Kozelsky.

"We're protecting you from your wife."

"You got no cause."

"We got plenty of cause. Walt?"

"In your statement, you admit to having unlawful sexual intercourse with an unmarried woman in a public place."

"Public! It was out in the desert!"

"Activity liable to corrupt anyone seeing you."

"Nobody did see us."

"Yes, they did," reminded Drummond. "That Indian. Yazzie."

"You indulged in a perversion with that poor woman," added Corbin. "Wait till the good ladies of Phoenix hear about that one. They'll be round here tomorrow with a pair of shears and a lynching rope. Yessir! You're going to be mighty thankful we got you somewhere safe and sound."

"What about the person who did kill Rosa?" said Kozelsky.

"We haven't forgotten him, sir, believe you me."

"Instead of hassling me, get out there after him."

We will," said Corbin, easily. "It may not look like it to you, but I got a feeling that we're closing in on him fast."

FRANK LLOYD WRIGHT was dominating a conversation yet again, and Tom Vernon was back to his old cheerful self.

"What really caught your imagination about Wright?"

"The Imperial Hotel."

"He often talks about that."

"When I heard that it had survived a major earthquake while buildings all around it tumbled down, I thought that this man had to be a phenomenon."

"He is. A titan."

"The Imperial Hotel must have been a joy to work on."

"That's not how he remembers it."

"Why not?"

"Japanese construction workers have strange habits," said Vernon. "Every time they got paid, they'd disappear for a few days to spend their money on having a good time. Then back they'd come to make more. Mr. Wright said it was an uphill struggle to get that hotel finished."

"I never realized that."

Vernon grinned. "There's always a story behind a Frank Lloyd Wright building."

"The Arizona Biltmore seems to have dozens."

"Yes. But it's not his."

"Technically."

"Or any other way."

They slowed down as they reached the site entrance. When Tom was recognized by the guards on duty, he was waved through and drove on to the parking area. Merlin hopped out of the car.

"I'll get that drawing for you."

"Let me come with you."

"No, you wait here. I know my way around in the dark better than you. I'll be back in no time at all."

Merlin trotted off across the camp until he reached the tent. Retrieving the drawing board, sketch pad, and other items he had borrowed, he took them back to the parking area. Moonlight showed him that Vernon had now removed his glasses and put them away in their case. He look somehow younger, and his skin had a college-boy freshness.

"Here it is," said Merlin, handing over his cargo. "The perspective is inside the sketch pad with a number of details I worked on just out of interest."

"I'll make sure Mr. Wright sees them."

"Thanks."

"As long as you haven't turned the Biltmore into a neoclassical temple. He wouldn't appreciate that." They both laughed. He put all the items on the passenger seat. "Well, since I'm here, why don't I let you take a proper look?"

"What at?"

"The concrete block system. Ingrid told me how inquisitive you were about it."

"What I wanted to know was why Rosa was so inquisitive. And George Imbert, that private detective from Los Angeles. Did Ingrid mention him to you?"

"Yes. A worrying development."

"Why?"

"I wish I knew. . . . Let's get across there, shall we?"

Merlin fell in beside him, and they strolled toward the factory with unhurried steps, chatting idly as they did so.

With the incentive of piecework, the night shift was working at a furious pace, shoveling sand, cement, and gravel into the concrete mixers, then adding water for the right consistency. The Mexican labor force made light of occupational hazards; deafening noise, filthy conditions, and dust in their eyes, noses and mouths were only minor irritations. Concrete that spilled, blocks that cracked, and stampings that failed were additional nuisances. A simple equation governed their life. More blocks, more money. They struggled on.

"How much did Ingrid tell you?" asked Vernon.

"She explained how Mr. Wright and his son had experimented with vertical and horizontal steel bars."

"That was the real breakthrough, in my view."

"Back in Wales," mused Merlin, "we use concrete for its strength, not for any decorative function. We'd never get away with a building like this in Merthyr."

"Your winters would crack it open like an egg."

"I was thinking of the rain, Tom. Those blocks are porous. They'd soak up the water like sponges and be discolored in no time. But here, they're perfect."

"That's why he chose them," said Vernon, reciting the words like a mantra. "There are four basic tenets to Mr. Wright's philosophy. Nature of the Site. Methods and Materials. Destruction of the Box. And what he calls Building for Democracy. Look at the plans for San Marcos in the Desert, and you'll see all four of those concepts brought into play."

They had reached the building and stood near a large window. Concrete blocks had been laid out to dry all around. A blaze of light in the darkness, the factory was louder than ever. Vernon had to raise his voice to be heard.

"Go as close as you like, Merlin,"

His hand gently pushed the other a couple of feet forward. Merlin now had an excellent view of operations, but he did not see anything of them. Angling himself carefully, he was able to watch the reflection of the man directly behind him. Lifting one of the concrete blocks from a nearby pile, Vernon raised it silently in the air to smash down on another unprotected skull.

But Merlin was no Rosa Lustig, absorbed in taking photographs. He was no young woman fresh from the arms of her lover. Though the roar of the machines banished all other sound, he could see quite clearly what Vernon was doing. Before the concrete block could fall, Merlin swung round, wrested it violently from his grasp, and hurled it to the ground.

Vernon went berserk. Hurling himself at Merlin, he got both hands around his neck and squeezed as hard as he could. Merlin took him by the elbows and pushed slowly upward, his greater strength breaking the stranglehold and sending the other stumbling back. Before Vernon could recover, a powerful crash tackle knocked the wind out of him and sent him flat on his back.

Merlin sat astride him, punching with both fists to subdue him, then holding his wrists to still the flailing arms. Vernon struggled wildly, but there was already a hopeless look in his eyes. As Merlin overpowered him completely, Vernon cried out in defeat and went limp. His chest was heaving.

"When did you know?" he gasped.

"As soon as you came out of the hotel."

"Something I said?"

"Your manner, Tom."

"Why didn't you challenge me earlier?"

"I had to be sure. And there's no surer proof than this." He looked down at his captive with utter disgust. "You murdered Rosa. You came into the tent that night to search for any photographs she might have, didn't you? But you couldn't find any. She'd already posted them."

"Rosa was a traitor!"

"When you realized that her camera was missing, you knew that she'd be down here. Taking photographs of every stage of the manufacturing process."

"She had to be stopped, Merlin. She had to be."

"So you killed her and threw the camera in the canal."

"Rosa had to die. Don't you understand?"

"You're sick in the head, Tom. Sick and vicious."

"Listen to me, Merlin. I had no choice. It was the only way

to save Mr. Wright. I couldn't let her do that to him. It might have ruined him."

"You're the one who's been ruined."

"No, no. I haven't. We can work out some kind of deal. I'll cut you in. I'll get you taken on as an apprentice by Mr. Wright. I'll have you—"

The punch stopped the flow of words in an instant.

"I don't want anything from you," said Merlin firmly, "and neither will Mr. Wright when he sees you for what you are. So don't drag his name into this as an excuse. You had your own reason for battering Rosa's head in."

"She wanted revenge," gabbled Vernon. "She thought Mr. Wright had turned down her designs and wanted to get her own back. There was a problem with the patent for the concrete block system. That's why she wanted those photographs. To show exactly what was going on out here."

"Who were the photos for?"

"Whoever was employing her. Someone who invented a similar system of construction and thought that Mr. Wright was infringing his copyright. Rosa was here to provide the evidence with which to sue Mr. Wright."

Merlin thought briefly of George Imbert, following up her inquiries and anxious to establish that the Biltmore was indeed the work of Frank Lloyd Wright, thus making him vulnerable to larger legal damages.

"Doesn't Mr. Wright have his own patent?"

"It hasn't come through yet. He's always been very casual about that sort of thing. A case against him might have ended in punitive damages. And made San Marcos in the Desert impossible, because it has the same block system. I had to protect Mr. Wright from that. It would have destroyed him."

"And you."

"I was thinking only of Mr. Wright."

"No, you weren't. You killed Rosa to save yourself. Mr.

Wright is all you have. You're not an architect, you're just a wafer-thin version of Frank Lloyd Wright. If he's put out of business, your career goes up in smoke."

The accusation stirred up such a frenzy in Vernon that he found a burst of energy to throw Merlin off and scramble up. Merlin caught him within yards, grabbing him by the collar and spinning him round and round with increasing force before releasing him in the direction of the window. Vernon's impetus took him headfirst through the glass, sprawling across a line of molds at the very moment when the thick, urgent concrete was pouring out of the mixer.

Within seconds his whole body was immersed, and he thrashed frantically about in the quagmire with a scream of fear that rose above the mechanical din. Police had to hose him down before the arrest could be made.

FRANK LLOYD WRIGHT worked quietly and methodically at a table in the Chandler office. He seemed unperturbed by the startling news about Tom Vernon. Like his own Imperial Hotel, he had survived the earthquake intact. His life had been one long series of seismic tremors, and they no longer hurt or alarmed him quite so much.

One of his apprentices had fallen by the wayside, but others were now arriving in Arizona to join him in the building of their camp. That was the project on which he concentrated all his energies. His pencil followed the darting genius of his imagination.

There was a tap on the door, and Merlin Richards came in. He waited patiently but nervously. Vernon had been arrested for the murder of Rosa Lustig only the day before, and Merlin was still shaken by the experience. There was another cause for anxiety. Laid alongside the plan on which Wright was working, Merlin could see his own his perspective of the Arizona Biltmore.

At length, Wright looked up quizzically at him.

"Ingrid said that you wanted to see me, Mr. Wright."

"Yes," said the other, solemnly. "We all owe you a profound debt of gratitude, young man."

"Thank you, sir."

"You helped to solve a murder at the Biltmore." He sniffed haughtily. "Of course, the hotel itself is an act of architectural homicide, but that's another matter. The point is that you got rid of a great cloud hanging over the project. It grieves me that it was one of own boys."

"Tom Vernon was the last person I'd have suspected."

Wright nodded soulfully. "There are times when we must part from those we love. One big consolation in life is that there are sometimes others to take their place." He regarded Merlin with new interest. "They tell me that you play the harp."

"Yes, Mr. Wright."

"Is it true you brought your harp all the way from Wales with you?" Merlin nodded. "Where is it now?"

"In a pawnshop in Madison, Wisconsin."

"Then we've got something in common," said Wright with a ripe chuckle. "I've spent most of my life dealing with the biggest pawnshop in the state. It's called the Bank of Wisconsin." He patted Merlin's arm. "Go and get the harp."

"Get it?"

"Yes. Ride the train up to Madison and redeem it."

"But I've got no money, Mr. Wright."

"We'll work something out," said the other casually. "Bring the harp here, Merlin. Its melodies will carry for miles across the desert. We're a musical family. I want my stepdaughter Svetlana to learn the instrument. Perhaps you could teach her."

"Me?"

"You'll be around, won't you?"

When he realized what Wright was saying, Merlin was thrilled. Having come to America with the sole ambition of meeting Frank Lloyd Wright, he would now be working alongside him.

Wright picked up Merlin's perspective of the Biltmore.

"This is excellent," he said.

"Do you really think so?"

"It's exactly the way I wanted it to be. You got right inside my head and designed it with me. That shows remarkable perception on your part. Congratulations!"

Wright tore the drawing into pieces and tossed them into the wastepaper basket before the astonished gaze of his new apprentice.

"Okay," said the architect seriously. "You've reminded me how well Frank Lloyd Wright can design. Now show me what Merlin Richards can do."

Postscript

ON FEBRUARY 23, 1929, the Arizona Biltmore was formally opened with a dinner for six hundred guests. Phoenix was heralded as a tourist gold spot.

ON OCTOBER 29, 1929, the stock market crashed, and bookings for the elegant new resort were badly hit. The Biltmore survived the storm, but plans for San Marcos in the Desert were abandoned. One of Frank Lloyd Wright's most inspired creations never left the paper on which it was designed.

EARLY IN 1930, Albert Chase McArthur received a letter from a Los Angeles law firm on behalf of another inventor of concrete blocks, William E. Nelson, who held two U.S. patents. The letter claimed that Wright's system was a violation of their client's. Wright later admitted that, for technical reasons, he had never managed to patent the system that he licensed to McArthur.